Praise for

The Unadoptables

'A high-speed, witty, absurd and joyful adventure.'
KATHERINE RUNDELL, author of *Rooftoppers*

'A compelling, gorgeously written story about the power of
friendship and the true meaning of family . . . perfection!'
ROBIN STEVENS, bestselling author of *Murder Most Unladylike*

'I adored this story from the very first page . . . A book to
absolutely fall in love with.'
CERRIE BURNELL, author of *The Girl with the Shark's Teeth*

'. . . one of the most satisfying endings I've read in a long
while . . . Bravo, Hana – what a book!'
EMMA CARROLL, author of *Letters to the Lighthouse*

'Effortlessly merging the gothic and ghastly with the eccentric
and absurd . . . complete with sinister supervillains, heart-in-mouth
cliff-hangers and lashings of evocative period flavour.'
The Best Children's Books to Look Out For in 2020, Waterstones

The UNADOPTABLES

Hana Tooke

Illustrated by
Ayesha L. Rubio

PUFFIN

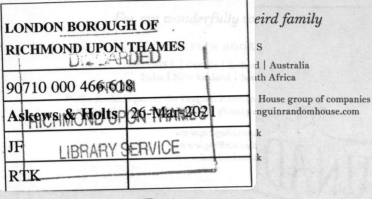

For a wonderfully weird family

PUFFIN BOOKS

... | Australia
... India | New Zealand | South Africa

... House group of companies
... enguinrandomhouse.com

... k

... k

Penguin
Random House
UK

First published 2020
This edition published 2021

001

Text copyright © Hana Tooke, 2020
Illustrations copyright © Ayesha L. Rubio, 2020

The moral right of the author and illustrator has been asserted

Set in 11/17.5 pt Monticello LT Pro
Typeset by Jouve (UK), Milton Keynes
Printed and bound in Great Britain by Clays Ltd, Elcograf S.p.A.

The authorized representative in the EEA is Penguin Random House Ireland,
Morrison Chambers, 32 Nassau Street, Dublin D02 YH68

A CIP catalogue record for this book is available from the British Library

ISBN: 978-0-241-41744-7

All correspondence to:
Puffin Books
Penguin Random House Children's
One Embassy Gardens, New Union Square,
5 Nine Elms Lane, London SW8 5DA

MIX
Paper from
responsible sources
FSC® C018179
www.fsc.org

Penguin Random House is committed to a
sustainable future for our business, our readers
and our planet. This book is made from Forest
Stewardship Council® certified paper.

AUTHOR'S NOTE

When I first began writing this story, several people told me that five main characters was too many and that I should consider having three or four at most. Initially, I nodded along to this advice, but Lotta, Egbert, Fenna, Sem, and Milou were having none of it. As Sem says in Chapter Nine: 'We do this together or not at all!' I realized there was nothing I could – or should – do to separate them. At the heart of this story is their unwavering loyalty for one another and their determination to show the world just how brilliant they each are. I became just as determined to do that too.

When I moved to England from the Netherlands in the 1990s, I never imagined that I too would have to prove myself to people who found it difficult to understand anyone that was different to them. With my foreign name, funny accent and wonky leg I really did stand out. Although a lot of people were really welcoming, there were many who weren't and (like Fenna) I ended up becoming a selective mute* from the age of twelve, right up into adulthood.

---

* Selective mutism is a severe anxiety disorder where a person is unable to speak in certain social situations.

What gave me the courage to be myself were the people around me who loved and celebrated me for who I am. This encouraged me to challenge peoples' expectations of what I was capable of and develop a fierce resolve to reach my goals, no matter how impossible they seemed. Slowly, I found my voice again and I wanted to write a story about children who don't usually get to be the heroes.

In this story, Lotta, Egbert, Fenna, Sem and Milou live in a time of extreme hardship and prejudice, but also one of emerging new ideas and exciting new technologies. You have people like Gassbeek and Rotman who want to keep things how they have always been, as a means to sustain their own cruel agendas, but you also have people like Edda Finkelstein who see a brighter future, if only people are willing to open their minds to new possibilities.

I love writing historical settings because it's a wonderful chance to see how much progress we've made since then, but also an opportunity for us to think about how much further we have to go to make our society fairer for all. Lotta, Egbert, Fenna, Sem and Milou's story is about them challenging the prejudices and expectations of the nineteenth century. Here in the twenty-first century, it's up to us to continue being as brave and bold as they are.

Lotta, Egbert, Fenna, Sem and Milou refuse to believe what Gassbeek says about them and instead they champion each other. As a result, not only do they go on the adventure of a lifetime, but they also carve out their own destiny. It's important to remember there are plenty of people who see that our differences are what make the world an interesting place; these are the people we should listen to.

So, I leave you with this quote from Edda: 'I think you're absurdly *magnificent*. All of you. The world needs more absurdity like yours.'

LITTLE TULIP ORPHANAGE, AMSTERDAM, 1880

<u>Little Tulip Orphanage</u>

<u>Rules of Baby Abandonment</u>

<u>RULE ONE</u>: The baby should be wrapped in a <u>cotton</u> blanket.

<u>RULE TWO</u>: The baby should be placed in a <u>wicker</u> basket.

RULE THREE: The baby should be deposited on the <u>topmost</u> step.

In all the years that Elinora Gassbeek had been matron of the Little Tulip Orphanage, not once had the Rules of Baby Abandonment been broken. Until the summer of 1880. Five babies were left at the Little Tulip in the months that followed and, despite the rules being clearly displayed on the orphanage's front door, not one of these babies was abandoned *sensibly*.

The first baby arrived on a bright morning at the end of August, as dew glistened on the city's cobblestone streets.

Swaddled in a pink cotton blanket, and placed on the appropriate step, was a baby with cocoa-bean eyes and blonde fuzz on its head. However, the way in which Rule Two had been disregarded left no room for forgiveness. The child was snuggled inside a tin toolbox, which had been wrapped with emerald green ribbon, as if it were a present.

'Ugh!' Elinora Gassbeek squawked, looking down at the toolbox-baby in disgust. She signalled a nearby orphan to retrieve it. 'Put it upstairs.'

The orphan nodded. 'What name shall I put on the cot, Matron?'

The matron curled her lip. Naming children was tedious, but necessary.

'She's got a lotta fingers, Matron!'

The baby was sucking its thumb, making loud slurping noises that sent ants crawling up the matron's spine. She counted the child's fingers. Sure enough, it had an extra digit on each hand.

'Name it . . . Lotta.'

The second baby arrived on a blustery evening in September, as a mischievous wind rattled the orphanage's many wooden shutters.

An orphan walked into the dining hall, cradling a coal bucket as if it were a bouquet of flowers. Something was whimpering inside the bucket. Peering in, the matron was displeased to find a raven-haired infant, wrapped in a soot-stained shawl, blinking up at her.

'Poor thing was abandoned beside the coal bunker,' the orphan said.

'Disgraceful!' Gassbeek screeched, referring to the breaking of Rule Two *and* Rule Three. 'Take it away.'

'A name for him, Matron?' the orphan asked nervously.

Elinora Gassbeek took another reluctant look at the coal-buckct baby, its charcoal-blackened nose and the shabby shawl that was wrapped snuggly round it. The cotton shawl looked like it had, possibly, been brightly coloured once. Now, however, it was a mottled shade of grey, with a barely discernible pattern of darker grey ovals. *Like rotten eggs*, the matron thought.

'Name it . . . Egbert.'

The third baby arrived on an unusually warm afternoon in October, as ladies with parasols paraded up and down the sun-warmed street.

Sitting on a bench outside, in her finest puffed-sleeve dress, Elinora Gassbeek opened her picnic hamper and was horrified to find a wriggling baby wedged in among the cheese sandwiches and almond cake. It had a shock of curly red hair and was babbling incessantly.

No cotton blanket. No wicker basket. Not on the topmost step.

The matron screeched shrill and loud like a boiling kettle. The picnic-hamper baby immediately fell silent, its eyebrows squeezing together in a frightened frown. Up and down the street, curious faces appeared in the windows of the tall, narrow brick houses and the strolling ladies came to a halt. Elinora Gassbeek gathered her wits and plastered on a smile for her neighbours. An orphan wove through the throng towards her.

'She wasn't in there a minute ago,' the girl insisted, picking the baby up delicately.

'Take it away,' Elinora Gassbeek said through gritted teeth.

'Yes, Matron. But . . . a name?'

The orphan rocked the now-silent baby, gently brushing fennel seeds from its hair. The matron shuddered.

'Name it . . . Fenna.'

The fourth baby arrived on a gloomy morning in November, as a blanket of fog curled over the canal behind the orphanage.

The delivery bell on the second floor jangled, rung from a boat on the canal below. Using the pulley system attached outside the window, an orphan hoisted the bucket winch up. As it emerged from the fog, Elinora Gassbeek's left eye began to twitch. Inside the bucket was a baby wearing a wheat sack and a sad frown. Two holes had been cut in the bottom of the sack to allow its unusually long legs to poke through.

The matron hauled the wheat-sack child inside, cursing the madness that had befallen her orphanage.

'Put some clothes on it,' she cawed to the orphan hovering beside her.

She looked at the baby's wonky ears, its gangly limbs and the wheat-coloured hair that stuck out from its head at the unruliest of angles. Printed on the wheat sack were the words: SEMOLINA FLOUR. The matron groaned.

'Name it . . . Sem.'

The fifth and final baby arrived under a full moon in December, as the constellations shone brightly above Amsterdam's skyline.

Elinora Gassbeek had sent an orphan out on to the Little Tulip's roof to investigate a strange noise. Wedged behind the chimney stack, inside a coffin-shaped basket, was a baby, cooing contentedly up at the starry night sky. It had hair as dark as midnight and eyes that were almost black.

Gingerly, the orphan brought the coffin-basket baby inside, where it immediately began to wail. Careful not to touch the infant, the matron reached down and pulled a toy from its clutches: a cat puppet made from the softest Amsterdam cotton and dressed in fine Lyonnais silk. A faint ticking noise emanated from the toy, but the matron was tutting too loudly to hear it.

'Ridiculous!'

She tossed the puppet back in the basket, on top of the black velvet blanket in which the baby was swaddled. On the corner of the blanket, embroidered in white thread, was a name:

Milou.

LITTLE TULIP ORPHANAGE, AMSTERDAM, JANUARY 1892

The Little Tulip Orphanage was an unusually tall house, wedged in the middle of a long row of unusually tall houses. In the small window of the very top floor, a girl with unusually dark eyes gazed down at the frozen canal below.

Milou tracked the falling snow as it settled over the ornate rooftops like a layer of cake icing. Crowds were gathering on the ice below, their pink-nosed faces beaming. Bicycles had been swapped for toboggans, clogs for skates, and cries of delight mingled with the neighing of carthorses.

The view became steadily more blurred as Milou's breath misted up the cold window and, with a final heavy sigh, she turned away. As she did so, a frozen piece of peeling paint on the wall beside her fell to the floor with a *clink*. Even the dormitory's floorboards were covered in a thin layer of frost, and Milou's eyeballs were so cold that it hurt to blink. The small fireplace on the adjacent wall was empty and dark, as always.

'Frozen orphan,' Milou said to the red-haired girl sitting on the bed opposite her. 'Sounds like some sort of fancy dessert, don't you think, Fen? I wonder if that's Matron's new plan: if she can't market us as potential sons and daughters, perhaps she hopes to sell us as ice cream.'

Fenna grimaced and rolled her eyes, then went back to feeding stale crumbs to a small grey rat nestled in her lap.

Milou scrunched up her nose and pushed her mouth into a pinched pout. 'Iced orphan!' she cawed, in a perfect copy of Matron Gassbeek's squawking tone. 'Come and get your iced orphan! Best iced orphan in all of Holland! Only five cents a scoop!'

Fenna relaxed her furrowed brow and the corners of her mouth twitched. Milou felt a twinge of satisfaction that warmed her gently from inside.

'We'd better hurry,' she said, turning serious. She rubbed a circle on the window and squinted at the clock tower at the other end of the road. It's only four more minutes until laundry inspection; Gassbeek will pull out our arm hairs if we're late again –'

A prickling shiver started at the tips of Milou's ears and ran down the back of her neck. It was not a shiver of cold, but a shiver of *warning*.

Footsteps sounded in the hallway. The girls shared a panicked look. Milou jumped down from the windowsill. Fenna rolled backwards over the bed, the rat clutched to her chest. As Milou grabbed an armful of laundry from the end of a bed, Fenna hid the rat in her picnic basket, a mere moment before the dormitory door burst open.

A boy's head appeared in the doorway with two oddly proportioned ears and a straggly tuft of blond hair. A gangly, spidery-limbed body followed immediately.

'There you are!' he said breathlessly, his long fingers fiddling with the hem of his grease-stained shirt.

'Oh, Sem, it's only you.' Milou breathed a sigh of relief. 'What is it?'

Sem grinned lopsidedly. 'We have *visitors*.'

He spoke with such breathless hope, a ghost-like fluttering started in Milou's belly. There was only ever one kind of visitor that could make Sem so eager.

Adopters.

'Visitors,' Milou repeated. Fenna gave a tiny gasp.

It had been months since anyone had come to the Little Tulip to look for orphans. What if today was the day? What if her parents had finally returned for her? She couldn't remember them, of course, but she had theories. An entire Book of Theories, in fact, which at that moment was tucked into the left sleeve of her smock. In all of them, her parents were clever and brave. In all but one, they were desperately making their way back to her. Perhaps, after twelve long years, they'd finally succeeded.

'Milou,' Sem urged. 'We need to hurry.'

'Just a moment.'

She clambered over three beds to get to the one she shared with Fenna and Lotta, reaching under the bed to pull out her coffin-basket. It was always packed and ready, just in case. Inside, on top of everything, was her cat puppet. Milou ran a finger over its foot, where the words *Bram Poppenmaker, Puppeteer* were written in swirling red letters. The puppet was cradling a lock of red, curly hair, which had been tied with an emerald green bow. Milou put it to one side and reached into the basket to move two pieces of paper: a charcoal portrait of herself and a poster advertising the famous Parisian circus troupe Cirque de Lumière. Tucked beneath these treasures was a neatly folded bundle of fine black Amsterdam velvet.

Sem sat on the bed beside her, his legs tucked up under his chin. 'Milou –'

'Just one minute.'

He gave her that look again; the one she knew said he thought she was silly for holding on to the hope that her parents would come back for her. He'd never felt like that: he'd only ever shown disdain for his birth parents. Milou reckoned that if *she'd* been left in nothing but a wheat sack she might have felt the same way. Sem didn't understand that she just *knew* she'd find her family one day.

It was a question of *when*, not if.

Milou slipped the black velvet dress over the stained cotton one she was wearing. If it *was* her real parents arriving, they should recognize her old baby blanket. It was rather snug; Sem had taken it out as much as he could over the years and soon the dress would not fit at all.

Sem looked at her outfit with a frown, then carefully adjusted the collar. Milou repacked her basket and grabbed her cat puppet, holding it over her thumping heart. When she'd been much younger, she'd been certain the puppet had a heartbeat of its own. It had soothed her through many cold, sleepless nights until, several years ago, it stopped and Milou realized that she'd likely imagined it all along.

Perhaps the cold, sleepless nights would finally end now. Perhaps today would be the day she finally left this place.

'Perhaps we should hurry?' Sem said impatiently, walking towards the door with Fenna.

Milou followed them. Their dormitory was on the fourth floor of the old, narrow canal house – a building mostly constructed of deep shadows and loose floorboards, and barely held together by peeling paint. They stomped down the treacherously steep staircases, past the mending room on the third floor, the laundry room on the second and the schoolroom on the first. Sem practically flew ahead of her, hopping down three steps at a time. Fenna seemed to glide, her feet as silent as they were nimble.

The ground floor was the only part of the orphanage that didn't look as if a mere sneeze would demolish it. In the main foyer, the marble floor was polished to a shine, the walls were painted a charming shade of violet, and a tall grandfather clock *ticked* and *tocked* in the corner. A motley collection of children were arranging themselves in a line against one wall: youngest at one end, older ones at the other. They were all frantically trying to make themselves presentable: rubbing at grease stains, tucking in shirts, adjusting petticoats, pulling up socks. But there was no disguising what they really were: scruffy, hungry, desperate orphans.

Sem and Fenna slipped into the line as three small brown rats darted across the marble floor in different directions. A girl with a waistcoat over her blue cotton dress was scrubbing at a raven-haired boy's sleeve. She shot Milou a worried look.

'What took you so long?' Lotta asked, then noticed Milou's dress and the cat puppet in her arms. 'Never mind. Quick, help me get this charcoal off Egg's shirt.'

Milou took Egbert's other sleeve and began rubbing at it with the inside of her sleeve. The charcoal smeared, leaving his shirt-cuff an interesting shade of grey.

'Gassbeek wanted another portrait,' Egbert said, his voice full of worry as he peeled his hands from theirs and carefully adjusted the soot-stained shawl that hung round his neck.

'Don't worry,' Milou said. 'It's just –'

The prickling shiver started at the tips of her ears again. The sensation intensified until it felt as if a thousand needles were jabbing at her earlobes. Milou pulled Lotta by the arm and shoved her in line beside Sem. She had just positioned herself next to Lotta when a familiar sound echoed out from the hallway leading to the Forbidden Quarters.

Click-clack-click-clack.

All twenty-eight children straightened as if pulled by invisible strings.

Click-clack-click-clack.

Twenty-eight staccato breaths were sucked in in quick succession.

Click-clack-click-clack.

Twenty-seven sets of wide eyes stared fixedly at the opposite wall. Milou peered through lowered lashes at the darkened hallway to her left.

Click-clack-click-clack.

Matron Gassbeek's boots emerged a moment before the rest of her: twin points of polished, blood-red leather, with low, pointed heels that were just as sharp as the expression on the matron's face when the rest of her appeared.

Every monster that Milou had made up for her bedtime stories was based in some way on Gassbeek: the brutal sneer of a gargoyle, the soulless eyes of a werewolf, the skin-itching screech of a banshee. If the matron hadn't been so filled with hatred and menace, she would probably have looked like any other middle-aged woman, but her vileness had transformed her features into something monstrous.

Gassbeek walked agonizingly slowly up and down the line, sneering with every *click* and scowling with every *clack*. Milou kept her eyes lowered and her spine straight, her shoulders not too low, but neither scrunched up to her still-tingling ears. Finally, the matron clucked her tongue in disapproval and stamped one boot.

CLACK!

All twenty-eight children flinched.

The doorbell *dinged* and then *donged*.

'Our guests are here, so do *not* disappoint me,' the matron cawed, already looking thoroughly disappointed in every single one of them.

Gassbeek *click-clacked* to the front door, paused to pat her tightly coiled hair and stretched her mouth into a hideous smile.

The door swung open and snow swirled in. Milou couldn't help herself. She leaned forward from her spot at the far end of the line as the adopters stepped over the threshold: two dark silhouettes in the midst of a snow cloud. Milou squeezed the cat puppet to her chest, right up against her jittery heart. Her ears tingled again; her breathing grew shallow.

The door slammed shut and the snow dropped to the floor, revealing two tall figures in black cloaks with hoods drawn over their heads. Even from the other side of the hall, Milou could see their cloaks were made of Amsterdam velvet; the subtle shimmer was unmistakable.

Her fingers sought the little label on the cat puppet's foot. Could this be Bram Poppenmaker? Had he brought her mother, too? She knew without doubt she would recognize them. They would look like her. *Different.*

As the couple reached for their hoods, Milou felt as if she had an entire graveyard of ghosts fluttering around in her stomach. But it was not midnight-dark hair and almost black eyes that emerged from those hoods. The ghosts in Milou's belly turned into solid, heavy tombstones.

Two heads of honey-blond hair.

Two pairs of ice-blue eyes.

Two *disgustingly* cheerful smiles.

The golden-haired strangers shook themselves free of snow and turned to face the line-up. Milou tried to ignore her deep disappointment and squeezed her cat puppet more tightly, staring down at her boots.

These weren't her parents.

'*Welkom!*' Gassbeek chirped, smiling like a wide-eyed marionette. '*Kindjes*, this is Meneer and Mevrouw Fortuyn. Everybody say *Goedemorgen!*'

'*Goedemorgen*,' chimed twenty-seven small voices.

Milou's tongue felt as if it were coated in cobwebs. She tugged on the collar of her baby-blanket dress, the tightness of which was now becoming suffocating. A hand reached into hers and squeezed, and Milou gave Lotta a tight smile.

'Come into the warm!' Gassbeek was cooing as she fussed round the visitors and ushered them across the marble floor. 'The *kindjes* are ever so excited to meet you.'

'*We* are ever so excited to meet *them*,' Meneer Fortuyn said.

He was a tall man and his wife was even taller. They stood in the middle of the foyer and ran their eyes up and down the line as if they were perusing a shop-window display.

'How delightful,' Meneer Fortuyn said.

'Delightful . . . indeed!' Gassbeek grimaced, her joviality slipping for an instant. Obedient, hard-working and well-mannered. And the older ones can all read and write.'

Mevrouw Fortuyn smiled brightly. 'Look, Bart, there are so many of them to choose from!'

Gassbeek's smile took a steep climb up her powdered cheeks. Milou dug her fingers deeper into the soft cotton of her cat puppet.

'Then by all means start your inspection,' Gassbeek cooed. 'We'll begin with the smallest.'

The first orphan, a small girl with blonde ringlets and an entire constellation of freckles on her face, took a hasty step forward. The matron lowered her reading spectacles on to the tip of her nose and squinted at her clipboard.

'This is Janneke,' Gassbeek squawked. 'Aged three-ish. She can count to ten and is beginning to wield a sewing needle without drawing blood. Janneke comes with a wicker basket and a yellow cotton blanket.'

The Fortuyns beamed down at the toddler. *'Hallo, liefje.'*

Milou felt a tug on her sleeve. She looked at Lotta, who was studying the Fortuyns with a thoughtful expression.

'I bet you a holeless sock they choose Janneke,' Lotta whispered. 'Seven times out of eight, they pick the youngest one. A child with freckles increases the odds. Mathematically speaking, we've lost this one already.'

'It's probably for the best,' Milou whispered back, eyeing the Fortuyns as they moved steadily down the line towards her. 'They look like grave-robbers to me.'

Lotta raised her eyebrows questioningly and Milou leaned in a bit closer to her. 'Black boots, dark cloaks. All the better for sneaking around at night, stealing corpses to sell for medical research. Perhaps they'll choose Sem, on account of those excellent shovel-wielding arms of his.'

Sem gave them a pointed look. Milou turned her gaze back to her boots.

Her Book of Theories suddenly felt like a dead weight in her sleeve. Perhaps her parents would arrive after the worst of winter had passed. It made sense. Travelling was difficult at this time of year, she reminded herself. She just had to be more patient.

'And what is your name, *liefje*?' Meneer Fortuyn said, now only a few children away.

Milou's stomach fluttered once more as she noticed Fenna fiddle with the hem of her apron.

'This is Fenna,' Gassbeek cawed, reading from her clipboard. 'Aged twelve-ish. Fully literate with adequate handwriting. Her cooking skills are second to none. Fenna comes with a picnic hamper, but, alas, *no* blanket.'

'What lovely red hair,' said Mevrouw Fortuyn, gripping Fenna's chin. 'It reminds me of my favourite shade of lipstick. Tell me, Fenna, do you sing?'

The foyer fell suddenly silent, except for the clunking gears of the grandfather clock. Mevrouw Fortuyn cleared her throat. Fenna's shoulders scrunched together; she squeezed her eyes closed.

'Oh, it's no good asking her questions,' Gassbeek sighed. 'She doesn't speak. *However –*' the matron's voice rose – 'she would make a gloriously *quiet* daughter.'

'A mute?' Meneer Fortuyn said thoughtfully. 'I suppose it might be good to have a silent child –'

'Oh, absolutely not, Bart!' his wife cried. 'What would our friends think?'

Fenna shuffled backwards as Egbert stepped eagerly forward. He wiped a charcoal-stained hand on his trouser leg, then held it out. The Fortuyns made no move to take it.

'This is Egbert,' the matron said. 'Aged twelve-ish, of unknown Asian heritage. He can name every capital city in the world and shows plentiful promise at both calligraphy *and* cartography. Egbert comes with a coal bucket and –' she scowled down at Egbert – 'that shawl.'

'An artist?' Meneer Fortuyn asked, and grimaced as he pointed to the stick of charcoal that was wedged behind Egbert's left ear.

'Egbert is, well, yes, he is *artistically inclined*,' Gassbeek said as if she were admitting that Egbert liked to eat dead frogs. '*However*, he'd be very useful for drawing portraits, or –'

Fortuyn held up a hand. 'We'd prefer a child with more sensible career aspirations.'

'Art is messy,' Mevrouw Fortuyn added, looking pointedly at the charcoal smears across Egbert's shirt. 'And frivolous.'

They moved down the line.

Sem tumbled forward as if the floor had suddenly tilted and the Fortuyns took a hasty step back. Sem managed to lock his legs rigidly and slap his arms to his sides. His nose turned bright red.

'This is Sem,' Gassbeek said. 'Aged thirteen-ish. An expert in dressmaking. Handwriting is . . . well, let's say his handwriting has *character*. Sem comes with a wheat sack, but no basket and no blanket.'

'I thought *girls* learned sewing?' Meneer Fortuyn said.

His wife turned to Gassbeek. 'Why is he not apprenticed if he's thirteen?'

'Clumsier than a three-legged donkey,' Gassbeek sighed. 'He keeps getting sent back from every job I've found him. *That said*, his height makes him my number-one cobweb duster. Very useful indeed. I could give you a discount on this one.'

Sem reddened in embarrassment and his smile faltered.

Mevrouw Fortuyn shook her head. 'I don't think so. Look at him, Bart. How would I ever find suitable outfits for such a beanpole of a boy? And don't even get me started on that disastrous hair. No. He won't do at all.'

Sem slunk back into line, his shoulders slumped lopsidedly. Milou let out a small growl, ignoring the sudden needle pricks on her ear tips telling her to watch herself. She shook her hair over her face. Peeking through a thin slit of ebony, she saw the adopters turn enthusiastically to Lotta. Mevrouw Fortuyn's eye twitched slightly at the sight of Lotta's waistcoat, but her friend's beautiful golden pigtails, tied with emerald ribbons, seemed to reignite the woman's interest.

'Lotta, aged twelve-ish,' Gassbeek sighed, reading from her clipboard in a monotone. 'Mastered the twelve times table by the age of four. She is familiar with concepts such as Pythagoras' theorem and pi. Lotta comes with an empty toolbox, a pink cotton blanket and three reams of emerald-green ribbon.'

Meneer Fortuyn scoffed. 'What use does a *girl* have for knowing about Pythagoras?'

Lotta's fists clenched at her sides.

'Oh, don't worry,' Gassbeek said quickly. 'I assure you, she's house-trained and docile, as a girl should be.'

Milou felt Lotta bristle beside her and the two girls shared a side-eyed look of contempt.

'That ghastly waistcoat will have to go, and the dress will need more frills.' Mevrouw Fortuyn bent down so that her nose was level with Lotta's. 'But, oh my, aren't you a pretty little doll?'

Lotta narrowed her eyes.

'Say *hallo*, Lotta,' Gassbeek warned.

'*Hallo*,' Lotta said in a voice as sweet as syrup. She raised one hand and gave them a six-fingered wave. Then she uncurled her other hand and made it a slow, twelve-fingered wave.

There was a long pause, in which Milou could hear some mumbled counting. Then the Fortuyns sidestepped hastily and, despite the wall of ebony hair covering her face, Milou felt their gaze land on her. It was time for her performance.

'This is Milou,' Gassbeek said. The matron cleared her throat, but Milou kept her hair over her face. 'Aged twelve-ish, she can recite the Grimm Brothers' fairy tales and has a pleasant enough singing voice. Milou comes with a small coffin, that strange little dress she's wearing and a puppet.'

'But does she come with a face?' Meneer Fortuyn asked.

'Milou?' The matron *clacked* her boot in warning. 'Move your hair immediately.'

'Mill-oo,' Mrs Fortuyn mused. 'What kind of a name is *Mill-oo*?'

'Not one I would have chosen,' Gassbeek sighed. 'You're more than welcome to pick a proper name for her.' *CLACK*. 'Move your hair, girl.'

Milou felt another prickle on her left ear, like a needle of cold air, but she ignored it. She didn't need her Sense to tell her that she was risking the matron's wrath.

'Is she deaf?' Mrs Fortuyn asked.

'No,' Gassbeek snarled. 'She isn't.'

The ear-prickling returned a mere moment before the matron seized a fistful of Milou's hair and pulled her head up. It was all the time she needed to rearrange her expression. She scrunched her nose, bared her teeth and, with her head tilted away from the light, she knew her almost-black eyes would look like dark, empty pits.

The Fortuyns gasped.

Milou smiled. It was not a sweet smile. There were no dimples. It was a smile the matron herself had taught her: all teeth and no soul.

'*Goedemorgen*,' Milou growled, using her best werewolf voice.

Their wide eyes roamed across her face, travelled down her ill-fitting black dress, then back up again. Milou stared up at them through spider-leg lashes. The Fortuyns shared a look: crinkled noses and a not-so-subtle shake of their heads.

'We'll take that one,' Mevrouw Fortuyn announced, pointing to a dark-haired boy in the middle of the line. 'He seems ever so sweet.'

Milou's heart did a little dance of triumph.

Gassbeek twisted her fist one more time, then let go of Milou and gave an oily smile.

'An excellent choice!' she cried in delight, *click-clacking* towards a side table upon which lay a huge, leather-bound tome. 'Let me prepare the adoption certificate for you.' Her smile vanished as she faced the orphans. 'The rest of you, back to your . . . studies.'

The grandfather clock *ticked* and *tocked*, rats scratched in the darkest corners of the room and the orphans moved on silent feet to attend to their back-breaking chores.

As they made their way up the stairs, Milou smiled to herself for a well-executed performance. Then she cast a sideways glance at her friends. Lotta was scowling, Sem seemed bewildered, Egbert was still trying to wipe charcoal from his cuffs, and Fenna looked like she wanted to climb into one of the many shadows and hide. Milou's smile slid to the floor.

'She won't forget what you did,' Sem said quietly. 'It'll be worse than head-shaving and caned fingers this time.'

Milou swallowed. 'I had no other choice. I can't get adopted; you know that. Whatever the matron does to me, I can take it.'

Sem didn't look convinced, but he gave her a small smile. 'I hope it's worth it.'

Milou clutched her puppet and ran her fingers once more over the label on its foot, ignoring the tiny stab of doubt that was trying to worm its way into her heart.

She hoped it was all worth it, too.

Hope was all she had left.

Milou's Book of Theories

Lotta says all theories must be based on evidence and that the power of deduction can solve any mystery. I was left here with more clues than any other orphan I've ever known. My family would never leave me without good reason.

<u>Cat puppet</u> made by Bram Poppenmaker.
Had a heartbeat.

<u>Coffin-basket</u>, with claw marks
down the left side of it.
A length of <u>white silk thread</u>
stuck inside the wicker weaving.

<u>Blanket</u> made of expensive
Amsterdam velvet.
Name stitched in <u>white silk thread</u>.
Two <u>drops of blood</u> on
blanket stitching.

Left on rooftop of
orphanage, under
a <u>full moon</u>.

My Sense, which warns me of danger.

The 'Werewolf Hunter' Theory

My parents are werewolf hunters (Sense, claw marks and full moon). They were being chased by werewolves, so they climbed to safety (rooftop). Worried that I might get hurt (babies do not make very good werewolf hunters), they decided to leave me somewhere until it was safe to return for me (orphanage). To let me know that they cared for me, they left clues to both my identity and theirs: they quickly stitched my name on to the blanket, pricking a finger in the process (thread and blood drops); and my father left me a clue to show he is Bram Poppenmaker (cat puppet). They'll return for me, no doubt, when I am old enough to train as a werewolf hunter.

3

After a meagre lunch of Fenna's signature cabbage broth, Milou spent an hour helping Lotta winch down bucketload after bucketload of clean laundry to a sledge waiting on the frozen canal. She then spent the following hour helping Lotta winch bucketload after bucketload of *dirty* laundry up from a different sledge. By the time the grandfather clock began to chime seven, Milou's arms felt like noodles and her hands were covered in friction burns.

'Holy Gouda, I can barely feel them any more,' Lotta said, wiggling all twelve fingers. 'At least if Gassbeek does cane you, you probably won't notice much.'

Gassbeek had gone into the city shortly after the Fortuyns had left and was yet to return. Even when the matron was gone, her malevolent spirit still filled every shadow-strewn nook and draught-battered cranny of the Little Tulip. It wouldn't have surprised any of the children if she had eyes in the walls or spies at the windows. If they slacked at their chores even slightly, Gassbeek would know. And so the orphans worked diligently, as if the matron were hovering over them, barking her endless orders.

Milou was growing increasingly anxious about what punishment Gassbeek had in store for her. The matron would be planning something terrible, Milou was certain of it. Her Sense was certain of it, too, it seemed. Even a mention of the matron sent a wave of shivers across the tips of her ears.

'Maybe she's fallen into the North Sea Canal,' Milou said hopefully, gazing out of the laundry-room window towards the smog-blurred docks to the north. 'She could be floating off to some faraway ocean as we speak.'

'Doubtful,' Lotta said as she retied a blonde pigtail that had come loose. 'Her buoyancy would be compromised by all those heavy petticoats she wears. It wouldn't take her long to sink.'

The grandfather clock continued to *dong* in thunderous tones, and Milou heard the hurried footsteps of orphans spilling out of rooms and hurrying upstairs. She closed the laundry-room window and then rubbed at her prickling ears.

'Come on,' Lotta said, a hint of exasperation in her voice. 'Let's get you to bed before your ears convince you that Matron is plotting your murder.'

Milou followed her out of the room, worry twisting her insides. When they reached the dormitory, there were ten children elbowing each other for room round the single bucket of water, into which they dipped their toothbrushes and hastily scrubbed their teeth. When the children moved on, Milou peered into the bucket. It was now slightly yellow with bubbles of spit floating on the surface.

She went to the open window and plunged her toothbrush into the snow on the window ledge. Egbert was sitting on the roof, his charcoal pencil scratching away on the corner of an old pillowcase. He lifted a makeshift telescope, made of metal piping and recycled spectacle lenses, and pointed it towards the horizon, seemingly unaware Milou was there. She put her toothbrush in her mouth, shuddered as the cold touched her gums, scrubbed, then spat into the snow.

'You're letting even more cold in, Egg.'

'Yes, but I've nearly finished adding the eastern docklands. Look.'

Milou peered over his shoulder at the pillowcase map. 'The tiny ships on the river look wonderful. With your leg shaking like that, it's as if they're bobbing up and down on the water.'

Egbert beamed at her, then shivered again. 'I suppose it is rather cold. I'll finish this tomorrow.'

He carefully handed her his map-making supplies and climbed back in through the window and closed it behind him. She tucked them into his coal bucket, then wriggled through the narrow gaps between the beds to the rear of the room. Bedsprings creaked as their inhabitants clambered in. Milou tucked herself in between Lotta and Fenna, then pulled her Book of Theories out from her sleeve.

'Could we have a cheerful story tonight?' Lotta asked, teeth chattering. 'I don't think I'm in the mood for ghouls or werewolves.'

Pale faces emerged from beneath bedsheets all around the crowded room to nod in agreement. Beside Milou, Fenna shivered, then snuggled in closer, and Milou felt the tickle of rat fur brush against her arm as her friend cuddled the creature to her chest.

'I've been working on a new theory.' Milou smiled, all thoughts of the matron vanishing the instant she opened her home-made notebook, flicking through its worn and scribble-filled pages. 'In it, my father, Bram Poppenmaker, is a puppet-maker by day, hot-air balloon aviator by night.'

As murmurs of interest rippled across the dormitory, Milou licked her dry lips and began her story.

'On a moonlit night, twelve years ago, a family of three sailed the skies above Amsterdam. They flew higher than the hawks, smoother than the starlings and faster than the falcons.'

Lotta coughed pointedly. 'I'm not sure that's how balloons work –'

'It's how *this* one worked.' Milou turned the page and resumed her storytelling voice: half raspy whisper, half sing-song. 'The balloon was midnight-black, speckled with silver stars. Below hung the grandest gondola there ever was. At its bow was a snarling wolf, carved from ebony, with giant emeralds for eyes. At its stern, dangling from a horizontal pole, was my basket, placed there so I could watch the stars twinkle above me.

'The Poppenmakers had just flown past Centraal Station and over the royal palace when suddenly and unexpectedly a storm blew up.' Milou's voice deepened. 'Lightning forked and thunder boomed. From the east came a swirling vortex of furious winds. My mother lowered the balloon, hoping to escape the worst of it, but the wind knocked the gondola into the rooftops. My basket caught on a chimney stack, wedged in so firmly that, as the hot-air balloon carried onwards, the ropes holding me snapped, and I was left behind.'

Milou paused for dramatic effect, then grinned behind her notebook at the sounds of breath being sucked in and then held. The rat in Fenna's embrace gave a little squeak as if it had just been squeezed. She let them wait another few heartbeats, then continued.

'There was nothing my parents could do. As the wind blew them further and further away from me, my mother did her best to try to turn the hot-air balloon round, while my father considered jumping out to get to me as soon as the balloon dropped low enough. But the storm had other ideas.

'The hot-air balloon was blown higher and higher, across oceans, spinning and turning until, a few days later, they crash-landed in the North Pole, surrounded by a family of very confused polar bears. The balloon had a huge tear in it and lay, deflated and limp, alongside the upturned gondola. My parents, with their quick wits and excellent survival skills, built a house out of ice. My father used old puppet strings as fishing lines and my mother befriended the bears by singing them lullabies.

'But it's hard to find balloon-fixing supplies in the Arctic. To this very day, they are still patching the balloon up and desperately trying to make their way back to me.'

'That doesn't explain why you were in a *coffin*,' Sem said, in a slightly muffled, disembodied voice from beneath the covers of the bed opposite hers.

'Well, yes, I'm still working on that bit, but –'

'Nor does it explain the claw marks,' Egbert added.

'I'll admit it's not my most convincing theory, but –'

Milou's words died away as her left ear began to tingle wildly. She looked at the closed dormitory door. A heartbeat later, a familiar sound echoed in the hall beyond it.

Click-clack-click-clack.

There was a collective rustle of bedsheets as the orphans ducked their heads under the covers again. Tiny rodent feet scampered up Milou's arm and over her head as Fenna's rat darted away. Milou heard a puff of air blown from small lips and the single candle that lit the room hissed and died.

Click-clack-click-clack.

The beds creaked and squeaked beneath shivering bodies.

Click-clack-click-clack.

The matron entered the room, and made her way past each bed, pausing every now and then.

Click-clack-click –

Through a hole in her blanket, Milou saw the pointed toes of the matron's boots stop adjacent to her bed. Her ears tingled as the boots turned, one at a time, to face her.

'Get up,' Gassbeek hissed, tearing the blanket from Milou's grip. 'Lotta and Fenna, you too.' She whacked the two lumps shivering in the bed opposite. 'Sem and Egbert as well.'

'Why them?' Milou asked, her heart thudding in double time as she staggered out of bed.

The matron merely smiled her signature smile, all teeth and no soul, then *click-clacked* out of the room.

In the pale light of the moon that streamed in through the threadbare curtains, her friends climbed out of bed with matching expressions of dread.

What was the matron up to?

Gassbeek was waiting in the foyer. There were dirty footprints leading across the marble floor towards the dining hall. The same floor Sem and Egbert had scrubbed clean earlier. Surely they wouldn't have missed such obvious marks. Was this what the matron had called them down for?

The five of them assembled in a line, shivering in their nightclothes. A strange, oily smell hung in the air, tickling Milou's nostrils in an unpleasant way.

'Your behaviour earlier today was unforgivable,' Gassbeek said, her gaze boring into each of them.

Milou frowned. 'But I was the only one who misbehaved, Matron.'

Gassbeek's eyes hardened. 'The five of you have been here *twelve* years. I have never had an orphan stay beyond ten before. No matter how hard I have tried, you have persisted in presenting yourselves as the unadoptable little brats that you are. And you, Milou, are the most irredeemably monstrous child I have ever had the misfortune of knowing.'

Milou took a shaky breath. Arguing with Gassbeek now

would only make things worse. Her friends looked terrified and it was her fault. The matron was going to punish them all, just to spite her.

Milou held out her hands. 'Please, just cane me. I'm the one who behaved badly. They've done nothing wrong.'

Gassbeek sneered. 'Oh, there won't be any caning today. I've realized that won't solve my problem at all. No, I have another plan. I've decided that the five of you have outstayed your welcome.'

Milou's heart thudded. 'What do you mean?'

'The law states that an orphan can remain until adulthood,' Lotta said. 'You can't just throw us out. The Kinderbureau would not allow it.'

'They only care about paperwork,' Gassbeek snorted. 'To them, you're nothing but names and numbers in a book. As long as the paperwork adds up, they won't look too closely. I can do whatever I please.'

'But that's illegal!' Lotta cried.

'I'll offer you one final chance at redemption,' the matron said, ignoring Lotta. 'I will allow you to attend *one* more line-up. Whomever is not chosen during the next inspection will find themselves nameless and homeless.'

'You can't do this,' Egbert pleaded. 'We'll starve, if we don't freeze first.'

'Perhaps you should have thought about that sooner.'

'It could be weeks before the next line-up,' Lotta said, turning to the others. 'Egg could paint some freckles on our faces perhaps? We'll just have to try harder.'

Milou kept her eyes on the matron. She knew there was something else coming before Gassbeek spoke. She could see it in the way her cruel mouth twitched at the corner. Milou looked at the footprints again. She realized then that they were far too large to be a child's and not pointy enough to be the matron's. She also noticed there were *two* sets of prints.

'Actually, Lotta *liefje*,' Gassbeek said, 'the line-up will begin right now.'

The strange scent of oil mingled with the ashy smell of smoke as Gassbeek led them down the dark corridor towards the dining hall. Adopted or banished, they would all be leaving tonight. Milou's parents would arrive one day and find her gone.

Milou clasped her cat puppet over her heart like armour, pretending that the pounding pulse she felt through it was its heartbeat returning, not just her own hammering hard enough for the two of them. Would it be better to go with this new family, to live who knew where? Or should she allow herself to be banished and try to find her parents herself?

She followed Gassbeek and the others meekly into the dining hall, where long, narrow tables lined the walls.

'Here they are,' Gassbeek announced to the visitors that

Milou still could not see beyond the matron's tall form. '*Kindjes*, form a line.'

A fire crackled at the far end of the room and Milou wondered who these adopters might be to warrant such a welcome from the matron. The unexpected fire did not, however, explain the oily smell of smoke that hung in the air, tickling Milou's nostrils unpleasantly.

'Quickly now.' Gassbeek grabbed Milou's arm and shoved her into place before spinning, with a rustle of her silk dress, towards the visitors. 'The oldest orphans I have, as you requested.'

With the matron no longer blocking her view, Milou saw that two men stood beside the fireplace. The taller one was wearing a finely tailored grey woollen suit, with a fur-trimmed tailcoat and a tall top hat. His face was half covered by a huge mustachios, which erupted from under his nose in two long curls and spread out towards his thick mutton chop whiskers. There were rings on almost every finger and a long tobacco pipe hung from his mouth. A younger man, barely into adulthood by the looks of it, was dressed in simple black trousers and a woollen coat. His bowler hat was tipped down so that the top of his face was in shadow, leaving only a pointed chin on display.

'At least she's bettered our odds by keeping the little ones upstairs,' Lotta whispered. 'We each have a twenty per cent chance now.'

'*Kindjes*,' the matron crooned. 'This is Meneer Rotman.'

She rolled the R in Rotman far longer than was necessary. Milou's ears tingled and she squeezed her cat puppet more tightly.

'*Goedeavond*,' the man with the mustachios said, his voice a deep baritone. 'It's a pleasure to make your acquaintances. My name is Meneer Bas Rotman and this is my apprentice, Pieter.'

Pieter nodded once, his face still hidden and his arms crossed behind his back. He didn't speak nor did he look up from the floor.

'Say *hallo*,' Gassbeek cooed and four croaked *hallos* sounded.

Milou had never seen her friends look so worried before. Their expressions pierced her heart. If only she hadn't angered the matron, they'd perhaps have enough time to find families that loved them for who they were. They'd at least have a *chance*.

The five of them stood, straight-backed and trembling, waiting for the matron to take out her clipboard, but Gassbeek merely crossed her arms. They'd be getting no help from her, Milou realized. If Milou wanted to be adopted, she'd have to make it happen herself.

'Meneer Rotman is a very wealthy sugar merchant,' Gassbeek said. 'And he is looking for an heir to join him on his many travels aboard his ship.'

In the flickering firelight, Milou saw her friends' faces waver between hope and despair. Their hands reached out towards each other, forming a line of solidarity, and a realization dawned on her. It wouldn't be right to take this one last opportunity for herself. They all deserved a fair chance at being adopted, of being *happy*. This was Milou's chance to make things right by one of them.

She had to do something. Something bold.

'Good evening, Meneer Rotman,' Milou said, giving him a small curtsy.

The others looked at her in surprise. The matron's eyes narrowed, but Milou knew it didn't matter if she angered Gassbeek further. The damage was already done.

'We are honoured to meet you,' Milou continued. 'Might I introduce us all?'

The merchant's mustachios twitched. 'That would be . . . *delightful.*'

He took a long drag on his pipe, then blew out a cloud of pipe smoke. As the smoke curled round them, Milou's ears began to tingle again. She looked down as she rubbed them and noticed that her shadow seemed to be . . . quivering. She frowned, wafted the smoke away and cleared her throat.

'This is Lotta,' Milou said, pushing her friend forward a step. 'The cleverest girl in all of Amsterdam. She's a mathematician *and* an engineer. She once made a telescope for Egg out of some old reading glasses and a metal pipe.'

'It's amazing what you can find in the canal,' Lotta said, beaming. 'I found a working compass in there once, too.'

'Her parents were undoubtedly well-regarded scientists from Bavaria,' Milou continued. 'It's the only explanation for her cleverness. And there is no knot that she cannot tie or untie. She would make a fine merchant's daughter, sir.'

Rotman's only response was more moustache twitching and a brief nod. Behind him, Pieter shifted slightly on his feet, but his gaze remained downcast.

Milou pushed Sem forward. 'This is Sem. The kindest boy in all of Amsterdam. He always puts others before himself, and those ears of his are a testament to how good he is at listening. What he lacks in grace, he more than makes up for with his sewing skills. I'm convinced his parents are dressmakers from Paris, who make magnificent haute-couture designs out of the most mundane materials. He fixes all our clothing and once even gave me stitches when I split my chin open. He would make a fine son, sir, if you ask me.'

'She's being a little too complimentary,' Sem said quietly, his cheeks flushed. 'I can fix clothes fairly well, though. And sails, too, probably.'

The matron clucked her tongue and Rotman's eyes narrowed. He nodded again and Milou stepped quickly over to Egbert and nudged him forward.

'Egbert is the most talented boy in all of Amsterdam,' she said. 'He has drawn an entire map of the city on an old pillowcase, just from sitting on the roof and observing his surroundings. It is remarkable, and covers the north of the city, all the way up to Centraal Station, the city docks, the Amstel river, and down to the watery flatlands of the polders to the south. No doubt he gets this talent from his parents, who were most likely travelling painters from the Far East. Surely a merchant like yourself would delight in having a son with such promising skills in cartography. He could help you explore the world.'

Egbert made a small noise, half giggle, half gasp, and Milou saw he was holding the corner of his shawl with a white-knuckled grip. He shot Milou a quick, grateful smile.

Rotman took another deep puff on his pipe and blew out a large cloud of smoke that hit Milou right in the eyes. As she fanned it away, she noticed her shadow elongating. It stretched across the floor until it hit the merchant's sealskin boots.

Milou frowned. Was it *pointing* at him? She checked behind her, but there was nothing there to cast such a shadow. When she looked back down, the shadow was still there, wavering in the last strands of smoke, like a long, shadowy finger pointing straight at Rotman's toes. Her ears tingled so suddenly and sharply that she let out a little gasp.

A sudden draught howled in through a crack in the wall, then the smoke was gone and so was the shadow. Egbert's elbow bashed her arm and Milou tore her gaze from the floor. Fenna was looking at her expectantly.

'And this is Fenna,' Milou croaked.

'I'm assuming Fenna is also an ideal child with impressive parentage?' Rotman asked.

There was cold amusement in his voice, Milou realized, as if he were laughing at her. As if he found her . . . *ridiculous*.

Milou stared at Rotman hard for a moment, trying to work him out. His extravagent dress sense was certainly befitting a rich merchant, as were the gold-plated teeth he displayed each time he opened his mouth. His features were neither handsome nor repellent, but there were deep lines on his forehead as if he spent a lot of time frowning. And his hands were clean and looked soft which, Milou thought, was odd for a seafaring man.

Rotman stared right back, unsmiling, and Milou's ears prickled uncomfortably.

'Fenna is the *sweetest* girl in all of Amsterdam,' Milou said finally, clearing her throat and making sure she held the merchant's gaze. 'She doesn't talk, but this is only because her parents were probably mime artists from London. She doesn't smile often, either, but when she does it's like an entire galaxy is twinkling in her eyes. She makes the best breakfast cake you could ever hope to taste. I imagine a cook would be very useful on a ship, sir.'

'That sounds wonderful,' Rotman said blandly, his mustachios twitching yet again.

To Milou's surprise, Fenna lifted her gaze to the merchant's and gave him a timid smile.

He puffed out another mouthful of smoke. 'What delightful little *creatures* you've raised, Matron.'

Milou looked from him to the matron, to the quivering shadow that was now wrapping itself round the merchant's ankles. Gassbeek looked thoroughly pleased with herself and Rotman's smile never waivered.

It was a parody of a smile, Milou realized, much like the matron's: all teeth and no soul. Something was wrong, but she couldn't work out what.

'And what about you then?' Rotman asked. 'What delightful skills do you have, young lady?'

'Me?' Milou said, her voice ragged. She lowered her chin and tilted her head just so, blinking up through spider-leg lashes. 'I'm the most irredeemably monstrous child you could ever have the misfortune of meeting, sir. You wouldn't want a child like me. Also, I think you smell funny, so I don't think I'd like you much as a father.'

Her friends gasped. The matron's eyes widened in fury.

Rotman tipped his head back and laughed. It was a strange laugh, like a seagull cawing. And it seemed to go on forever in which time an unshakable worry settled over Milou like an itchy blanket.

Rotman did not behave like any adopter she had ever met before. He didn't coo over them. His smile, and his laugh, seemed ... wrong. He was looking at them in the same manner that Gassbeek did: as though they were *things*. *Creatures*, he had called them. Why would a man who so obviously disliked children want to adopt one?

'Pieter!' Rotman said, holding his hand out towards the younger man. 'Pass me a handkerchief, would you?'

Pieter reached into the inside pocket of his coat and pulled out a white handkerchief, which he held out for Rotman to take. Milou saw that there were scratches all up the younger man's arms. Some were scabbed over; some seemed fresher. As if sensing Milou's gaze, Pieter quickly put his arms behind his back and resumed staring at his feet.

As Rotman's chuckling subsided, Milou noticed her shadow was still twitching and stretching outwards, pooling thickly at the merchant's boots. Her ears tingled. It couldn't be a coincidence. Her Sense had never failed to warn her of danger before, but now it seemed to be trying to warn her more urgently.

'Well, Matron,' Rotman said, wiping a tear of mirth away with his handkerchief, 'I am most impressed. It's just as you said – the most remarkable orphans I have ever come across.'

Gassbeek preened at his words and Milou felt queasy.

'Now.' He clapped his hands together. 'I suppose I must choose which of you I shall take home. My ship, *De Zeehond*, is spectacular. It's the fastest vessel in all of Europe and has sailed every ocean in the world. It might be an unusual home, but I guarantee it will be full of surprises.'

'Would I really get to travel?' Egbert asked.

'Oh yes,' Rotman said, smirking. 'We will visit places you've never even heard of.'

'What about a mother?' Sem asked. The hope in his voice made Milou's heart ache.

Rotman's mustachios twitched again. 'You will have a female . . . guardian. Her name is Dolly.'

Pieter's shoulders immediately stiffened, Milou noticed. The others were looking at Rotman with awe-filled gazes and hopeful smiles. They didn't seem to notice anything strange about him.

'It is *such* an impossible choice you give me, Matron,' Rotman said, taking another long drag on his pipe, blowing smoke out in a thick and disgusting plume right in their faces.

As the oily cloud of smoke dissipated, Milou realized the merchant was staring at her. He smiled that foreboding smile of his. Then he gave her a wink.

'I suppose I shall just have to adopt all five of them.'

5

Milou stared at the others. In the flickering light, their smiles were wide enough to swallow the moon. She gaped at Rotman.

He wanted all five of them? He wanted to adopt . . . *her*?

Milou blinked up at him. She wanted to say something, anything, to make him change his mind and leave, but her tongue felt too heavy to move.

'Are you . . . sure?' Gassbeek squawked, her expression one of utter shock. 'You want . . . *all* of them?'

'Oh yes, I'm quite serious, Matron,' Rotman said, his smile now gone. 'This little girl has convinced me, well and truly, that these children are perfect. In fact, I find them all *adorable*.'

He said 'adorable' in the same way that someone might describe a bad smell. He was, Milou decided, a terrible performer, uncommitted and arrogant.

A six-fingered hand grabbed Milou's arm and gave her a little shake. Lotta smiled delightedly. She wrapped her arms round Milou's middle. 'Oh, Milou,' she whispered. 'Thank you.'

Milou opened her mouth to respond, but all that escaped her lips was a strangled croak.

'Well,' Gassbeek spluttered, her mouth flapping, 'that's marvellous!'

Rotman took another long drag on his pipe. In the cloud that enveloped them, Milou watched her shadow tremble. Her ears didn't tingle – they *burned* icily. A wave of panic washed over her. This was wrong, all wrong. What had she done?

'Pieter!' Rotman barked, snapping his bejewelled fingers at his apprentice. 'Go and ready the carriage while I discuss the *transaction* with the matron.'

Milou stepped aside to get out of Pieter's way as he marched swiftly and silently from the room, the scratches up his arms hidden once more.

'*Kindjes*,' Gassbeek said. 'Go and pack your belongings. Wait in the schoolroom until I call for you. Meneer Rotman, we have *much* to discuss. Please follow me to my office.'

Without a backward glance, Gassbeek and Rotman strode out of the dining hall, towards the Forbidden Quarters, leaving a trail of oily smoke and five stunned, silent orphans in their wake. Down the hallway, the grandfather clock *donged* once to mark the half-hour.

'I don't believe it!' Sem said happily.

'Neither do I.' Egbert grinned. 'We're going to travel!'

Lotta beamed. 'We're free!'

Fenna let out a tiny giggle, no louder than a hiccup.

But Milou shook her head. 'No. We can't leave with him. He doesn't like children.'

Lotta frowned. 'What are you talking about? He's just offered to adopt all five of us. That suggests he likes children very much. *Five times* as much as your average adopter, in fact.'

'He's not what he seems,' Milou insisted. 'There's something wrong about him. I'm not quite sure what, but he definitely wasn't telling the truth. Perhaps he's a pirate, or a smuggler. He might even be worse than the matron.'

'Enough of your theories.' Egbert let out a sigh. 'Milou, I know you thought your parents would come for you if you stayed long enough, but you don't have a choice any more. This is our only way safely out of here. That doesn't mean you have to give up. Perhaps Meneer Rotman can help you find them, like he'll help me find my real home. He seems *nice*.'

'No, he doesn't,' Milou said. 'I think his apprentice is scared of him. Pieter barely looked up from the floor. And did you see the scratches on his arms? They were the kind you might get in a sword fight. Or from a whipping.'

'Milou,' Lotta said, 'you're being overdramatic. And why are you rubbing your ears like that?'

'You know why. My Sense has been warning me. I thought at first it was telling me not to anger the matron by speaking up, but then I realized it was Rotman it wanted me to be wary of. That man is the very definition of creepy. Dangerous even.'

'Holy Gouda.' Lotta rolled her eyes. 'Not that again. Your ears do not have magical danger sensors, Milou. It's scientifically *implausible.*'

'Why would he come so late at night if he wasn't up to no good?' Milou said. 'And why wouldn't Gassbeek have the other orphans come down, too? She looked so smug, as if there were some secret that we weren't in on. This whole line-up is what's implausible. Adopting all five of *us*?'

'He requested the oldest ones,' Egbert said.

'No one has *ever* requested the older ones,' Milou said. 'Not once.'

Milou saw it. The tiniest flicker of doubt in Lotta's eyes.

'And no one has ever called us a *transaction*,' Milou added. 'That's a business word, not a parenting word.'

Sem's eyebrows furrowed.

'This is silly,' Egbert said. 'Let's just get our things and wait in the schoolroom like the matron told us.'

He turned back towards the foyer, tugging Fenna and Sem along with him.

'No one has ever said we're *adorable*,' Milou called after them.

It was Fenna who faltered this time.

'Something's not right about him,' Milou pleaded. 'You have to believe me.'

'Milou, you have no proof that he's lying,' Egbert said, turning to glare at her. 'All you have is a wild imagination that *always* gets us into trouble. We aren't in one of your spooky stories now. This is real life. And this is the first time we've been offered a chance at a proper home. I'm not giving it up because your ears told you to.'

And, just like that, the others turned away, too. Reluctantly, Milou followed them into the gloomy darkness of the foyer. She looked back at the hallway that led to the Forbidden Quarters. Soon Rotman would have the paperwork he needed to take the five of them away, to whatever fate he had in mind for them. She had to do something. But what?

Milou could still see the wispy trail of oily smoke leading beyond the red line on the floor, past the iron plaque on the wall that read: NO ORPHANS BEYOND THIS POINT.

Beneath the last curls of smoke, she thought she saw a thin, finger-shaped shadow pointing shakily *over* the red line.

'If it's proof you need,' Milou called as her friends began climbing the stairs, 'then I'll get you proof.'

Sem turned, his eyes widening as he realized what she was about to do. In three long strides, he was down the stairs and reaching for her, but Milou had already crossed the hallway and stepped over the red line. Sem hovered on the threshold, still with his arms outstretched, and the others appeared behind him.

'Milou,' Lotta whispered, 'you can't. If Gassbeek catches you –'

'Any punishment would be worth it to prove to you that Rotman's promises are emptier than our hungry bellies,' Milou said. 'He may have convinced you with his pretty words, but I don't trust him.'

Sem reached for her again. 'Please, Milou –'

She took three steps back down the corridor before he could grab her. The others stood on the other side of the line, too scared to step over it. Fenna shook her head at Milou, pleading with worried eyes.

'I promise I'm not overreacting,' Milou said. 'And I would *never* lie to you. But, if you don't believe me, then I'll have to convince you.'

Milou's Book of Theories

The 'Secret Spy' Theory

My parents are spies. They were posing as undertakers that night (coffin-basket) when they were attacked by an assailant with a metal hand (claw marks). One of them was injured (blood drops) and the narrowly missed having their arm ripped off (snagged white thread). They climbed to safety (rooftop). Worried that I might get hurt (babies do not make very good spies), they decided to leave me somewhere until it was safe to return for me (orphanage).

Orphanage's rooftop

Milou's secret spy parents

Coffin Basket

assailant

metal hand

For them to have been gone this long, they would have been given an extremely dangerous mission, like keeping the young Princess Wilhelmina safe from an evil villain perhaps. I haven't heard any of our neighbours gossiping about this, but that's the thing about spying: it's all top-secret. Spies are stealthy and brave. They do the jobs no one else dares do, to protect others.

6

The orphans of the Little Tulip had often discussed what might lie beyond the shadowed hallway of the Forbidden Quarters. The only thing they knew for certain was that the matron's chambers were situated in the only place no orphan had been before: deep down in the Little Tulip's underbelly. Milou's theories ranged from a dark dungeon filled with preserved rodents floating in glass tanks to a factory that turned rat hides into pointed leather boots, dyed crimson with mouse blood. No one had ever been stupid enough, or brave enough, to step over the red line to find out until now.

The only thing keeping Milou's heart from bursting out of her ribcage was the fact that she had her Sense to help her. In the pipe smoke that still curled down the entire length of the long, dark corridor, that thin, shadowy finger seemed to keep beckoning her forward. Milou tiptoed, one hand brushing along the wall to steady herself, the other clutching her puppet, towards a thin strip of light at the far end.

Onward she crept until, finally, she reached the small, flickering oil lamp beneath which lay a wooden staircase that spiralled down into a gloomy abyss. Milou flinched as the first step creaked beneath her. Her breath stuttered as the second one groaned, but she knew turning back was not an option. The spiral stairs wove downward, drawing Milou towards who knew what, until she finally emerged in another hallway. She stopped on the threshold. Dumbstruck.

It was as long as all the orphanage's many hallways, but twice as wide. The walls were covered in a blue-and-white floral wallpaper – no peeling paint in sight. Along one wall there were two large bookcases filled with ornaments, and a chest of drawers with an elegant oil lamp and vase placed on top. On the opposite wall were three doorways, the furthest of which was outlined by a ring of light. Next to the stairwell was a coat stand laden with fur coats. The air was warm and toasty, filled with the scent of burning coal.

No pickled rodents. No glass tanks. No cold.

As the heat seeped into her frozen limbs, fury began to burn inside her. How could the matron let them freeze and suffer above while living a life of luxury underneath their feet?

In the walls beside her and under the floorboards, Milou could hear the telltale *pitter-patter* of small, rodenty feet, the sort that sent Gassbeek into fits of terror. It seemed she wasn't the only thing making its way towards the cosy warmth of the matron's office. Milou felt a slight twinge of satisfaction that Gassbeek was, through her own sheer greediness, provoking her own phobia by luring the very creatures she feared so greatly toward her private quarters.

It still wasn't enough to dull Milou's rage, however, and she swallowed down an angry lump in her throat. The warmth of the hallway wrapped round her shoulders and ankles, drawing her towards the furthest door. She crept up to the very edge of the doorway and pressed her ear against it.

'You drive a hard bargain, Matron,' Rotman was saying. Milou heard him blow out a puff of smoke. 'You want money *and* my help in exterminating your rodent infestation? That was not in the advertisement.'

'The rats are all over the house now,' Gassbeek said, her voice tinged with barely contained panic. 'I cannot . . . bear the foul creatures. I hear ships are often riddled, too. You must have a better solution than traps that don't work. Furthermore, I should think it a bargain considering you're getting five able-bodied workers out of this. Had I known you would take them all, I would have asked sooner. It's merely a favour I ask of you, in honour of our new partnership.'

Partnership? Milou's fingers gripped her cat puppet tightly.

'Not to mention that by taking on multiple new apprentices every year you will rouse immense suspicion,' Gassbeek continued. 'Especially if the Kinderbureau were to investigate and find those children had all . . . vanished. I am the only matron in Amsterdam who is not only capable of but willing to eliminate that suspicion for you, Meneer Rotman.'

'Oh? And how will you do that?'

'How I do it is none of your concern. You need only worry about paying me *adequately* to do it.'

'Very well, I will return to the city docks this evening and send my rat exterminator to you. Though it's probably best that your other orphans don't meet Dolly. No point frightening them.'

Milou frowned. The woman he'd claimed would be their mother was a rat exterminator?

'Excellent,' Gassbeek squawked. 'We have a deal then?'

'They were all quite pale and skinny. Working a ship like mine isn't for the weak, Matron. It would not do if I had to throw them overboard before the journey is even over. I need them to last long enough to pay off the investment before I come back for more.'

Milou's grip on her cat puppet tightened. She had been right about him then. He wanted cheap, disposable *workers*, not heirs. A rat skittered past her toes and darted under a bookcase.

'When will you return?' Gassbeek asked. 'I can ensure the next batch are fattened up a little.'

'I have a tight schedule this spring,' Rotman said. 'I'll return in August. But I must ask. The dark-haired girl, the one who looks like she should live in a graveyard. Is it likely she'll give me much trouble? Her little performance just now makes me think she's not one to toe the line.'

'Milou?' the matron scoffed. 'Don't worry about her. As long as you have the others under your thumb, she'll follow. Sentimental little brat, that one.'

'Then we have a deal, Matron. In return for a steady supply of orphans each year, I will provide you with coin and rid this place of vermin: both the rodent variety and the urchins you can't shift.'

'I'll need an hour to sort out the paperwork.' Gassbeek sounded supremely satisfied, Milou thought furiously. 'Will that be long enough for you to retrieve Dolly?'

Milou had heard enough. She had an hour to tell the others what she'd learned and to formulate a plan. She turned back towards the stairs, coming to a sudden halt when she realized her friends had tiptoed down the hallway and were standing right behind her.

'Milou?' Sem said.

'Sem!' Milou hissed. 'What are you doing here!'

'We came to get you –'

Behind her, Milou heard Rotman and Gassbeek get to their feet, the floorboards groaning beneath them. The office door creaked open and light and smoke spilled out into the hallway, a shadowy outline of Rotman stretching up the wall.

'It's been a pleasure doing business with you,' Rotman said, his booming voice filling the hall.

Milou realized they would never make it up the stairs without being seen or heard. The others seemed to come to the same conclusion. They stood, staring at each other in wide-eyed horror.

Milou's Book of Theories

The 'Baby Phobia' Theory

Perhaps my parents have some unfortunate medical condition that means they are temporarily unable to look after me. This could even be a phobia of some kind. Like a fear of babies and young children. Gassbeek's fear of rodents turns her from an evil witch to a quivering wreck any time she even hears a rat. And Egg has a phobia of earwax. Even just saying the word makes him tremble. Babies are a bit like earwax: sticky and weird-smelling.

My parents will just be waiting until they are well enough to look after me again. Or until I'm old enough not to give them nightmares.

otman stepped out of Gassbeek's office, preceded by a dense fog of pipe smoke. Milou shoved at her friends. The children moved quickly and silently. Fenna curled under the chest of drawers, Egbert tucked himself between the two bookcases, Sem and Lotta slid into the first doorway, and Milou buried herself in the thick fur jackets on the coat stand. Something small and hairy shuffled past her ankles.

Milou heard the matron's *click-clacks* accompanied by the heavy *thud-thud-thud* of sealskin boots go past. She had never been as thankful for the deep and hungry shadows in the canal house as she was then. Still, her heart thumped painfully against her chest.

'I'll have them ready and waiting,' Gassbeek squawked, her voice echoing down the stairwell.

'I can see myself out from here, Matron. You get started on that paperwork. I need it looking believable when it comes to sneaking them past the customs officials.'

'Don't worry, my paperwork is always flawless.'

Click-creeeeak-clack-creeeeak. Gassbeek's footsteps retreated down the stairs.

Milou carefully made a peephole in the coats. She noticed a thin arm sticking out from underneath the chest of drawers, reaching towards a little grey rat.

Fenna.

Click-creeeeak-clack-creeeeak.

Fenna grabbed the rat round the middle, but the beast twisted and sank its teeth into her hand. Fenna's arm disappeared back under the chest of drawers as the rat scurried up and over it, narrowly dodging the oil-lamp before knocking into the vase and making it wobble.

The matron re-emerged from the stairwell and looked around suspiciously.

Milou adjusted her peephole. Gassbeek stood there, her face lost in shadow, out of reach of the flickering oil-lamp light.

Click.

Clack.

Click.

Clack.

Gassbeek approached the chest of drawers and stilled the vase. Then she bent down as if to look underneath. Thinking of her friend hiding mere inches from the matron's boots, Milou quickly drummed her fingernails against the wall behind her. Gassbeek stood bolt upright. Milou added a small rat-like squeak.

With trembling fingers, the matron lifted the vase and held it over her head, like a weapon. Milou stopped drumming. She had hoped Gassbeek would simply run back to her office in fear. Closing her peephole, Milou pushed herself against the wall and held her breath. She tried to push herself further back. Her head hit the wall with a small *donk.*

Click.

Clack.

Click.

The fur coats were wrenched away.

Milou blinked up at the matron, whose face contorted from fear to fury. 'You!'

Gassbeek reached out and grabbed the cat puppet. Milou tried to clutch it to her chest. They struggled, Gassbeek growing increasingly red-faced with fury as Milou refused to let the puppet go. Then, with a sickening ripping noise, the matron tore the cat's head right off.

'No!' Milou watched in horror as Gassbeek threw the

puppet's head aside and raised the vase above her head, ready to strike.

Milou's eyes squeezed closed. Gassbeek let out a blood-curdling scream. Not a scream of fury, Milou realized, but a scream of utter terror. Milou's eyes snapped open again.

The matron was staring at the wall next to her, eyes like full moons. Her shrill scream continued. A movement by the chest of drawers caught Milou's eye. Fenna's little grey rat was once again standing atop it, directly in front of the oil lamp. Milou turned to look at the wall beside her, to where the rat's shadow stretched across the wall: a huge twitching nose with whiskers as long as swords. It opened its mouth, teeth like daggers, and raised its paws, claws like scythes.

Gassbeek's scream was suddenly cut short. The vase dropped from her hands and rolled across the floor. The matron fell forward, crashing into the wall. She clutched her chest, gasping and croaking.

Milou took a hesitant step towards her.

Gassbeek slid down the wall and landed with a thud on the floor. The hallway fell silent except for Gassbeek's gurgling – the same sound water makes as it disappears down a clogged drain. *A death rattle*, Milou thought. The gurgling stopped abruptly, Gassbeek's hand fell slackly to her side and she stared blankly up at the ceiling.

She didn't move again.

Milou's Book of Theories

The 'Unthinkable' Theory

What if I truly am an orphan? A proper orphan, I mean. Perhaps the only way my parents would have ever given me up was if they were dead.

   Until the other theories are disproven, however, this theory is not worth even thinking about.

   Dead parents don't climb roofs.

   Dead parents don't leave clues.

   Dead parents don't come back.

8

The matron lay, limbs splayed awkwardly like a discarded marionette, on the polished wood floor of the Forbidden Quarters. She stared unblinkingly at the ceiling, her neck twisted to the side and her mouth open in a silent scream.

Milou held the headless body of her cat puppet to her sputtering heart. A door creaked open beside her, then stopped with a *thunk* as it hit the matron's supine body. Lotta peeked out, looked down and gave a yelp. Sem's head emerged from the doorway above her. Egbert appeared from between the bookcases and, one bony limb at a time, Fenna crawled out from under the chest of drawers, clutching her rat-bitten hand. The five of them stared down at Gassbeek.

'Is she dead?' Sem asked finally, looking at Lotta. 'Check to see if she's alive.'

'No –' Lotta hiccuped loudly. 'I don't want to touch her. You do it.'

Sem paled. 'I'm not touching her!'

Fenna shook her head as she stared down at Gassbeek.

'Neither am I,' Egbert added. 'She looks dead. Milou, you touch her. You like dead things.'

'I don't like *real* dead things. I . . . oh, fine.'

Milou knelt beside the matron, extended a hand, then hesitated. She *really* didn't want to touch the matron, either. Instead, she waved a hand in front of the matron's face, but Gassbeek didn't blink. Milou stood and quickly backed away; the others followed suit.

'Can someone really be frightened to *death*?' Egbert asked.

They all looked to Lotta, who merely shrugged. 'I'm a scientist, not a doctor.'

The little grey rat emerged, darting over the matron's dress and off towards the office's open door. Milou thought she saw the matron's foot twitch, but, when she looked again, Gassbeek was still lifeless. Fenna made as if to chase the rat, took one step closer to the matron, then shook her head and hurried back to huddle between Lotta and Sem, who both wrapped an arm round her.

Lotta hiccuped once more, then turned to Milou. 'What did Rotman mean about *believable* paperwork and *sneaking* us past the dockyard's customs officials?'

'He and Gassbeek struck a deal,' Milou said quietly and flatly. 'He pays her to make all records of us disappear, then he'll work us until we're broken or dead. And in August he'll come back for a fresh group of orphans.'

They all stared at her.

Lotta shook her head in disbelief. 'But that's against the law.'

'Since when has Gassbeek cared about any laws but her own?' Sem said quietly, staring around at the opulent hallway, then down to the lifeless form at their feet.

'I should have known. A *girl* would never be allowed to be an engineer on a ship,' Lotta huffed. 'He'd no doubt have had me doing his laundry. We should have listened to you, Milou.'

Wordlessly, Milou reached out and squeezed her friend's hand.

'Well, we can't stay here,' Egbert said. 'The authorities might think we killed her.'

'We can't just run,' Lotta said. 'The Kinderbureau will send a new matron. Perhaps we could explain –'

Sem shook his head. 'You really think they'll believe us? We can't take that chance. Egg's right, we need to leave.'

'But we've got nowhere to go.'

No one spoke, and the silence hung heavy in the still-oily air.

Milou held her puppet's body tight, then went to pick up its head. As she leaned forward, something small but heavy fell from the open neck, landing between her feet with a soft thud. The tips of her ears turned icy cold, and she sucked in a short, sharp breath.

A round piece of silver glinted in the lamplight, and Milou sank to her knees in front of it.

'Milou?' Egbert dropped down on one side beside her, Fenna on the other. Milou's throat felt too tight to get words out. With trembling hands, she put her puppet aside and picked the glimmering item up.

'What is it?' Sem asked, and he and Lotta crouched in front of her. Milou swallowed and they all leaned in.

It was roughly the same diameter as a guilder coin, and the thickness of Milou's little finger. The surface was of tarnished silver, which was inlaid with a neat line of tiny crystals, shimmering like stars, round which curled a golden crescent moon. There was a loop at the top, with a thin chain running through it, and, at the bottom, the smallest clasp she had ever seen. Milou lifted the lid and found an intricate clock face, each Roman numeral sitting below a tiny golden star. In the middle was a painted blue disc, only partially visible from behind a cut-out in the clock face, displaying the sun and moon cycle.

The pocket watch's gears had long since fallen silent and the hands were completely still.

'Well, that explains the puppet's supposed heartbeat,' Lotta said. 'I told you there is *always* a logical explanation.'

Milou turned the watch over in her hand, revealing a delicate inscription, so small she had to lean right in to read it:

> *Beneath the stars I found you.*
> 52.284040, 4.784040
> *Under the moon I lost you.*

The icy chill spread from her ears, down her neck, to her shoulders as she read the inscription again.

> *I found you.*

The chill grew heavier, colder, pricklier.

> *I lost you.*

Where the first two lines had been engraved in a neat typeface, the final line had been scratched on to the back of the watch.

'Geographical coordinates,' Egbert said, almost reverently, pointing at the numbers.

Coordinates. Milou's breath hitched inwards once more.

I lost you.

She ran her fingers shakily over the coordinates. Things that were lost could be found again – if you knew where to look.

'I'm leaving!' she said, the words finally bursting from her lips. Four shocked faces turned to her. 'This is a message from my parents – and, before you say anything, this isn't one of my wild theories. This is *proof.* I'm going to find them. And I want you to come with me. Let's leave this place together and never look back.'

'Milou,' Lotta said softly, despairingly, 'we need papers. The only realistic way out is adoption and no one except that horrid merchant wants to take us.'

Milou uncurled the watch's chain and slipped it over her head, a plan already blossoming in her mind. Her Sense gently tickled her ears in encouragement.

'Then we'll just have to adopt ourselves.'

9

As the oil lamp flickered, the rats scratched and Gassbeek lay lifelessly still, Milou, bright-eyed and tingly-eared, faced her friends and began to explain.

'It's simple really,' she said, her head swirling as if she'd just spun in a thousand circles. 'And so obvious. We know Bram Poppenmaker, my father, made this puppet. Which means, most likely, he or my mother made this watch. They must have hidden it because they knew an orphanage matron might steal it, and they were definitely right about that. My point is, it's a proper clue. On its own, the puppet was useless at telling me how I could find them, but together –'

'Milou!' Lotta said, exasperated.

'Yes?'

'You still haven't explained how you plan to get us out.'

Milou shook herself, trying to calm the maelstrom in her mind. 'It's easy. We write ourselves an adoption certificate, using my father's name, and then we just *leave*.'

Egbert frowned. 'And go where exactly?'

Milou held up the pocket watch and pointed at the numbers etched on the back of it. 'Here, of course!'

'But where do those coordinates lead?' Sem asked.

'Gouda knows,' Lotta said. 'It could be anywhere in the world. Milou, we need a *proper* plan. Rotman will be back soon. I suggest we go back up to the dormitory and pretend to be asleep. In the morning, we can act as if –'

'Actually,' Egbert said, eyes agleam, 'those coordinates are within a hundred-kilometre radius of the city.' He held Milou's pocket watch up for them to see. 'Amsterdam sits just over fifty-two longitude, and just under five latitude. It took me seven attempts and twice as many canings to get that information out of Gassbeek when I started making my map. I didn't think she'd ever tell me, but I guess she wanted to shut me up – anyway, it was worth it. But we'd need a much more detailed map than mine to find the exact location of these coordinates.' Egbert's smile widened. 'Just as well I know where we can find one.'

Milou hugged him.

'Wait,' Lotta said. 'Even if we do find this location, there's no guarantee that it'll lead us anywhere useful.'

Milou was about to argue – to point out that her parents wouldn't have left her coordinates that led nowhere – but stopped herself just in time. Lotta needed logic in order to be convinced, not optimism.

'If we stay, we'll be in trouble no matter what we do,' Milou said softly. 'If we leave, there's a chance – maybe just a small one – that we can be rid of this place, rid of the chores, rid of the *line-ups* – forever.'

They all looked at Gassbeek. The grandfather clock chimed the quarter-hour.

Sem got to his feet. 'We need to decide now. Milou's right. We'll never have a chance like this again.' Milou beamed at him, but her smile faltered slightly as he shook his head gently. 'I'm not coming just to help you find your birth family, Milou. You know how I feel about the people who *discarded* us here. I'm agreeing because it's the only chance we'll ever get to leave this place on our own terms.'

Milou swallowed hard. 'I understand.'

Egbert stood, too. 'I've never belonged in this place,' he said, glaring at the matron. 'None of us have. There's nothing but pain here.'

He and Sem looked expectantly at the girls.

'We do this together or not at all,' Sem said. 'I'm not leaving any one of us behind.'

Fenna stood, too, and nodded in agreement.

Lotta sighed, holding out a hand for Milou to pull her up. Then she nodded. 'All right, I'm in.'

Lotta, Sem and Fenna left to gather everyone's belongings and to forage for supplies. Milou took Egbert's hand and dragged him towards the matron's office, carefully stepping over her body. The door to Gassbeek's office opened with a creak that sent goosebumps up Milou's arms.

'Quiet!' Egbert hissed. 'You'll wake every dead dog in the neighbourhood.'

Milou pushed the door fully open. Egbert edged around her into the warm glow where, mere minutes ago, Gassbeek and Rotman had been plotting their nefarious deeds.

Milou stepped in behind Egbert. It was like walking into a wall of warmth; a large fire burned brightly in a huge fireplace made of marble and iron, above which hung a charcoal portrait of the matron in a gold-painted frame. A huge oak desk dominated the centre of the room, two elegant oil lamps at either end. And in the middle of the desk lay a thick, leather-bound book, with the words LITTLE TULIP ORPHAN RECORDS stamped across it in bold letters.

'There it is!' said Milou.

'This stuff looks like it belongs in a mansion,' Egbert said, loosening his shawl slightly. 'Those lamps alone could have paid for new clothes for every one of us.'

The UNADOPTABLES

'Gassbeek was as crooked as a corkscrew,' Milou said, her lip curling in disgust. She looked at the crackling fire. 'It's so warm in here and yet she left the rest of us to freeze.'

'Let's be quick,' Egbert said, sitting down in the desk chair, his feet dangling high above the luxurious grey carpet.

Milou opened the record book to the most recently written-on page, which showed the name of a girl who'd been adopted six months earlier. At the bottom of the adoption certificate, Gassbeek had signed her name in a scratchy scrawl.

'Why isn't the Fortuyn adoption from this morning listed in here?' Egbert asked.

'She was clearly too busy trying to find someone to sell us off to to record it. Can you copy her signature?'

Egbert pulled out a blank sheet of paper from the desk, took a quill from the ink pot and made a few practice squiggles.

Milou looked between Egbert's paper and the record book. 'Outstanding! I can't tell the difference at all.'

Egbert gave her a bright smile and turned the page over to a blank form. His quill hovered over it. 'Are you sure your parents will agree to this?'

'Of course,' Milou said without hesitation. She placed her cat puppet on the desk in front of him and pointed at the label sewn into its foot. 'Here. This is how you spell Bram Poppenmaker.'

Egbert gave her a small smile and began filling out the adoption certificate. He finished the final signature, blew on the ink, then tore off the top sheet, leaving the certificate's imprint on the pink sheet below.

'We are officially no longer orphans,' Milou said, her mouth stretched into a grin that nearly met her ears.

'Well then, Milou *Poppenmaker*,' Egbert said, returning her grin, 'shall we get out of here?'

'Just a moment.' Milou snapped the record book closed, heaved it up and stepped out into the hallway.

She nudged the next doorway open. The matron's bedroom was as luxurious as the rest of the Forbidden Quarters, but Milou didn't pause to examine it. She skirted round the large four-poster bed towards a more familiar-looking woven laundry basket. Pulling dirty dresses and underskirts aside, she buried the record book at the bottom.

'Just in case.' She grinned at Egbert. 'I reckon that'll take the next matron a while to find!'

The grandfather clock struck the ninth hour, the first *dong* rattling the ceiling. Milou and Egbert were running up the spiral staircase as the second *dong* rang out. As the third strike ricocheted off the walls, they were over the red line and back in the cold gloom of the foyer, shivering as they ran. The others were already waiting.

Sem had his wheat sack slung over his shoulder, Milou's coffin wedged in his left armpit, her Book of Theories tucked under his chin, and Egbert's coal bucket dangling from his long fingers. Lotta was clutching her tin toolbox and an armful of the matron's fur coats. Fenna held her picnic basket.

'It doesn't feel right,' Lotta whispered as the fourth *dong* rang. 'Leaving the other orphans behind.'

Egbert took his coal bucket from Sem. Milou gathered her own coffin-basket into her arms, then tucked her Book of Theories into her sleeve once more.

'We don't have a choice,' Sem said.

The *fifth* dong echoed across the marble floor.

Fenna lifted the lid of her picnic basket, revealing a bundle of mostly mouldy vegetables and some stale bread.

Lotta handed out the matron's coats, three in total. Fenna and Egbert huddled into one, Sem had one to himself, leaving Lotta and Milou to share the last one.

'That's it then,' Milou said. 'We're ready to go.' The certificate of adoption was tucked into her breast pocket and she held a hand over it. She took one last look round the foyer as the sixth *dong* chimed. 'Ready?'

The others nodded eagerly, and they hurried to the front door as the seventh *dong* rattled the room.

This was it; they were finally escaping. Milou was going to find her parents.

Sem's hand clasped the door handle as the eighth *dong* struck.

Milou heard a loud whinny from outside and her ear tips were assaulted by a pinch so sharp she cried out. 'Sem, don't –'

But Sem had already yanked the door wide open, letting in a cloud of oily smoke.

A large, ring-bedecked hand wafted the smoke away and a moustachioed face grinned down at them.

'Ah, *kindjes*,' Rotman said. 'I see you're all packed and ready to go.'

10

The children stared up at the merchant in silent horror as the ninth and final *dong* echoed round them. Milou clasped the pocket watch as her Sense prickled frantically at her scalp and neck.

The merchant's gold-toothed smile tightened. 'Aren't you going to let me in?'

A wave of icy shivers, colder even than the winter air blowing in from outside, ran down Milou's spine and urged her forward. She nudged Sem aside and glared up at Rotman.

'No,' she whispered.

Rotman's mustachios twitched.

'No,' Milou growled. Then, more bitingly: 'NO!'

She grabbed the edge of the door and swung it closed, but it crunched on something before she could close it fully. On the other side of it, Rotman roared in pain. Milou looked down to see the merchant's sealskin boot half inside, wedged at the ankle. He pushed at the door, knocking Milou backwards into Sem.

'You little –'

Hands appeared from behind her, reaching out to force the door back. The five of them pressed forward. Milou kicked at Rotman's foot until, finally, the sealskin boot was pulled away. The heavy front door closed with a thunderous *thunk*, rattling the windows and shutters to either side of it.

Sem slid the bolt across and they all took a step back.

Rotman pummelled the door. 'Open up!'

Milou peered out of the side window at him. He looked nothing short of murderous as he battered his fists against the door. Window shutters opened on the house across the road. Then more followed. Realizing he was being watched, Rotman stopped banging the door and straightened his tailcoat. He shot Milou a furious glare. Adjusting her coffin-basket on her hip, Milou closed the shutter again, looking helplessly at the others.

'There's no other way out,' Sem said. 'We're trapped.'

The doorbell *ding-donged*.

'The bucket winch!' Lotta said, spinning on her heels and dragging Milou towards the staircase with her.

Ding-dong-ding-dong.

They hurried up the steep stairs, baskets creaking, bucket and toolbox clunking, and wheatsack swinging as they ran. Milou grabbed the banister as she and Lotta skidded round the corner and thundered up the next set of stairs. The laundry room was lit by a thin column of moonlight streaming in through a broken slat in the shutters. It was a narrow squeeze past the tubs and tables to the small window.

'It'll probably take two at a time,' Lotta said, opening the window with an ear-splitting screech. The laundry bucket was already suspended on the other side, illuminated by the moonlight and swaying in the icy wind that blasted in at them. 'Egg and Fenna, you first.'

Egbert peered eagerly over the window ledge. He held a hand out to Fenna. 'Ready?'

The doorbell *ding-dong-ding-dong-ding-donged*.

Rotman was going to wake the other orphans at this rate. Not that they would be brave enough to go and investigate. They didn't know the matron was dead.

Fenna climbed up next to Egbert, the suspended basket swayed and the rope groaned. They climbed into the bucket together. It was a tight squeeze, especially with a picnic hamper and coal bucket in there, too.

'Ready?' Lotta said, then she began turning the crank handle.

Milou watched as the bucket descended with a *creeak-clunk-creeak-clunk*. She let out a long breath when it touched the ice and Egbert and Fenna began to climb out.

Lotta's arms spun quickly, the winch crank squealing as she wound it back up again. Milou slipped out of the coat they shared, her skin erupting with a million goosebumps.

Sem peered nervously over the edge. 'But the canal –'

'It's frozen, Sem,' Lotta said impatiently. 'If it can hold a hundred ice-skating families, it can hold five children. Now shush yourself and get in the bucket.'

Sem climbed in and Milou followed quickly behind, careful to keep her eyes only on the round bucket, ignoring the height and the biting wind that stabbed like an icy dagger at her exposed skin. The basket swayed from side to side and Sem wrapped half of his stolen fur coat round Milou's shoulders. Lotta passed them their coffin-basket and wheat sack, then piled her toolbox into Milou's arms.

'See you in a minute,' Lotta said.

'What about you?' Milou asked, suddenly fearful. 'You can't operate the crank and lower yourself down.'

Lotta gave her a wry smile. 'I'll need you to unlatch the bucket and then attach the hook, nice and taut, to the railings on the other side of the canal. OK?'

'But how –'

With a sudden grinding squeal, the bucket began to lower them down towards the canal. Sem's arms tightened round her so much Milou could barely breathe, but, before she could wriggle enough to get room to tell him off, the bucket hit the ice with a scratchy thud.

They scrambled out, Sem's limbs tangling with hers, and unhooked the bucket.

'I hope she has a plan,' Milou rasped, the cold night air catching in her throat.

They slipped and slid across the width of the frozen canal. Fenna climbed up the stone bank first, pulling Egbert over the iron railings. Milou gave her the hook and she clicked it on to the topmost rail.

'I'll help you up,' Sem said.

But Milou shook her head. 'Lotta –'

Lotta was a dark silhouette in the laundry-room window. Milou watched in awe-filled horror as Lotta reached up towards the taut line of rope, her hands wrapped in something Milou couldn't quite make out. Then she leaped into the air.

A scream lodged in the back of Milou's throat, but she swallowed it down. Lotta knew what she was doing. Lotta *always* knew what she was doing.

Lotta's coat billowed out around her as she slid down the rope and glided over the canal like some sort of nightmarish wraith. Milou's swallowed scream resurfaced as a delighted giggle. Lotta was *spectacular*. She hurtled down towards them at a dizzying speed and, just as her maniacally grinning face came into view, she let go and dropped to the ice. She landed, tangled in a mass of skirts and fur, with an *oof*.

'Stupid dresses,' she huffed as she straightened herself out. 'So impractical.'

Milou and Sem slid over to her and pulled her up. 'Are you all right?' Milou asked.

Nodding happily, Lotta stood on shaky legs, her pigtails in disarray and a wet rag in her left hand. She nodded and threw the rag aside. A few streets away, a whistle blew, then another.

'Rotman stopped ringing the doorbell,' she said, her face turning serious. 'We need to run.'

Sem boosted Milou up on to the pavement, then pulled himself up after her. Together they hoisted Lotta over the railings. Frost glistened on the cobblestones and the street was deserted, except for the wind that whistled over the canal and through the tiny gaps between the towering houses. The air was sharp, stinging Milou's lungs. The cold enveloped every part of her, clinging to her cheeks like tiny claws of ice. It made her jaw ache and her shoulders squeeze up towards her ears. She wriggled into Lotta's fur coat.

The five of them stood at the canal edge, staring up at the towering form of the orphanage just across the way.

'We're free,' Sem said, his voice a disbelieving whisper.

Milou hoisted her coffin-basket on to her other hip and used her free hand to tuck the pocket watch under her collar. 'Not quite yet. Which way next, Egg?'

Egbert had his pillowcase map held out in front of him and Fenna, his brown eyes glinting as he surveyed it. Then he tucked it under his arm and nodded towards a bridge at the other end of the street. 'That way.'

They had made it only a few steps when Milou's ears prickled urgently. A chill blew over her forehead. A mere moment later, they heard cartwheels scraping on nearby cobbles and a whip cracking.

She tugged Lotta towards a narrow gap between two houses, nudging the others ahead of her. Rotman's carriage rattled round the corner just as Milou pushed herself into the darkened alleyway. The horse snorted, its hoofbeats slowing. Peering carefully round the wall, Milou watched as Pieter pulled the carriage to a stop next to the railings, where the bucket-winch's rope was still hooked.

The door opened, emitting a puff of smoke, and Rotman stepped out. He limped up to the railings, reaching out to touch the rope which led right up to the still open laundry-room window. He looked up and down the street, the moonlight casting a silvery glow over his furious expression.

Milou ducked her head back into the shadows, her heart galloping.

'He knows we've left,' she whispered. 'And he's blocking our route.'

'We'll just have to go the long way round then,' Egbert whispered back. 'Follow me.'

They hurried through the narrow alleyway, huddled closely together in their fur coats. Egbert paused at the end and they all strained their ears. A cart passed by, its wheels squeaking with each rotation.

'That wasn't him,' Egbert whispered softly. He leaned forward. 'I think it's clear now.'

Milou felt a little tingle at the base of her spine. 'Go. Quick.'

They darted across the street, their boots tapping a hurried rhythm, and into the next alleyway. They walked quickly with Egbert and Fenna at the front, over bridge after bridge, each canal a frozen sheet of glimmering ice. The canal houses had always reminded Milou of Sem: tall, gangly, peculiarly proportioned, yet full of character and charm. But she realized that looking down at Amsterdam from the dormitory window was one thing. To be walking its streets for the first time in her life was something else entirely. From down on the ground, the pointed, jagged roofs loomed like gaping jaws. Milou felt as if they were being swallowed up by the city. The canals all looked identical, as did the bridges. It was as if they were running round in circles, trapped in a maze, but Egbert led them with confidence, turning his pillowcase map this way and that.

After a short but heart-galloping while, Egbert came to a sudden halt. His face was lost in the shadows, but Milou heard his sharp intake of breath.

'We're here,' he said, pointing to a canal house across the street. 'Kerkstraat 189.'

Much like the Little Tulip, Kerkstraat 189 was built of black bricks, its windows painted white in contrast. An octagonal sign dangled from a wrought-iron bar sticking out above the door. Milou squinted up at it.

BRAAKENSIEK EN ZOON

Lithographer &
Maker of Maps

'I heard one of our neighbours talk about this place a few months ago,' Egbert said. 'It took me weeks to find. I had to climb across four other rooftops to spot it and add it to my map. Look.'

There, in the ground-floor window, lit up by the moonlight, were several large maps.

Tingles danced across Milou's ear tips and a giggle escaped her lips. She and Egbert shared a delighted smile. They checked the street was empty, then emerged from the alleyway and huddled in front of the window. Egbert's expression was nothing short of reverential.

'Is that really what *Nederland* looks like?' Milou asked, pointing to one of the maps. 'It's a bit like a rabbit's head.'

'That's just the northern province,' Egbert said, setting his coal bucket by his feet. 'Here, we want this one.'

He pointed to a map of Amsterdam, running his fingers over the glass as he surveyed it. Finally, he jammed his finger on a point south-west of the city. 'That's it right there. We can follow the Amstel River down here for a few kilomctres, then head west. If I copy this section of the map, I can probably get us fairly near to your coordinates.'

'Fairly near?' Milou asked, clasping the pocket watch tightly. 'How are we going to find the exact spot?'

Lotta stepped up beside Egbert. She tapped her forefinger against the bottom corner of the map. 'Using this scale.' Then she tapped a point near the coordinates, at a tiny junction. 'Egg just needs to get us to the start of this road here. I can get us to the exact spot.'

'How?'

Lotta smiled. 'Maths, of course.' She took a tape measure out of her toolbox and handed it to Sem. 'Here. Measure my stride, from rear heel to front toe.'

Lotta stepped one foot forward and held her pose as Sem measured the distance between her feet. Milou rubbed her arms for warmth as Lotta and Sem repeated their measurements a few more times. After just a few minutes, Egbert had finished his map and Sem was handing the tape measure back.

'Don't you need to make your ... calculations?' Milou asked Lotta.

'It's fine. I'll do the maths while we walk. Come on, we should hurry.'

They were already limping by the time they reached the Amstel River, just as a distant church clock tower chimed ten o'clock. Milou felt as if her coffin-basket had a heavy body inside it; her arms ached as much as her empty stomach. The river meandered past factories and warehouses. Every now and again, they would hide behind whatever they could find as a boat went past, but, for the most part, the snow-shrouded streets were empty as the people of Amsterdam sought shelter from the cold.

Milou and Lotta leaned heavily on each other as they crossed a bridge on the very outskirts of the city, and finally stepped out into the first slice of open country they had ever seen.

'It's like the fields have been rolled flat with a giant rolling pin,' Milou said. She blew snow from her eyelashes and huddled closer to Lotta.

'And the c-canals drawn in precisely with a g-giant ruler,' Sem said, teeth chattering.

Now that they'd left the city the air no longer smelled of stagnant water and horse dung. It was so fresh it tickled Milou's nostrils. They shuffled along deserted dirt road after deserted dirt road for what felt like hours, the houses becoming shorter and wider and spread further apart the further they got from the city.

They were halfway down a painfully long, completely houseless road when Egbert came to a sudden halt.

'Here's your junction, Lot,' he wheezed and pointed down a road that ran perpendicular to the one they were on. 'Milou's coordinates lead that way.'

The road stretched endlessly ahead of them, flanked on either side by criss-crossing canals and a patchwork of fields, with a smattering of farmhouses that Milou could just about make out by the light from their windows. She had spent her entire life wanting more space, but right then she'd have given anything to not have to walk another step more.

'Have you worked out the distance?' Milou asked Lotta breathlessly.

'Of course I have.' Lotta swayed slightly with exhaustion, but she shook herself and straightened up. 'One thousand, four hundred and seventy-three strides.'

Four groans sounded.

Lotta took a step forward, wobbling precariously. Milou grabbed her elbow with her free hand, careful not to get her feet in the way of Lotta's stride. They walked on, feet dragging and breathing raggedly, as Lotta counted quietly, then silently, to herself.

As they passed a pyramid-roofed farmhouse, Milou's heart gave a little flutter of anticipation. Further down the road, they passed another farmhouse, smoke pluming out of its chimney, and Milou's hope burned stronger.

The mist rising from the canals thickened as they walked, first curling round their ankles, then up to their knees. Then it seemed to draw over them from the horizon. Soon they would only be able to see the next farmhouse when they were right beside it.

'We'll be warm soon,' Milou promised. 'They probably have fresh, creamy milk we can heat up. And plenty of blankets and a roaring fire. I'm a little tired, so I might not be able to tell a bedtime story, but I'm sure either my mother or father will.'

They passed another farmhouse. It had the same pyramid-shaped roof as the others, but, instead of brown thatch, this one had a bright copper roof. Instead of the usual red and white, its shutters were a bright, bold blue. And, instead of a plain wooden gate at the end of its bridge, it had a stone gargoyle on each post.

It looked both ridiculous and wondrous at the same time, and nothing like anything Milou's imagination could have conjured up after a lifetime of seeing nothing but towering townhouses. Her heart sank just a little when they walked past it without stopping.

They didn't make it much further down the road, however. Lotta came to a sudden halt mid-step, leaning heavily on Milou.

Milou sagged beneath the added weight. 'Come on, Lot, it can't be much further.'

Lotta shrugged herself free. 'No. We're here.' She lifted an arm and pointed weakly to the side of the road. 'Your coordinates,' she said breathlessly. 'Right there.'

Milou looked to where she was indicating and frowned.

Lotta was pointing to a tree.

12

Tingles erupted all over Milou's scalp as she craned her neck to look more closely. The top half of the tree emerged from the mist in long, twisting, gnarled branches. It was leafless, frost-covered and entirely not what Milou had expected. She shook her head. This couldn't be right.

'Maybe you miscounted –'

Lotta huffed indignantly.

'I did *not* miscount.'

Sem sighed heavily.

'It must be the copper-roofed farmhouse,' Milou said, ignoring him. 'This tree is so close.'

'Milou,' Sem said half impatiently, half pityingly. 'I'm sorry, I really am, but this so-called clue of yours is futile. There's nothing here.'

'No!' A shiver of despair coursed through her. 'You're wrong, Sem. There must be something –'

'Over here!' called a disembodied voice from the mist beyond. 'I've found it!'

Milou looked at the others. Egbert and Fenna had been standing with them moments before, but now they were gone.

'Just carry on further down the road a little way!' he called out. 'Hurry, I'm freezing!'

Milou, Lotta and Sem shuffled forward, as quickly as their aching legs could manage, and found Egbert and Fenna standing at the canal edge in front of a set of gates. The gates were not like any of the others they had passed, not even the one with the gargoyles. They were, Milou decided, like the gates of a graveyard. Her heart felt like it was about to leap out of her mouth.

Rusted iron railings rose like spears from the ground, their painted-gold tips gleaming in the moonlight. Ivy creepers curled round the two tall posts on either side and a heavy rusted padlock hung from a chain that had been wrapped round the middle of the gate several times. Above it was a weathered wooden sign. Milou stepped closer and saw that it said: POPPENMILL. Except the word POPPEN had been scratched out and replaced with GHOST. And then below that, in the same scratchy scrawl, someone had etched: DANGER! KEEP OUT!

She pressed her face up against the gates and squinted into the gloom, but the mist was now too thick. She couldn't see any red-and-white shutters, nor a triangular roof.

'Where is it?' she asked in frustration.

'Look up,' Sem said breathlessly.

Milou followed his wide-eyed gaze to where the mist had opened slightly above them. Emerging through the gloom, further back from the road than the farmhouses had been, was the shadowy cross of skeletal sails.

A thrill coursed through Milou's aching body as she realized what she was seeing.

It wasn't a farmhouse at all. It was a *windmill*.

The fog drew back in, and the windmill's sails disappeared again, but this did nothing to cloud Milou's delight. The pocket watch had led her *home*.

Goosebumps danced all over her arms and neck and her ears tingled pleasantly. Not a warning this time, she thought, but an encouragement, urging her forward. She had a good feeling about this place.

'I have a bad feeling about this place,' Lotta grumbled beside her. 'It looks –'

'Old,' Sem whispered.

'Haunted,' Egbert said, eliciting a tiny gasp from Fenna.

'Perfect,' breathed Milou.

'I was going to say uninviting,' Lotta said. 'The gate's padlocked, there are no lights on and the sign isn't exactly welcoming.'

'They've probably just gone to bed. Come on, there'll be food and warmth inside.'

And my parents, she thought.

She resisted shooting Sem an I-told-you-so look and, instead, approached the thin canal that ran either side of the entrance and underneath the wooden bridge upon which the gates stood. Hefting her coffin-basket up on to her shoulder, she edged herself and Lotta towards the ice. It was too low for her to step down on to, so, hoping for the best, she jumped down, pulling Lotta with her. Their feet landed with a solid thud, but the frozen canal did not crack.

'Milou!' Sem called out. 'I'm not sure this is a good idea. The sign says –'

'That sign is for other people, not family,' Milou said over her shoulder. 'Come *on*.'

The sound of feet dropping on to the ice behind her was the only response she received. With her free hand, Milou grabbed the iron post and pulled herself and Lotta up on to the bank on the other side of the gates. Egbert, Sem and Fenna followed a moment later. Fresh snow crunched loudly beneath them as they edged almost blindly towards the mill.

As they got closer, all Milou could see was the red brick wall of the lowest level.

It took them a few minutes to find the front door. There was a scratch and a hiss as Sem struck a match and passed a candle to Milou. She held it up. The door was made of equal parts thick oak and peeling black paint. Two glass lanterns, held up by iron hands, hung on either side, unlit and shattered. In the middle of the door was a knocker, an iron ring gripped in the mouth of a lion.

A thrill of delight ran through her. This was the moment she had waited twelve long years for. Her family were a mere heartbeat away.

Milou had to stretch up on tiptoes to reach the knocker. She wrapped her frozen fingers round the ring and gave three short, sharp knocks, loud in the eerily calm night. She held her breath, listening intently for the sound of approaching footsteps, trying to picture the look of surprise on her parents' faces when they opened the door and found her standing there. Would it be her mother or her father who answered? Would they recognize her? Of course they would. Just as she would recognize them.

She waited, biting her lip, but the silence rang on, loud and deafening. Her smile faltered. She rattled the handle and the door swung inward, groaning as it opened fully. Darkness greeted them and the candle puffed out.

'I don't want to go in there,' Egbert whispered nervously, his and Fenna's worried faces peeking out of the top of their shared coat.

'There's nothing to worry about,' Milou said and stepped out of the furcoat she was sharing with Lotta, ignoring the sharp sting of cold.

'Hang on,' said Sem.

Milou thought he was going to try to stop her, and she readied herself for another argument, but he just rummaged in his wheat sack and produced some more matches and candles, handed them out to the others, then relit Milou's and gave her a smile of encouragement. Huddling close, they held their candles above their heads, forming a halo of light around them, and stepped inside.

They entered a small, square hallway. A row of clogs hung from hooks beside the door. Milou took another step and caught sight of a figure in the deep darkness beside a cupboard. Her candle flickered as she spun towards it, shadows dancing wildly across the stone floor.

'Papa . . .?'

Her voice died as the shadows stilled. Milou realized it wasn't a figure at all, but a coat stand, a cap balanced at a jaunty angle on top.

She hurried onward, through a low doorway to the left that led into a kitchen that was not quite a semi-circle.

Against the middle wall was a stove, pots and pans dangling from hooks above it. A small table with two chairs sat beneath the window. Milou held the lantern higher. A tall wardrobe and two smaller cabinets were lined neatly along one wall, next to a sink. And a cupboard bed, its doors wide open, took up almost the entirety of the other. Milou could see it was empty, its bright green quilt tucked neatly in.

Milou licked her dry, cracked lips. 'Papa? Mama? It's me . . . it's Milou.'

She put her coffin-basket down on the table and ran her finger over the back of one of the chairs. Her fingertip came away coated in a thick layer of black dust. She squinted into the deep shadows and took another step; something crunched beneath her boot. Smashed crockery littered the floor.

'What a mess,' Lotta said. 'I wonder what happened.'

'They're probably just too busy to clean,' Milou said. 'They'll be thrilled to know I can help them with the housework now that I'm back.'

She walked briskly towards the next doorway, into a similarly proportioned living room. There was a fireplace in the middle wall this time, cold and empty, its mantel just as bare. Two rocking chairs sat opposite it, in front of another window, blankets draped over the backs and thick cushions on the seats. There were bookcases filled with tomes and another cupboard bed, its mahogany doors closed.

Giving Lotta her candle and opened the cupboard-bed doors. She found herself staring at a red quilted bed this time, as cold and empty as the first one. A small gasp of despair left her lips.

'Milou,' Egbert said. 'Perhaps we should come back –'

But Milou was hurrying through the next door, only to find herself back in the hallway they had started in, having lapped the ground floor entirely.

She looked despairingly at her friends. 'They'll be upstairs no doubt.'

Then she took the candle back from Lotta, hurried towards the ladder and climbed, breathless and swaying with exhaustion, up to the next floor. The walls were rounder upstairs, with a small landing and a single door blocking off the room beyond.

Milou pushed it open. A white face greeted her from beyond the door, its head flopped slightly to the side. Milou's heart seemed to stop entirely.

Then she saw that the face had a snout.

And pointed ears.

And . . . stitches all over its . . . *cotton* skin.

Milou squinted at the figure. Its eyes were painted. On the tip of its snout was a button. There was stuffing sticking out of the side of its neck and it was wearing a finely tailored suit of soft Amsterdam velvet, in a deep shade of burgundy.

Lotta and Sem emerged from the ladder shaft to stand beside her, their faces as pale as the one before them.

'It's a puppet,' Milou said, a giggle of hope bursting from her lips. 'A fox puppet.' She could see strings now, suspending the puppet from a hook on the side of some shelving. 'This is definitely the right place.'

She stepped in and looked round the circular room. The dust was thicker up here and Milou gagged on a cloud of it, waving it away from her candlelight to get a look at the room. Running down the middle, from a hole through the ceiling, was a thick, square wooden shaft. The rounded thatched walls were covered in puppets of all shapes and sizes. There were rolls of fabric, spools of string, tools, a desk filled with paintbrushes and paint pots, and a cast-iron sewing machine.

Bram Poppenmaker's puppet-making workshop.

'We're only halfway up the windmill,' she whispered, the room swaying beneath her weary legs. 'They'll be upstairs.'

They had to be.

With renewed hope, Milou ran across the room towards a ladder that led up to a large, rectangular hole in the puppet-room ceiling. Her arms and legs ached as she hauled herself up on to the first rung, her candle nearly losing its flame.

Lotta reached for her. 'Milou –' But Milou was already scaling the ladder.

As she crawled through to the next level, her head hit something hard as she tried to stand. Milou hissed, dropping to a crouch and feeling her way towards an empty place to sit. As the dust settled and her candle flame stilled, Milou realized why there was barely any room to move: huge wooden cogwheels interconnected, horizontally and vertically, in a complex array from the ceiling right down to the floor.

There was a thud and then another hiss of pain as Lotta emerged through the hatch and crawled towards her.

'Holy Gouda,' Lotta breathed, staring up at the mechanisms with her mouth hanging open.

Milou stood, carefully, and held the candle up to the domed ceiling, illuminating more shadows and more dust, but no ladders or stairwells.

This was the very top of the windmill; there were no more rooms for her to search.

Milou shoulders drooped, as if her invisible puppet strings had been snipped clean, and her legs finally collapsed under her. Her knees hit the floor hard, but the pain of it hurt less than the way her heart seemed to be squeezing in on itself.

'Oh, Lotta,' Milou said, her voice cracking. 'They're gone.'

13

Milou was only vaguely aware of being led by Lotta and Sem back down to the kitchen. Her eyes were wet and, despite the fur coat now draped round her shoulders, a numbness had settled heavily over her, making it almost impossible to walk.

Sem had been right. She'd come all this way for nothing. The Poppenmakers were gone.

Her friends' voices sounded muffled behind the raging despair in Milou's mind.

'What's wrong?' Egbert was asking.

'Milou needs to sleep this ordeal off,' Lotta was saying. 'Help me get her into bed.'

Milou was ushered into the green-quilted cupboard bed by Lotta and Sem. It smelled musty, but it was softer than anything she had ever laid on. Fenna was already in there – she pulled Milou close and wrapped her arms round her, resting her chin on Milou's brow. The blankets were heavy, but not scratchy in the slightest. Despite all this, Milou still could not stop shaking.

'They're gone.' The voice sounded like her own, but it was far too high-pitched and raw to be, surely?

Egbert's face appeared. 'It'll be all right, Milou,' he said softly. 'We'll be all right. I promise.'

Then Lotta was beside her, too, more arms enveloped her, and Milou's tear-blurred eyes lost their battle to stay open.

Milou woke to sunlight. She'd somehow slept through the dawn bell. Gassbeek was going to kill her. Panic filled her and she scrambled backwards, blinking furiously, trying to work out why the dormitory seemed much, much smaller and her bed much, much bigger. Gone were the draughty eaves, replaced with a low, mahogany ceiling. The brown, threadbare blanket she was used to had somehow been transformed into multiple layers of blanket and a bright green quilt.

The memory of the previous night came creeping back.

Gassbeek was dead. Milou was home. Her family were gone.

Just as her heart began to break again, she spotted that above her head, sitting on a low shelf, was her cat puppet, its head sewn back on so deftly that it could only have been done by Sem. She shuffled upward and pulled the pocket watch free from beneath her collar, rubbing a thumb over the inscription.

> *Beneath the stars I found you.*
> 52.284040, 4.784040
> *Under the moon I lost you.*

Even after following the coordinates all this way, Milou was still lost to them.

Fenna and Lotta stirred, looking up at her through sleep-heavy lids.

'Milou?' Lotta spoke gruffly, one pigtail sticking out vertically from the side of her head, the other loose entirely. 'What is it?'

'Nothing,' Milou whispered, climbing over Lotta. 'I just need some fresh air.'

Lotta yawned in response, her lids drooping closed again. Fenna, however, scrambled out to join Milou as she peered through the doorway into the next room. The boys were still sleeping soundly in the other cupboard bed in the living room: Sem face down, one long arm dangling to the floor, and Egbert resting his head on his carefully folded, soot-stained shawl. Milou closed the door quietly again so as not to disturb them.

Compared to the gloominess of the night before, the kitchen looked radiant. The shadows were gone, but the thick dust remained, curling round the shafts of sunlight and sticking to every surface.

Milou began opening smaller cupboard doors near the sink. There was no food; only more dust. She tiptoed over to the wardrobe and opened one door. Her breath caught at the sight of the clothing that hung on one side. Men's shirts, jackets, trousers – all finely made, practical and gentlemanly. On the other side, Milou found an entire rail of dresses, cloaks and scarves, again finely made, but surprisingly small and . . . youthful-looking.

Sighing, Milou gazed round the sun-dappled, debris-strewn room. Her ears, neck and shoulders tingled in a way she had never felt before; she felt a coldness that somehow, impossibly, warmed her – easing the tightness in her chest ever so slightly.

At least she was *home*, she told herself, even if her parents were not.

'I'm going to find them, Fen,' Milou whispered. 'I've a whole windmill full of new clues now, which means I'm closer to finding them now than I was yesterday.'

Milou reached into her mother's side of the wardrobe and selected a long green cloak – which was only slightly too big for her – and wrapped it round her shoulders. Then she found a red one for Fenna to wear and thick cotton socks to cover their frozen feet. She cast a quick look at her sleeping friends and then took Fenna's hand.

'Come on, let's search this place from top to bottom.'

The mechanism room was still dark, still empty. Despite this, Milou and Fenna climbed up and round every single cogwheel to check for clues. But there were no stray midnight-dark hairs or hidden messages carved into the wood for Milou to find. The walls groaned and, high up in the dome, something scratched and shuffled in the thick thatch.

The only thing Milou could find of any interest was a small, square door in the wall. She had to work the latch with all her strength. It finally slid open and she carefully pushed at the door – which opened out into the sky. Cold air rushed in and, when Milou saw just how high up she was, dizziness overwhelmed her.

The low-lying land of the polder looked entirely different in the light of day: a milky patchwork of frostbitten fields, criss-crossed with canals. Thatched barns were dotted around between the farmhouses, cows grazed in the icy fields and cyclists moved slowly up and down the road, waving to one another as they passed. Everything was so spread out and peaceful, unlike the crammed, busy city she was used to.

From this distance, Amsterdam was just a line of grey with a cloud of darker grey above it. Had they really walked all that way?

Milou closed the door, sealing the outside world off once more. She saw that Fenna had climbed to the very top of the room, her gaze fixed on the noise above.

Scratch. Scratch. Scratch.

'It's probably just a bird's nest, Fen,' Milou said. 'A pigeon most like.'

Fenna sighed and nodded, then clambered back down, wiping dust from her legs.

'I think we can safely say there are no clues up here,' Milou said. 'Let's go and find something *useful.*'

Milou nudged Fenna towards the ladder, down to the puppet-making workshop. She had been steeling herself to explore this room, but, even so, the sight of the puppets her father had crafted sent fresh waves of despair coursing through her. Everything was left out just so, as if the Poppenmakers had merely stepped out for the day. And yet the thick dust coating everything showed that it had certainly been much longer than a day, or a week, or even a year.

Milou approached the desk – and something lying beside it caught her eye. It was a picture frame, its glass fractured as if it had been thrown to the ground with force. She picked it up carefully and blew the dust away.

Inside was a child's portrait of a man. His face was potato-shaped, one eye twice as large as the other. His nose was a backwards L, and he was either wearing an upside-down bucket on his head or a top hat, Milou couldn't quite tell. The only thing she could see for certain about this man was that he was happy; his banana smile stretched all the way up to his plum-sized ears. Below the portrait, in scrawling writing, was a poem:

Dearest Papa,
Your smile is the stuff of which dreams are made,
Your eyes are two shimmering stars,
Your heart is my centre of gravity,
And no love is as huge as ours.

In the corner of the page, in a slightly messier hand, someone had written:

By Liesel, 1872, aged 10

The portrait was twenty years old. Milou's ear tips prickled. Her breath hitched.

'I . . . I think Bram Poppenmaker has another –' Milou swallowed. 'He has another daughter.'

She handed the picture to Fenna, who read it silently.

'I suppose that explains the dresses.' Milou bit the inside of her cheek to stop more tears from falling. 'I have an older sister. A daughter he *kept*.'

Once again, her ears prickled sharply and unpleasantly. Milou rubbed them hard, determined not to cry. There would be a logical explanation for all this. Somewhere. She just needed to keep searching.

She turned back to the room and rummaged through every drawer, every shelf, every nook. There were no letters, no photographs, no personal documents at all. She dug into the stuffing of every puppet, looking for more hidden items or messages, but found nothing. She checked for loose floorboards or other secret compartments.

Nothing.

And it was as if her mother had never existed in the first place. No poems, no portraits, nothing at all to suggest a third person lived here. Nothing to suggest a baby – her – had lived here, either. Milou's fingers shook as she wrote down the few clues she had found. Then she snapped her Book of Theories closed and headed down to continue her search in the kitchen.

By now the others were awake, and dressed in Bram and Liesel's clothing.

'I hope you don't mind,' Sem said, sheepishly tugging at the collar of the striped shirt he wore. 'It's just so cold.'

'Of course not,' Milou said, rummaging through the drawers beneath the green quilt bed. There had to be more clues somewhere. 'I'm sure my father won't mind, Sem.'

'I found this,' he said, sitting on the bed beside her.

He was clutching a small stack of newspapers. Milou took them from him, blowing off the dust.

'They're all dated 1880,' Sem whispered. 'The most recent one is December 1880,' he added. 'When you were . . .'

Milou nodded in understanding, her throat constricted with emotion. They'd abandoned the windmill the very month Milou had been left on the Little Tulip's rooftop.

'Thanks, Sem,' Milou said, jotting it down in her notebook. 'That helps a lot.'

He gave her a tight, uneasy smile. 'I still think you should be prepared for disappointment –'

'I've had nothing *but* disappointment up until now, Sem, so what's a little more going to matter? Good or bad, I *need* to know what happened. I need answers.'

'There are so many books here,' Lotta said, as she peered through the doorway into the other room. 'It would take me months to read them all.'

'Well,' Milou said, pulling herself together and standing, 'you've got plenty of time to read them now we don't have to break our backs doing chores all day, every day. Though, of course, this place does need smartening up –'

'We can't stay here,' Egbert said. He was sitting by the window, paper on his lap and a charcoal stick in his fingers, drawing.

'What do you mean?' Milou asked.

Egbert grimaced. 'I'm sorry, Milou, but we can't stay if your parents aren't here.'

'But –'

'Egg's right,' Sem said. 'Five orphans living in an abandoned windmill with no adult in sight is going to draw attention from the neighbours.'

'We can just tell them that my parents –'

'They won't believe us.'

'Then we'll just keep ourselves hidden,' Milou insisted. 'No one needs to know we're here.'

Lotta shook her head. 'We can't hide smoke from the fireplace, and we can't stay indoors indefinitely. It's just not practical and it's too big a risk. There may not be as many neighbours here as we had in the city, but there are enough of them to ask questions.'

'But –'

'They might alert the Kinderbureau,' Egbert said. 'If your parents aren't coming back any time soon, then there's no one to stop us being dragged back to the orphanage and blamed for Gassbeek's death.'

Milou didn't have an answer to that. Her parents were supposed to be have been here to solve everything for them.

'There's no harm in staying one more night,' Lotta said. 'That gives Milou time to search for clues, for us to gather what we can to take with us, and an opportunity to think of where on earth we should go next.' She blew out through pursed lips. 'I suppose I can at least read a few books in that time.'

Milou sank on to the window ledge by Egbert, resigned and defeated. She pressed her cheek against the cold glass and peered out at the winter-ravaged polder, which now seemed as utterly miserable and desolate as she felt. The only colour in sight was the strange copper roof of the farmhouse next door.

'It's a shame we can't stay,' Egbert said softly. 'There are so many wonderful things to draw and paint. Like that barn. I wonder why the Poppenmakers used such grand doors for an outbuilding. They're nothing like the simple wooden doors on all the others.'

Milou looked at his drawing, then out of the window and saw that he was right. The Poppenmill barn did have unusually ornate mahogany doors carved with swirling, flowering vines, much like the ones on the cupboard beds.

Tingles erupted all over her scalp and, before she even realized it, she was running out of the front door, the wind whipping at her as she hurried down the weed-ridden gravel path to the barn door. Panting and shivering, she tugged on it. The hinges screeched, and dust erupted around her.

She stepped inside, her feet touching a spongy floor. Milou looked down at the red carpet. She waved cobwebs away as she took another step forward, only to bump into something. A velvet chair.

She blinked her eyes until they adjusted to the gloom, then realized there wasn't just one velvet chair, but rows and rows of them. Milou staggered past them, down a narrow aisle, and stopped in the middle of the barn, directly beneath a huge gaping hole in the ceiling, through which the morning sunlight streamed. At the far end was a huge stage, its tattered, moth-eaten curtains closed.

Milou's heart skipped in double time when she realized what she was seeing.

It was a theatre. And there, behind the curtains, was the unmistakable silhouette of someone standing on the stage, arms stretched out towards her.

Milou's Book of Theories

New Evidence

- My parents left me a pocket watch engraved with a riddle and coordinates, hidden in my cat puppet. It led me home, but they're not here.
- Front gates chained with a rusted padlock. The sign has been vandalized, claiming that this windmill is haunted and dangerous.
- The windmill is empty of people, but not empty of their belongings.
- Clothes belonging to a man, my father, and to a girl, my sister.
- Portrait and poem made by Bram's other daughter, Liesel.
- Newspaper stack by front door: all dated from twelve years ago ... the year and month I was abandoned.

<u>Missing Evidence</u>

- No hidden messages.
- No photographs.
- No hint at where they have gone.
- No sign of my mother.
- No sign of a baby (me).

Perhaps, if I solve the pocket-watch riddle, I'll know how to find them.

14

Milou ran down the theatre aisle and leaped on to the front of the stage. The withered curtains fell from their rails as she tugged them open, draping over her. She frantically disentangled herself.

A girl stood before her: feet pointed, arms held out in a ballerina's pose.

A girl with large, unblinking eyes and bright pink lips.

A girl made of cotton and suspended on strings.

A puppet.

Milou silently scolded herself. She was a fool to have thought it could be anything else. Or any*one* else.

Warm, salty tears slid into the side of her mouth.

'Milou!' Lotta called out from behind her. 'What were you thinking? You could have been seen – Holy Gouda!'

Milou quickly wiped her cheeks and faced the others. They were all gawking at the theatre.

'This place is amazing!' Egbert said, turning in slow circles as he made his way down the aisle.

Sem was the only one looking at Milou. 'Are you all right?'

He glanced at the ballerina puppet, his worried expression transforming into a sympathetic one.

Milou blushed, then stepped round the puppet and into the shadowed area of the stage. To one side was a pile of wooden planks and half-finished set pieces – all stacked up precariously. On the other side there was a large wooden ladder leading up to a puppeteering platform above the stage. Milou made her way towards it, then stopped, her ears tingling from tip to lobe.

A lump of blankets lay, crumpled and frosted over, in the far corner of the stage. Milou's ears prickled sharply and her heart thumped. She nudged the pile with her foot and it rolled open, revealing nothing but more blankets.

Milou rubbed at her ears. Her Sense didn't seem to be helping much at the moment.

'Look,' Sem said, his voice tight.

He pushed the blankets further aside and Milou gasped. Claw marks. Just like the ones on her basket.

'What if I'm too late?' Milou said quietly. 'What if they're –'

'If they were dead, the windmill would have been cleared of their stuff and sold,' Sem said. 'And they wouldn't have left you the pocket watch to find them, either.'

Milou hoped he was right.

'It's all so . . . confusing,' she said. 'I need to find out what happened.'

'I know you do.'

'This place really is full of possibility,' Lotta said, sitting down on one of the many velvet chairs. 'It's a shame we can't stay. I'm certain I could get the mill working again. Imagine all the things you could bake, Fenna, if we could grind our own grain.'

Fenna smiled ruefully.

'I'd love to learn how to use that sewing machine in the workshop,' Sem said. 'I've always dreamed of having one.'

'If only I'd found the pocket watch sooner,' Milou said glumly. 'Perhaps my father might have still been here. It's not fair that I've finally found my home and I can't even stay in it.'

Silence fell, dust motes danced, the frost-covered marionette sparkled.

'What if Bram Poppenmaker *was* here,' Egbert said suddenly. He had climbed on to the stage and was circling the puppet.

'But he *isn't*,' Lotta said.

Egbert grinned. 'But what if he *was*.'

'Egbert!' Lotta looked up at the hole-riddled ceiling in frustration. 'You're making less sense than a square cheese.'

'What are you thinking, Egg' Milou asked, recognizing the glint in his eye. It was the same look he got whenever he thought up a new project or painting.

Egbert reached up and tugged on the puppet's string, making her wave. 'We could *make* a father.'

They all frowned up at him.

'A *puppet* father.' Egbert's smile turned wistful. 'Do you remember that time I painted a gaping wound on Milou's forehead and Lotta nearly fainted when she saw it?'

Lotta huffed. 'It looked real.'

'That's my point,' Egbert said. 'We could create a convincing illusion.'

'Like when the matron –' Sem started, then stopped.

Silence fell as they all thought back to the awful events of the previous night. Gassbeek had been so convinced by a mere shadow that she'd been frightened to death.

'We trick people into thinking Bram has returned?' Milou said. 'And, that way, the neighbours will leave us be?'

'What about Rotman?' Sem asked. 'Suppose he comes looking for us? He's lost his workforce, and we hurt his foot – he didn't seem too pleased about that.'

'Rotman needs doctored paperwork to get us past the dock officials,' Lotta said. 'With Gassbeek gone, he doesn't have that option. And he wouldn't risk exposing their *deal*.

No, I think our biggest concern is the Kinderbureau. If they ever found out what we've done –'

'There's no reason for them to doubt the record book,' Milou said. 'As long as our neighbours don't suspect anything, the Kinderbureau will have no reason to come here – they'll be far too busy trying to deal with replacing Gassbeek anyway. All we need to do is convince people here that he's come home, and that he's taken us all in.'

Lotta's mouth opened as if to protest, then snapped closed again.

'That might actually work,' she said finally. 'We could make sure he's just visible through the windows, as long as we don't let anyone get too close a look. If anyone does come around, we'll have to make sure they don't step foot inside the mill.'

'If nothing else,' Milou said, 'it will buy me more time to find my parents. Once they're back here for real, we'll be safe.'

'And it gives us more freedom to work out another plan if we do have to leave,' Egbert added.

'We need money for food,' Sem said gravely. 'There's no food here and Fenna only managed to grab a stale loaf of bread, a few potatoes and a carrot before we fled. It's all very well having shelter, but that won't stop us from starving to death.'

'We could sell some stuff,' Egbert suggested. 'The silverware maybe?'

'No!' said Milou. 'We can't sell anything that doesn't belong to us.'

'We could make something to sell at the market,' Sem offered. 'Some puppets perhaps?'

'There's two problems with that,' Lotta mused. 'Firstly, selling Poppenmaker puppets will draw too much attention to us. Secondly, the markets are in the city. If we go into Amsterdam, we risk being recognized by any adopted orphan that still lives there, or anyone else who knows us from the Little Tulip – the deliverymen, for example.'

'If we dress smartly and make sure our faces are partially covered by scarves, no one will recognize us.' Sem smiled. 'I could make dolls to sell instead of puppets. We have all the materials for that and we can always restock Meneer Poppenmaker's supplies as soon as we can afford to.'

'So, we won't leave?' Milou asked. 'I'll find my parents, and we'll sell dolls to make money in the meantime. Everyone agreed? Fen?'

Fenna nodded a yes.

'What are we waiting for?' Milou said, a thrill blooming inside her still-aching heart. 'Let's go build ourselves a father!'

They sneaked back into the windmill, ducking briefly behind the oak tree to avoid being seen by a passing cyclist, and then filled their empty bellies with the last of the stale bread that Fenna had taken from the Little Tulip's kitchen.

'Is this the only picture you could find?' Egbert asked dubiously, holding Liesel's portrait of Bram.

Milou nodded. 'Yes, that's all I have. Sem, you can use some of my father's long johns for the body. Egbert, use whichever paints you need. I'll find him an outfit to wear.'

'Fen and I will remove the padlock from the gate and then clean,' Lotta said. 'We can't live in all this dust. And I'm going to start a fire. I'm fed up with not being able to feel my toes.'

By the time dusk settled, flames were popping and crackling in the fireplace, casting an amber glow around the kitchen, and the children's puppet-father ruse was almost complete.

Lotta hummed happily as she placed another log on and held her hands up to the heat. 'Holy Gouda, that feels good,' she sighed, wriggling all twelve fingers. 'Perhaps we could heat enough water for some baths tomorrow.'

Milou's skin tingled with both warmth and delight as she stood back to examine Sem and Egbert's handiwork.

'I think you got the potato-shaped face just right, Sem,' Milou said. 'And Egg, the eyes you painted are perfectly mismatched.'

The puppet-father was as tall as Sem, with long limbs made of long johns filled with stuffing. Using Bram's sewing machine, Sem had stitched the head from a plain piece of cotton, and Egbert had painted its features. The puppet was wearing brown wool trousers, a green button-down shirt, a woollen hat and a black velvet jacket.

'It'll do nicely,' said Milou. 'If you squint, he looks real.'

Lotta came to stand next to her and Milou noticed her friend's eyes had gone slightly watery.

'He looks splendid,' Lotta said, taking the puppet's hand in her own and placing a kiss on it. 'It's a pleasure to meet you, Papa.'

Sem lifted Puppet-Papa from a hook on the wall and sat it in a chair by the kitchen table. Milou climbed on to the table and grabbed the two wooden crosses from which twelve strings connected to Puppet-Papa's limbs. She flicked one of the crosses upward and Puppet-Papa's arm lifted. With a couple of gentle manoeuvres, the puppet was picking its nose.

Sem rolled his eyes as Lotta laughed.

'Can you make him walk?' Egbert asked.

Milou held her arms wider, in a proper puppet-master pose, and began to jiggle the crosses. After a few moments of Puppet-Papa looking like he was frantically trying to shake a spider from his person, Milou had him moving in a stationary walking position.

'Bravo!' Egbert giggled.

Milou smiled. 'Watch this.'

She jiggled the crosses some more until Puppet-Papa was doing something that resembled a dance – arms waving above his head and legs hopping from one foot to the other.

'Where's Fenna?' Egbert asked. 'She's been upstairs for ages now – she needs to see this!'

As if in answer, something *clomp-clomp-clomped* down the ladder and into the kitchen. Fenna, feet swamped in wooden clogs and arms cradling a bundle of cloak, was staring open-mouthed in the doorway. Milou turned Puppet-Papa to face her and lifted his head.

'*Hallo*, Fenna,' Milou said, in her deepest voice. She moved the strings so that Puppet-Papa gave a small bow. 'I am your papa.'

Fenna smiled, bright and rapturous. The bundle in her arms wriggled and emitted a loud *Screeeeeeeeech!*

'What was that?' Lotta asked.

Screeeeeeeeech! HooOOooOOoo!

Fenna made a small gap in the cloak bundle. A round face appeared, the colour of parchment, and two huge dark eyes blinked up at them.

'Where on earth did you find an owl, Fen?' Milou asked, climbing down from the table to get a better look. Fenna pointed up and Milou remembered the scratching noise they'd heard in the windmill's dome. 'Not a pigeon then. Did you pull it out of the roof?'

Fenna shook her head, then made a few gestures.

'He fell?'

Fenna nodded sadly, rocking the owl gently in her arms.

Screeeeeeeeeech! HooOOooOOoo!

Lotta stepped forward and peered beneath the cloak. 'He's no bigger than a fledgling,' she said. 'He must have been born very late in the year. And his left wing looks malformed. I bet he was abandoned. Poor thing looks half starved and completely spooked.'

'He's an orphan?' Egbert asked quietly. 'Like us?'

'Well, little owl,' Milou said, stroking the soft feathers on its head, 'I suppose we can make room for one more orphan in this windmill.'

Fenna's smile lit up the room, and Milou's heart gave a little stutter at the sight of it.

'He'll need a name in that case,' Lotta said. 'How about Bartje?'

Fenna's nose crinkled. The owl snapped its beak.

'Wouter?' said Egbert.

Fenna shook her head and the owl screeched.

'Screechy?' Milou suggested.

Fenna rolled her eyes.

'No,' Sem said, looking thoughtful. 'He needs a name that suits him –'

SCREECH!

All of them, except Fenna, plugged their fingers in their ears.

'How about we call him Noisy then?' Egbert said.

SCREEEECH!

Sem broke out a big, lopsided smile. 'Do you remember when Gassbeek thought she might be able to get rid of us more easily if we learned to play a musical instrument?'

SCREEEEEECH!

Sem's grin widened as the others nodded. 'He sounds just like that noise Milou made on the violin.'

'That wasn't *noise*,' Milou huffed. 'It was *Mozart*.'

SCREEEEEEEEEECH!

'Well, how about we call him Mozart?' Sem asked Fenna, eyes twinkling as he gazed down at the bird.

The owl turned its head 180 degrees to look at him, then gave a little musical chirp. A giggle burst from Fenna's lips, a raspy trill that seemed to fill the room.

They all stared at Fenna, who clapped a hand over her mouth, her cheeks turning a shade of red to match her hair. A lump caught instantly in Milou's throat.

'Mozart needs a nest,' Lotta said finally. 'Why don't we build one above the wardrobe?'

Fenna tucked the bird gently into her chest and nuzzled it. Then she lifted her head and nodded, smiling brightly.

The lump in Milou's throat hardened as a new, unwelcome realization settled over her. If her plan to find her parents failed, if they were dragged back to the Little Tulip, then she might never see Fenna smile – or hear her giggle – that way again.

Milou's Book of Theories

The Puppet Theatre

Observations:

- The windmill barn has been partially converted into a puppet theatre.
- Holes in the roof, tears in the seats, crumbling curtains.
- Marionette dangling from puppeteering platform.
- Building materials and stage props piled to stage right.
- Pile of blankets to stage left.
- <u>Claw marks next to the blankets. A match to the ones on my coffin-basket.</u>

Are these werewolf marks?
Did something terrible happen?
Are my family still alive?

15

After a pitiful meal of potato stew, the children settled down beside the fire in the living room. Puppet-Papa was sitting in the bigger rocking chair, one leg propped up on his knee and a pair of thin wire spectacles balanced on his cotton nose.

'Another log for the fire, please, Sem,' Lotta said in a deep voice, pulling Puppet-Papa's head-string to nod at the fireplace. 'And Milou, *darling*, clear those plates away, would you?'

'Of course, Papa,' Milou giggled.

Fenna smiled as she took off her apron and hung it on a peg on the wall. She had made a nest for Mozart out of puppet-stuffing on top of the wardrobe, and now she clambered up to drop him a handful of worms she'd gathered from inside the barn. Wedging herself into the chair with Puppet Papa, Milou couldn't have wiped the smile from her face if she'd tried. This was, she thought, the most perfect evening of her life so far.

No matron.

No shivering.

No fear.

Sem finished hanging a thin cotton curtain across the window and drew it closed, sealing the rocking chairs, Puppet-Papa, the fireplace and the five of them behind it.

'It works!' Egbert announced with excitement, shouting from the other side of the glass. A few moments later, he was inside again, beaming. 'I could see your silhouettes, but that was all. Puppet-Papa looks like a real person.'

It had been Milou's idea to hang a thin curtain at each window, and another across the cupboard bed they would put their fake-father in should anyone come inside the mill. Any passing neighbours wondering if Bram Poppenmaker had really returned would see the evidence of it clearly: smoke curling up from the chimney and light pouring through the downstairs windows. If they came closer, they would see a family of six around the fire listening to a story. That was what families did in the evenings. Milou was sure of it.

'Excellent,' she said. 'Then it's time for Papa to tell us a story.'

'Ooh!' Lotta said, standing beside one of the bookcases. 'Speaking of stories, I found two books we could read tonight.' She dropped a huge tome into Milou's lap.

'*A Medical Guide to Consumption*? I'm not sure this would make for an exciting bedtime read.'

'Ugh, fine, I'll read it myself later then,' Lotta said, taking the book from Milou and placing a small leather journal in her lap instead. Her eyes twinkled. 'You'll like this one.'

'What is it?' Milou asked.

Lotta smiled. 'Just open it and see.'

Milou turned to the first page and chills erupted all over her skin. There was a pencil drawing of what looked a lot like the tree outside, except its trunk was more gnarled. The topmost branches twisted upward into two jagged lines of writing:

A Carnival of Nightmares
by
Liesel Poppermaker

Milou ran her fingers over the page. Her sister was a storyteller, just like her.

'There are more of her stories in that bookcase,' Lotta said. 'They're all romantic ones, though, except for this one. It seems you and your sister are both very alike and very unalike.'

The next page had only one line, a dedication that Liesel had written:

For Thibault

Milou swallowed. Who was Thibault?

Whoever he was, he had known her sister. He knew what she looked like, how her laugh sounded, maybe even what had become of her. Milou couldn't help but feel a sting of jealousy at the thought of Liesel writing a story for him instead of her.

Sem and Fenna sat on pillows on the floor. Egbert followed a moment later, climbing on to the other rocking chair beside Lotta.

'Milou's going to read us a story,' Lotta said brightly. 'Aren't you, Milou?'

All Milou could manage was a quick nod as her fingers fumbled to turn the page. In a shaky voice, she began to read.

'*When darkness falls, the nightmares come. There is no hiding from them. Once they sink their claws into you, once they have drunk from your soul and tasted your fear, they know exactly where to find you.*

My own nightmare has plagued me for weeks.

I lie awake in my bed, knowing that they are waiting. My battle to stay awake is futile, of course. I am drifting down into the murky fog of sleep before I even realize that my eyes have closed. The walls of my bedroom disappear, replaced with endless dark. The warmth leaches away and I am left shivering. Thunder roars and lightning whip-cracks above me, birthing a pale moon in the dark, starless sky.

I am standing on a tundra. The grass at my feet has shrivelled and died. This bleak land stretches to the horizon in every direction, lit only by that faraway moon. I realize I am clutching something to my chest and, when I look down, I find a rusted iron cage; inside it is my own beating heart.

Thud-thud. Thud-thud. Thud-thud.

Shadows slither round my feet, pulsating in time. Tendrils reach up towards my heart-cage and I bat them away. Something booms, shaking the ground beneath me.

In the distance, a tall, gnarled tree rises from the barren ground. Its branches reach upward and outward like tentacles and I have to crane my neck to see the top of it. I wrap my arms more tightly round the heart-cage as the tree's ascent comes to a shuddering halt.

The Night Tree is grotesque: branches made of bones and leaves made of talons. My feet immediately start walking towards it, as they do every time I come here. I do not control my feet any more, the shadows do. As always, I stop after a hundred and seventy-five steps, just a few paces from the trunk.

There are faces carved into the gnarled bark: some I know only vaguely; others are of the people I love most. All except one, of course.

"Let me be!" I yell at the shadows, the tree, the faces.

"You can't escape this any longer, Theodora," the faces speak as one monstrous voice. "The carnival awaits, and you must enter."

"No."

"Theodora."

I startle at the sound of my name, now spoken so sweetly, even though I know it is coming.

A boy stands beside me. His ears have sharp points and tufts of brown fur covering both lobes. His eyes are yellow, and his nose is more like a snout. When he smiles, I catch a glimpse of his dagger-sharp teeth.

"Werewolf," the faces in the tree growl.

I clutch my heart-cage tighter and shake my head. The boy's face returns to that of a normal boy, and he smiles at me – half boyish, half wolfish, but wholly familiar and comforting.

"Hendrik," I whisper as the shadows slither ever further up my legs. "Help me, please."

As soon as his hand grips mine, the shadows loosen their grip and I am able to kick them away. Hope blossoms inside me and soon the heart-cage in my arms is wrapped in bright, flowering vines. Hendrik and I turn our backs to the Night Tree and flee.

Suddenly we are running along a path made of grave-mud. The Night Tree is gone and there is nothing left but this vast and dark wasteland, and Hendrik and me, and my beating heart.

I count our steps. Each night we get two steps further. Last night we made it to six hundred and sixty-three steps. With every step, the beat of the caged heart quickens. At six hundred and sixty-five steps, we come to a halt. I blink until my vision clears, my pulse a staccato in my ears.

Just a pace away is a gate. Huge iron bars painted black, their tips bright gold. I can see monsters beyond the bars. They are dancing, singing, calling my name. Claws, teeth, talons, snouts, whiskers . . . I see so many grotesques, they seem to blur into one horrifying being. There is music playing, but it's unlike any music I've ever encountered before. Sounds clash together, as if each note is battling to be heard. Violins screech, drums thunder, a flute wails in agony. Shadows spill out and wrap round my ankles once more. I want to cover my ears, but I can't. I want to run away, but I can't.

This is when I usually wake up again, gasping for breath and batting away invisible monsters, but tonight I can tell the shadows will not let me go. Tonight will be different.

"It is time," the nightmares call.

Hendrik tugs at my hand, trying to pull me away again, but this time the shadows only grip tighter, pulling me towards

the gates. More appear, reaching out to the heart-cage, and I
realize that there is only one thing that I can do.

I look up at the gates, letting my fear wash over me. Then
I uncurl my fingers from Hendrik's and push the heart-cage
into his arms, giving him the bravest smile I can muster. He
looks at me, confused and scared, but, before he or I can
speak, a wind rushes at me, tearing me off the ground,
pushing me forward, away from him, away from my own
beating heart.

I pass through the gates and . . .'

An ember popped loudly in the fireplace. Milou's friends
blinked up at her, leaning forward in eagerness.

'And?' Lotta asked eagerly. 'She passes through the gate
and then what?'

Milou turned the page, but the next one was blank.
'There's no ending.' She flicked through the remaining
pages. 'The rest of the book is empty.'

'What?' Egbert cried. 'But it *must* have an ending!'

'Fancy not finishing a story,' Sem said. 'Surely, if you
start a story, it must be easy enough to finish it?'

'It's fine.' Milou smiled. 'I shall just make up my own
endi–'

Her ears prickled an instant before they all heard the
sound of rattling at the window.

Milou jolted upright, slamming the book shut in her lap. They all peered round the curtain. A shadow passed by the window. A person-shaped shadow.

'Who was that?' Lotta gasped.

Sem picked up a candlestick and was across the room, into the hallway, and opening the door in just a few long strides. Milou raced after him. They stepped out into the frozen night, snow swirling down in delicate little clusters. The night was black, and the mist hung thickly above their heads, blocking out the moonlight. Sem held the flickering candle closer to the snow-laced ground.

Footprints – under the window – leading off towards the gravel path that led to the barn. Milou followed them, tugging Sem along with her. The prints turned, not towards the front gate, but off the path and down towards one of the smaller canals that lay behind the windmill.

'Who's there?' she called. 'Show yourself!'

The only response was a whistling howl from the wind.

Milou bent down to examine the prints. She'd scrubbed enough shoe and clog prints from the Little Tulip's foyer floor to recognize the kind of footwear that made them. These prints were rounded at the toe, with a thick, wide heel, both of which suggested a man's boot.

The prints were small, however. A boy then?

'Show yourself!' Milou called again, anger and panic raging through her.

How much had this boy seen? How long had he been standing there, watching them? After Sem had hung the curtain to shield Puppet-Papa? Or before?

She hadn't expected anyone to come trespassing right up to their window. The sign on the gate suggested people were scared of the mill; the unbroken lock showed that they kept their distance. But it seemed at least one neighbour was brave enough to venture closer and it would only take one to ruin everything.

'Let's go back inside,' Sem said.

Milou made to follow the prints. 'But –'

'Whoever it was,' Sem said, pulling her back towards the windmill, 'they've gone now.'

Milou's Book of Theories

Liesel Poppenmaker

- She is a storyteller, like me.
- She writes poems for our father.
- She writes stories for her friends.
- She wears overly frilly aprons.
- She is thirty years old now.
- She is lucky to have grown up here.

Perhaps Liesel got married and moved away. Maybe my parents went to visit her and her new family and just haven't come back ... in twelve years.

Perhaps Liesel got a job writing operas for a theatre in Italy. Maybe my parents went to see her there and just haven't come back ... in twelve years.

It doesn't make sense.

Nothing makes sense.

Where are they?

16

Morning brought both sunshine and gloom. The polder was aglow with a sun-speckled frost, the main canal glittering like a long sliver of diamond. Milou, however, felt as if the world were grey and morose. She was still worried about the boy-spy from the night before, as well as frustrated with her lack of progress in solving the mystery of her family's disappearance. Deciding that sleep was a lost cause, she climbed out of bed and tiptoed into the living room to curl up beside Puppet-Papa, her Book of Theories open in her lap. Mozart flew down in a haphazard spiral from his wardrobe perch to watch her.

'Oh, Mozart,' Milou whispered as the bird stared at her from the arm of the rocking chair, 'I don't suppose you have any clever revelations that will help me find my family?'

Mozart blinked. Milou sighed and went to tickle his head feathers.

Screeeeeeeeeech!

Snap!

She whipped her fingers away just in time. A blanket with legs and a blonde head appeared in the doorway.

'Morning, Milou, morning, Papa,' Lotta whispered, giving Puppet-Papa a kiss on the forehead. A six-fingered hand emerged from the blanket to stroke the owl. '*Hallo*, Mozartje.'

Screeeeeeeeeech!

Snap!

Lotta's hand retreated to the safety of the blanket.

'I think he's hungry,' Milou said, closing her Book of Theories so that Lotta wouldn't see her failure of an investigation.

'He needs more meat. Gouda knows where we'll find any. We'll all be eating worms soon at this rate.'

'Sem will have some dolls ready tomorrow. I'll go with him to Amsterdam. Maybe we can buy some meat then.'

Their stomachs growled in unison.

Lotta went over to the window to peek through the curtains.

'How many?' Milou asked. Lotta held up a hand. 'Six!' Milou groaned. 'There were only three a few minutes ago. Nosy farmwives. Haven't they got anything better than to do than just stand there, gawping?'

She went to peer out of the window. Six ladies stood by the gate, their winged-bonnet-clad heads together. On the canal, a few children slid to and fro on skates, making sure to remain within sight of the mill. Two men had stopped to fix their bicycles on the road just a bit further down, but Milou didn't think bicycle-fixing also involved staring at the windmill. She had expected people to be curious about the mill being inhabited again, but she hadn't expected them to gawk quite so openly.

'We need to do something,' Milou said at last.

'What kind of something?' Lotta asked.

'Something *normal*.'

'Normal?'

'Yes. Normal families don't hide behind curtains. We're making ourselves stand out.'

'And what is normal, loitering by someone's front gate, having a gossip?'

They watched as the women by the gate pretended to chat, while sneaking glances at the mill, no doubt hoping to be the first to spread the gossip about Bram Poppenmaker's return.

'Gossip!' Milou said. 'Of course!'

These people might have important information that could help her.

'I have an idea,' she said brightly.

Milou opened the door leading from the puppet workshop out on to the high balcony that wrapped round the windmill's entire circumference. Icy air blew in and a clothless sail groaned just in front of her. She peered out and saw that the farmwives were still watching the downstairs windows.

'Quick,' she whispered to the others. 'Now.'

Fenna and Lotta carried out Puppet-Papa's rocking chair. They had wrapped him up in a thick coat, hat, gloves and a scarf that covered most of his cotton face. They set him down against the wall, under the window, and Egbert draped a blanket over the lower half of his body. Milou covertly fed the puppet strings through the top of the window, to where Sem was waiting.

'Oh, Papa!' Milou yelled, casting a quick glance at the spectators below, who all started at the sound of her voice. 'Isn't it a wonderful morning? Look, there are our neighbours! Why don't you give them a wave?'

The farmwives squinted upward. Puppet-Papa lifted an arm and waved. Tentatively, the women waved back. Further away, on the main canal, the skaters came to a halt.

'Now you can watch us skate,' Milou said, her voice carrying across the polder. 'And the fresh air will do you such good.'

Puppet-Papa nodded, as did Milou to Sem whose face was only just peeking out from behind the curtain. Then she, Fenna, Lotta and Egbert headed back downstairs. Milou had found three pairs of skates in the wardrobe. They weren't the booted skates that Milou had seen in Amsterdam, but rather skate blades that strapped to the bottom of shoes.

As soon as they stepped out of the front door, the gossiping ladies made a hasty retreat and the two men cycled off. Milou frowned. At least the three children on the ice hadn't run away. Milou hoped they had enough gossip to help further her investigation.

'Do you mind if I skip the skating?' Egbert asked as they reached the main canal. He had his coal bucket slung over his shoulder. 'We've been cooped up all morning. I'd like to map the area.'

He sat on the bank and unrolled a piece of parchment. The girls carried on, wobbling towards the canal edge on skate-bedecked feet. The children on the ice snuck glances their way, but made no move to come closer. Spurred on by a gentle ear-tingle, Milou took a deep breath and jumped down, swinging her arms to propel herself forward. Her skates landed on solid ice, and her momentum sent her careering forward.

On.

And on.

And on.

It was both terrifying and exhilarating, as if she were a marionette being dragged forward by invisible strings. And, as her scream died away, so too did her momentum.

The others were still standing at the canal edge, staring at her. Milou took another step and wobbled. Her right leg shot one way, the world tipped upside down and the canal rose up to meet her back. All the air left her lungs and she lay there, gasping, for several long moments.

'That was an interesting skating technique,' Lotta giggled, her face blotting out the sky as she leaned over Milou.

Fenna appeared next to Lotta. They hoisted Milou to her feet. She looked at the skating spectators. They were all still huddled and gawping, hiding their giggles behind mittened hands.

'This is impossible!' Milou said. 'The skates just make it *more* slippery.'

'It is not impossible, silly. Your mistake was throwing yourself around like a rag doll. Watching you was a lesson in how *not* to do it. Here, look.' Lotta let go of Milou and slid in a circle round her and Fenna, swishing her feet and holding her arms out. 'Keep your back straight, but lean ever so slightly forward. Find your centre of gravity and it will provide you with the necessary equilibrium to stay upright.'

Milou blinked at her. 'You can turn everything into a science lesson, can't you?'

'That's because science is *in* everything.'

The girls linked arms, with Milou wedged in the middle.

'Ready?' Lotta asked.

Milou groaned, then nodded. They set off, feet sliding from side to side in unison, up and down the canal. Lotta suddenly let Milou go and gave her a push.

'*Gaah!*' Milou instinctively began to windmill her arms again.

'Stop panicking!' Lotta cried.

Milou straightened her back and leaned into her wobble, holding her arms out to balance herself. She grinned, then peered over her shoulder. The other children were skating again, closer to the canal bank this time.

'I'm going to talk to them,' Milou said.

Lotta nodded, then she and Fenna gracefully glided away. Milou's ears tingled. If she made a mistake, their ruse would be exposed. Wobbling much less than before, Milou skated over to the children.

The two girls were about Milou's age, and the boy looked to be a few years younger. One girl was short and dark-haired, the other was nearly as tall as Sem, with hair the colour of honey. The boy looked like a miniature version of her, clearly a sibling. They stopped skating as soon as they saw Milou approach.

'*Goedemorgen,*' Milou said brightly. 'I'm Milou Poppenmaker. Pleased to make your acquaintance. Those are my sisters, Fenna and Lotta.'

'I'm Sanne,' said the honey-haired girl as she looked down her long nose at Milou. 'This is my brother, Arno, and my friend, Kaatje. You don't look like sisters.'

'We're *adopted* sisters.'

'Is Meneer Poppenmaker really back then?' Arno asked nervously.

'Of course,' Milou replied. 'He's up there watching us, see?'

She waved at Puppet-Papa, who instantly waved back at her.

There was a long silence as the children looked from Puppet-Papa to one another, then back again.

'But my mother said the Poppenmakers were dead,' said Kaatje. 'She said they died of the White Plague and that their bones are lying in their beds to this day. My brother said he's heard their ghosts wailing at night.'

Milou smiled through gritted teeth. 'Clearly, your mother was wrong.'

If this was the only kind of gossip they had, it would be of no help to her.

'That can't be right,' Arno said. 'My mother reckons Meneer Poppenmaker was in trouble with the law. Our father said he saw the Poppenmaker carriage hurrying away in the dead of night, years ago. It was a full moon in December, so he could make out Meneer Poppenmaker's face clearly. He looked terribly unhappy apparently. He's been on the run from authorities ever since. Everyone knows that. Liesel too.'

Milou's ears prickled in warning, but it was too late.

'You don't know *anything*,' she spat.

The boy flinched. His sister, Sanne, pulled him towards her and shot Milou a furious glare.

'We *know* that Liesel Poppenmaker was a lovely *fair-haired* beauty,' Sanne said, eyeing Milou from head to toe with an incredulous smirk. 'We *know* that she hung around with undesirables. We *know* she stopped my father from shooting that huge, beastly dog that terrorized the neighbourhood all those years ago. We *know* this place has been much more pleasant since the Poppenmakers left because that's what everybody around here says. And we *know* that it's not normal for a father and daughter to just disappear one night.'

Milou swallowed, her ears on fire now.

'The only thing we *don't* know,' Sanne continued, 'is where they've been all these years and why Meneer Poppenmaker had repeatedly refused to sell the mill to decent working folks like my parents. Something suspicious *must* have happened.'

Milou took a steadying gulp of air, her mind swirling with anger, confusion and a thousand more questions. Questions she couldn't ask without arousing suspicion.

'It was nothing suspicious at all,' Milou said with a forced smile. 'He and my sister just decided to explore the world. Liesel is still travelling, of course. She'll probably be climbing an old volcano in Italy right about now.'

Sanne scoffed.

'And my *father*,' Milou said, forcing all her conviction into that single word. 'My *father* decided to adopt some orphans from the city and return home to give them a better life, so here we all are. That's all you need to *know*.'

Milou and Sanne glared hard at one another, the others glancing nervously between the two of them. They only broke their staring contest when Lotta and Fenna skated up beside them.

'It's nice to meet you,' Lotta said, holding a hand out for Sanne to shake.

Arno and Kaatje gasped at the sight of Lotta's fingers. Sanne recoiled. They all turned their attention hastily to Fenna, who, to Milou's surprise, held the blonde girl's gaze with a steady one of her own. She did not, however, smile.

'Who is that?' Arno asked.

Milou turned to see Egbert standing behind them at the canal's edge. His head appeared from behind his map and he pulled his shawl away from his face to offer them a small smile.

The polder children stared at him. Milou could almost hear the hinges of their jaws as they dropped.

'Where did Bram Poppenmaker find a child like *that*?' Sanne asked, not bothering to lower her voice. 'Clearly, he's not from *Nederland*.'

Egbert's smile disappeared; he hid once more behind his map. Milou's anger flared.

'That's our brother Egg – he's a cartographer,' she said proudly, squaring her shoulders. 'Sem, our other brother, is inside, making dolls.'

Sanne narrowed her eyes at Milou. 'I suppose it does make sense that a man as peculiar as Meneer Poppenmaker would adopt an entire circus of freaks.' She grabbed her brother's hand and turned away from them. 'Come on, Arno, let's go and skate further down the canal.'

'Hey!' Milou yelled, ignoring the sudden prickling on her earlobes. She bent down and picked up a handful of snow from the canal bank, squashing it into a ball.

'Milou, don't,' Lotta whispered.

Sanne turned. 'What –'

Milou's snowball caught her right in the face. Sanne spluttered and gasped, scraping the snow from her face. She blinked at Milou with a mixture of surprise and fury. Milou's ears tingled, but she didn't regret what she'd done. She wouldn't let anyone speak about her friends that way.

The two girls stared each other down. Then Arno giggled and a snowball caught Kaatje's chin, then one hit Lotta's chest.

An eyeblink later, more were flying in every direction, hitting shoulders, heads, legs, punctuated by shrieks of delight. Milou stood rigid, even as Sanne started laughing and slinging snow at her friends, her fury still gripping her tight. Something cold and hard hit her on the cheek.

'Hey –'

Milou suddenly found a snowball in her mouth instead of words. She spat it out, coughing, and found Fenna grinning before her. Milou gathered a handful of snow from the side of the canal and launched it at Fenna's head, but she ducked just in time. The snowball flew right over her and hit Lotta on the forehead instead.

'Oops!' Milou said.

Lotta charged at her, a wild grin on her face. Milou flapped her arms in panic and turned to run. She made it three desperate steps before her feet slipped beneath her. She flew forward and slid across the ice on her stomach for what felt like an infinity, snow spraying into her face.

On.

And on.

And on.

And on.

Her squeal of delight was cut short as she slammed into two adjacent lamp posts.

'*Oof!*'

There weren't usually lamp posts in the middle of canals as far as Milou was aware. Her eyes were blocked with snow and ice, so she reached out a hand and gasped when she realized the lamp posts were both warm and seemed to be wearing trousers.

Milou blinked snow from her eyelashes and found herself face to shin with a tall figure silhouetted by the bright winter sun. Her gaze followed the long lamp-post legs up, noticing the outline of a tailcoat and a stiff peaked cap. Milou's own hat had fallen off and, as she reached down to pick it up, she noticed the figure's boots: men's boots, small, with rounded toes and a wide heel. Her heart leaped into her throat.

The spy.

17

The figure loomed above her. As she struggled to her feet, Milou noticed silver buttons on the jacket, military style, and a belt round the middle with a baton wedged firmly in it. A uniform, she realized in horror.

'I'm so sorry ... uh ... Meneer,' Milou spluttered, staggering up on to her skates.

'I am not a Meneer,' said the tall figure in a stern, but decidedly female, voice.

'Oh, *goedemorgen*, Mevrouw.' Milou's ears prickled steadily. 'I'm so sorry I bumped into you.'

Milou looked down at the women's boots again. She couldn't be a hundred per cent certain, but they looked like a match for the prints she'd seen outside the house the night before.

'That was a remarkable impression of a dancing octopus,' the uniformed woman said. 'I've never seen anything quite like it.'

Milou rubbed at her ears. She blinked up at the woman, who gazed down at her with an amused expression. She wasn't an old woman, perhaps in her early thirties, but her eyes did crinkle at the corners and she had a thin streak of grey in the middle of her light brown fringe. A large gold locket hung from her neck and in the crook of her left elbow was tucked a wicker basket, its contents hidden beneath a double hatch lid. The woman arched a single eyebrow high up her forehead and Milou realized she was gawping. She shook herself and held out a gloved hand.

'My name is Milou Poppenmaker. It's a pleasure to meet you.'

The woman's raised eyebrow twitched. A hand clad in soft black leather shook Milou's, firm and strong. Milou couldn't help looking at the uniform again.

'Edda Finkelstein,' the woman said, tipping her peaked cap in greeting. 'Polder Warden for these parts. I'm sure your father has mentioned me.'

Polder Warden. Was that like a police officer?

Milou gulped down a mouthful of nervousness and stretched her smile even wider.

'Of course he's mentioned you,' she said, her mind clunking like a broken clock. 'He's said such wonderful things about you, Mevrouw Frankenstein.'

The woman's eyebrow rose higher.

'It's *Finkelstein*. So, Milou Poppenmaker,' Edda Finkelstein said brightly and Milou knew another question was coming. It was the woman's unwavering eyebrow that told her – her Eyebrow of Curiosity. 'Where has the elusive Bram Poppenmaker hidden himself away all these years? I'm dying to hear all about it.'

Milou opened her mouth to spin her wild but convincing tale again when a warm, herby smell tickled her nostrils. A growl thundered out from the vicinity of her belly button. The deep, rumbling type of growl that can only be made by the emptiest of stomachs.

Edda's other eyebrow rose.

Milou felt a blush burn her cheeks. 'Pardon me,' she said, the belly grumble still rolling on and on. 'I'm afraid we were so excited about skating that we forgot to have breakfast.'

With a final gurgle, the belly-rumbling stopped. The herby smell lingered, making Milou feel suddenly, overwhelmingly dizzy.

The warden narrowed her eyes slightly. 'You look vaguely familiar, Milou. Have I met you before?'

Yes, Milou wanted to say, *you spied on us last night. That's why I look familiar.*

Instead, she smiled brightly and said, 'I am Bram's youngest daughter. No doubt that's why I look familiar.'

'I see,' she said, the Eyebrow of Curiosity rising once more. 'And the other four, are they the long-lost offspring of Meneer Poppenmaker as well?'

Four. She knew exactly how many of them there were. It must have been her. Milou's ears prickled again.

'Those are my best friends,' Milou said, trying to keep her voice from shaking. 'I asked my father to adopt them.'

She summoned what she hoped was a confident smile, and held it in place as Edda Finkelstein cast a curious glance at the windmill. Milou took a calming breath in through her nose. If the Polder Warden had seen them assembling Puppet Papa, then surely she'd have arrested them by now?

'And where, um, where is Liesel?' Edda asked, her smile tightening slightly.

'Travelling,' Milou said. 'With her friend. She's quite the adventurer.'

'Yes, of course.' Edda's smile faltered completely. Her gloved hand reached up to the locket, then fell to her side.

Milou inhaled deeply to quell her nerves, but that warm, rich aroma still hung in the air.

'Why are you dressed like a police *man*?'

Milou started. She hadn't heard Lotta skate up to them. Milou peeked behind her quickly to find that Fenna and Egbert had both gone back indoors. Up on the balcony,

Puppet-Papa appeared to be looking at them, his head tilted towards the canal.

'I'm dressed as a Polder Warden actually,' Edda said matching Lotta's inquisitive expression.

'But you're a woman.'

'Correct.'

'That's impossible. They don't let women join the force.'

'It's *improbable*,' Edda said. 'Not impossible.'

'How did you convince them? Were you a soldier once, too? Have you –'

'This is Lotta,' Milou interrupted. 'Lotta Poppenmaker.'

'You're very curious, Lotta Poppenmaker. Tell me, is that oil I see on your cheek? And a waistcoat over your dress?'

'It seems you're also curious.' Lotta crossed her arms, but Milou could see a glint of awe shining in her friend's eyes. 'As you avoided my questions by asking more of your own.'

Edda smiled. 'It seems there are lots of questions in the air today.' She patted her basket. 'I made some food as a homecoming offering for you. How about we go inside? Your father can tell me all about his wild adventures.' Edda skirted round Milou. 'The food won't stay warm out in this cold.'

The woman's legs were exceedingly long and quick. She was halfway towards the canal bank before Milou had even managed to turn and take a single step.

'No!' Milou cried. 'Stop!'

A sharp warning prickled her ears, but Milou didn't need her Sense to tell her she'd made a mistake. Edda stopped mid-stride, one leg already up on the bank, and turned. The Eyebrow rose once more.

'He's contagious,' Lotta blurted out.

'Contagious?' The Eyebrow of Curiosity climbed higher. 'Then why was he out here in the freezing cold?'

Milou shot Lotta a worried look.

'I have the situation perfectly in hand,' Lotta said confidently. 'He's wrapped up warm and our brother Sem is up there with him.'

'And what ailment is it Bram is suffering from?'

'Bacterial tuberculosis,' Lotta said. 'Or, as most laymen call it, consumption. He was seen by a fantastic microbiologist in Berlin who performed ground-breaking treatment to weaken the offending bacteria. We think he's over the worst of it and should be well again come spring.'

Milou tried not to gawk. What was Lotta doing? What was she saying? Half the words didn't even make sense.

'I don't suppose you know what a microbiologist is or the nature of bacteria,' Lotta continued animatedly, 'but, I assure you, a little fresh air will do him good.'

'It's best you don't come too close,' Milou interjected. 'We wouldn't want you to catch it.'

Edda's mouth twitched again. 'No, we wouldn't want that at all.' She sighed, then lowered her Eyebrow. 'Well, I suppose you'd better take this. Perhaps it will help make Bram feel better.'

Edda opened the lid of the basket and held it out for Milou and Lotta to see. The smell was so intoxicating, Milou felt dizzy again. Beside her, Lotta gave a low groan of longing.

'Smoked sausage with plenty of potatoes, some carrots and an aubergine I bought at the market.' Edda handed the basket to Lotta. 'This is far too much for me to eat alone so you may as well have it. I live just over that little bridge.' She pointed towards the copper-roofed farmhouse. 'You can return the dishes to me tomorrow.'

Milou responded with another belly growl. Lotta's stomach joined in. They both quickly wrapped their arms round their middles and peered in the direction Edda was pointing – at the copper-roofed house, separated from their mill by a thin canal, a narrow field and the skeletal oak tree.

'Thank you,' Milou said. 'We'll see you tomorrow.'

Edda bowed in farewell, then set off across the icy canal in a lope so long-strided it would have made a giraffe jealous.

Milou turned to Lotta. 'How did you –'

'I read that medical book last night. It's fascinating. As is Mevrouw Finkelstein. A female Polder Warden. Isn't she splendid?'

Milou's ears tingled as she glanced back over her shoulder, to where a line of small, wide-heeled footprints followed in Edda's wake.

'Yes, splendidly troublesome.'

With the kitchen cleaned, the fire roaring in the next room and Edda Finkelstein's feast laid out on the Poppenmakers' finest crockery, the children gathered round the kitchen table. Puppet-Papa watched over them from the rocking chair, wrapped in a corduroy dressing gown, smiling his banana-shaped smile, as they stared at the food.

'It's beautiful,' Sem said. He went to sit down, but Milou put an arm out to stop him.

'Maybe we shouldn't be eating this,' she said.

They all shot her an incredulous look.

Sem's eyebrows crinkled. 'Why on earth not?'

Milou waved her hand at the food. 'It could be a trap.'

Egbert laid his shawl on the back of his chair and sat down. 'I doubt those carrots are going to jump up and drag us back to the Little Tulip.'

Milou was still unconvinced. Worry gnawed at her, despite her eerily unprickly ears. 'What if she's just trying to gain our trust so she can hand us over to the authorities and claim a reward?'

'If she had seen anything incriminating last night, we'd be back in Amsterdam by now,' Lotta said. 'And anyway you don't know for certain it was her at the window last night.'

'What if the food's poisoned?'

'Then we'll die incredibly happy,' Sem said, sitting down beside Egbert.

'But what if –'

Egbert held up a hand to silence her. 'What if we just eat this before it all goes cold?'

As if in reply, all five stomachs gurgled in unison, like an entire orchestra of drainpipes.

Sitting themselves down on velvet chairs borrowed from the theatre, the others began to pile their plates high with food as Milou reluctantly sat down too. Fenna took her plate and filled it with sausage, carrots, potatoes and a strange purplish vegetable she hadn't seen before.

Then her friends dived straight in, slurping, gulping and scraping cutlery.

Milou stabbed at a piece of pink sausage. It wasn't grey like the occasional scraps of meat they'd been fed at the orphanage. She bit into the end of it, hot juice spilling all over her mouth, and groaned with pleasure. Warmth radiated from her scalp to her shoulders and an unfamiliar sense of calm washed over her.

Any nefarious plot Edda Finkelstein might have had in mind by offering them this food was worth risking for the unrivalled joy of the flavours that were now dancing across her tongue.

'I could eat a hundred mouthfuls of this,' Egbert said, holding up his forkful of aubergine. 'Even if it does taste suspiciously of eyeball.'

Fenna held a strip of sausage meat up in the air, then grinned in rapturous delight when Mozart spiralled down and took it from her fingers, nipping them as he did. Fenna sucked her finger where the owl's sharp beak had caught her and turned back to her food. With a muffled *HooOOooOOoo*, Mozart flew in circles back into the shadows.

Soon their plates were licked clean and the five of them were leaning back in their chairs, rubbing their rounded bellies.

Lotta slurped at all twelve fingers, then licked at the sauce that had dribbled out each side of her mouth. 'Holy Gouda, that was good.'

'This is what it's like then,' Sem said.

'What what's like?' Egbert asked sleepily.

'Being a *normal* family.'

For the first time since meeting Edda, Milou smiled.

Milou's Book of Theories

Gossip

Useful intelligence:

- They speak as if Bram and Liesel lived in the windmill alone: no mother or baby mentioned.
- Bram was seen leaving the windmill one night, in December, under a full moon.
- Bram refused to sell the windmill.
- Liesel was a 'fair-haired beauty' who hung around with 'undesirables'.
- A 'huge, beastly dog' used to terrorize the neighbourhood. Could this have been a werewolf? If Sanne's parents are as ridiculous as she is, I bet they wouldn't be able to tell the difference between a large dog and a werewolf.

Nonsense:

- Rumours about plague, ghosts and criminal activity.
- Sanne and her silly, smirking face.
- Sanne's suggestion that Egbert doesn't belong here.

What other reason would my father have to refuse to sell the mill, other than because he intends to return one day?

Perhaps they really have just gone travelling. Or did the werewolf chase them away, despite my sister having saved its life? Why would she save its life? Perhaps, like Fenna, she is just too kind-hearted to see any creature come to harm. Maybe my parents are still hunting it down.

The children woke before dawn, and ate leftovers for breakfast on the windmill's balcony, all ten legs dangling over the balcony's edge and all five sets of shoulders wrapped in thick wool blankets. Afterwards, they sat and watched the sun rise over the seemingly never-ending landscape. Birdsong drifted up to them in sweet trills and, with freshly licked lips, Fenna began to tentatively whistle each trill back to them. Sem was stitching dolls, Egbert was drawing and Lotta was gazing happily across the polder, her legs clad in newly fashioned trousers inspired by the Polder Warden's. Mozart nestled in Fenna's cloak, sleeping soundly.

Milou was the only one not smiling. She was watching Edda Finkelstein's copper-roofed farmhouse, certain she could see the Polder Warden's curtains twitching.

'I'm glad we decided to stay,' Lotta said. She waved to a passing farmer, who tipped his hat in return. 'Our neighbours are lovely.'

Milou knew Lotta was really referring to Edda.

'Not all of them are,' Egbert muttered, and Milou gave his hand a squeeze.

'Milou and I can head into the city this afternoon to sell the dolls,' Sem said. 'Perhaps we'll earn enough for a feast like the one we had last night.'

In his lap was a duck doll wearing a pale blue, puffed-sleeve dress and a lacy winged bonnet. Sem was stitching the bottom of its left foot closed, with Fenna tucking the stuffing in as he went.

'First, we'd better return these dishes,' Lotta said gleefully, getting to her feet. 'We should all go over and thank Mevrouw Finkelstein.'

'That woman is far too curious,' Milou said. 'We should just leave the dishes by the front door.'

'That's not how *normal* neighbours behave,' Lotta said. 'It would only encourage her inquisitiveness.'

Milou sighed dramatically. Lotta was, of course, right.

No matter how much Milou wished to, there was no avoiding Edda Finkelstein.

*

They dressed neatly. Fenna plaited Milou's hair and Sem wore one of Bram's bowler hats to cover his ears, which Milou snatched right off his head again.

'There's nothing wrong with your ears, Sem.'

Cheeks reddening, Sem nodded. 'I just thought ... well, you said we needed to appear more normal.'

'Milou's right,' Lotta said. 'But I'm not sure bringing Mozart is going to help us appear normal.'

Milou turned to find Fenna tucking the owl into the front of her cloak. Her friend responded to Lotta's statement by clutching Mozart more tightly and narrowing her eyes in a decidedly defiant manner.

'Suit yourself,' Lotta replied. 'I suppose there's only so much normal the five of us can realistically get away with. Just don't let him out of your cloak if you can help it.'

Fenna smiled and nodded.

They set off to Edda Finkelstein's house, passing Sanne and Arno who were skating on the canal again. Egbert pulled his shawl up to cover his face, trying to hide from their blatant staring, which only soured Milou's mood further. She linked arms with him and marched past as if the two siblings didn't exist. They passed under the oak tree and skirted around a raised flower bed rimmed with a stone border. Milou led them over a little bridge and stepped on to a neat stone path that wound its way towards Edda's farmhouse. The two pigs in the pen were snuffling the frozen mud, and clucking noises emanated from the chicken hut just beyond.

'It's really quite inspiring to see a woman have all this on her own,' Lotta was saying. 'I didn't see a wedding ring on her finger, so she must be a spinster.'

Milou looked at her friends and was disappointed to find they all seemed impressed.

Fenna's smile was almost touching her ears as they approached the Polder Warden's brightly painted front door. The doorbell was a small brass peacock. Fenna giggled softly, then pulled the peacock's legs and a tinkling arpeggio of chimes sounded. Milou scowled as a traitorous bubble of awe tickled at her insides.

'Um, Milou,' Egbert whispered, tugging her arm urgently. He nodded to a metal plaque on the front door, upon which was written:

E. FINKELSTEIN
CLOCKWORK ARTISAN

Her friends turned to her, mouths agape, then looked down at the pocket watch dangling from her neck. Milou clutched it tightly, suddenly feeling dizzy.

'Do you think she's your –'

'*No*,' Milou said, the mere thought of it twisting her insides. 'It must be a coincidence. She can't be –'

'Poppenmakers!' Edda's voice boomed suddenly out of nowhere.

They all jumped, Fenna gave a small gasp of surprise.

'Where's her voice coming from?' Egbert whispered.

'Speaking tube,' Edda's tinny voice sing-songed. 'Next to Lotta's elbow.'

Lotta let out a half-gasp, half-squeal. She put her face close to a round metal grille. 'I've heard about speaking tubes,' she shouted, 'but I've never seen one!'

'Ow!' Edda said. 'Clearly not. Come in, the door's unlocked.'

Lotta pushed it open and they stepped inside.

Tick-tick-tock-tock-tick-tick-tock-tock.

It sounded like a thousand tiny metal feet dancing a chaotic rhythm. They walked into the middle of a square hallway, surrounded by clocks. They were nothing like the plain grandfather clock in the Little Tulip, nor were they like the fancy mantelpiece clock in Gassbeek's office. Each one was an intricately built sculpture in the form of an animal.

A metal bear, head fashioned from an old saucepan and a body made of bicycle parts, loomed in the corner closest to the door. Its jaw was open in a silent roar and nestled in its mouth was a clock face. A row of metal cats hung in a line along one wall, their long tails *swishing* and *swooshing* and their eyes *ticking* left and then *tocking* right.

There were ducks with tiny clocks for eyes; an octopus whose eight arms pointed towards either the year, month, day, hour, minute, second, mealtime or bedtime; a pig in a copper top hat with a clock for a snout; and a windmill, as tall as Milou, whose sails whooshed at a dizzying speed round a clock face made of a metal polished to such a shine she could see her own dumbstruck face reflected right back at her.

'Holy Gouda,' Lotta said, spinning in a slow circle. She and Fenna collided mid-spin as they took in the strange sight. Mozart let out a disgruntled *HooOOooOO*.

'That's an odd lamp,' Egbert said, pointing to a glowing glass orb that hung from the middle of the ceiling by a thick wire. 'It's like fire, but . . . not.'

'*Electricity*.' Lotta breathed the word out like a prayer.

'Indeed, indeed,' Edda's tinny voice sounded from a large speaking tube located in the middle of the bear-clock's belly. 'Now close the door, would you – the bear's cogs squeak most unpleasantly when it gets too cold. Take the first doorway on your right and up the stairs.'

Behind the door was a staircase, lit by more electric bulbs all the way up. Lotta took the lead eagerly, climbing up and round until they finally emerged in a large, open room. More clocks, in various stages of assembly, lined the walls and worktops. Tools were scattered on every surface. There was so much stuff everywhere that Milou didn't notice Edda immediately. Then she saw the familiar streak of grey through light brown hair bobbing behind a metal elephant head. Edda peered round the side of it, her face appearing just below its curved trunk.

Milou quickly shoved the pocket watch under her collar. It pressed, cold and seemingly heavier, against her now racing heart. She stared at the Polder Warden, a thousand questions pressing against her skull, though one was much louder than the others:

Could *Edda Finkelstein be her mother?*

She wasn't old enough to be her mother, surely?

'Ah, *welkom*.' Edda's left cheek had a thick smear of oil across it and her fringe was sticking up behind a pair of goggles that rested on her forehead. 'You've arrived at a most fortunate time. My sleeve is caught inside this clock and I can't move or the whole thing will collapse.'

Edda raised one of her eyebrows, which were far lighter than Milou's black ones. Not to mention that Milou did not possess the ability to raise one eyebrow at a time.

'Cogs ... sprockets ...' Lotta spoke fervently. 'This ... wow.'

Milou had never seen Lotta look so filled with wonder.

Edda's bright *blue* eyes danced in delight at Lotta's awed expression.

You look vaguely familiar, Edda had said yesterday.

Milou stared at her, examining every centimetre of her face, but there was nothing familiar about Edda Finkelstein.

'This is Sem, Egbert and Fenna,' Milou said croakily. 'We're just here to return your dishes. We'll be immediately on our way, so as not to disturb you.'

Milou set the dishes on a worktop and tugged at Sem's elbow, intending to drag them all straight back to the windmill.

'Oh, don't be silly,' Edda said. 'You're not disturbing me at all. In fact, I could do with an extra hand here.'

Lotta was suddenly elbowing her way past Sem and Milou in her eagerness to help Edda. Milou reached out to grab her, but missed.

'I've also dropped a cog,' Edda said. 'If I hold this, can you reach in and find it?'

Lotta nodded enthusiastically.

A large tabby cat was curled up on the windowsill. Fenna used her Mozart-free hand to scratch the cat's forehead, provoking a grumpy yowl from the beast.

'Ah, Fenna,' Edda said. 'That is Meneer Catticus. If you scratch behind his left ear, you'll earn his adoration very quickly. That's it, Lotta, that cog just there.'

Fenna beamed. As did Lotta. Sem and Egbert wandered, wide-eyed, round the room, but Milou just stood there, trying to keep the questions from bursting from her lips. She couldn't just ask Edda outright, not without the Polder Warden immediately realizing Milou hadn't been telling the truth about who she was. If she wanted answers, she'd have to ask *careful* questions.

Milou gave Edda a bright, dimply smile. 'Do you make these clocks for your children?'

The Eyebrow of Curiosity shot upward.

'There are no children here.'

'Elsewhere then?'

The clockmaker sighed. 'I don't have any children,' she said. 'How's your father feeling today, Milou?'

Milou hid her frustration at Edda's deflection by brightening her smile further.

'He's resting in bed with a book.'

'I'm glad to hear Meneer Poppenmaker is feeling well enough to read,' Edda said, the left side of her nose twitching slightly, as if she were trying to stop a sneeze. Or a sneer. 'Perhaps, if he's well enough tomorrow, I could visit –'

'Got it!' Lotta said, holding up a small metal cog.

'Excellent work,' Edda said. 'You have twelve exceedingly nimble fingers! You would make a fine clockmaker.'

Lotta grinned so delightedly, it made Milou grimace.

'Do you make watches, too?' Egbert asked, with a pointed look at Milou. 'I only see designs for more clocks.'

'Hmm? Oh no. I've always preferred making larger pieces of clockwork – Oh dear. I seem to have torn my sleeve –'

This time it was Sem hurrying across the room to Edda's rescue, a needle and thread already in his hands. 'Here, let me.'

'Oh no, really, it's –'

'It's the least I can do after the wonderful meal you cooked us.'

'In that case, you are my hero, Sem. My sewing abilities leave a lot to be desired if I'm honest. My, you're very adept. I have plenty of mending work for you should you wish to earn some extra coin?'

Sem beamed.

Milou turned away, walking up and down the narrow gap between the workbenches. She picked up a small clock face and pretended to examine it, trying to think of what questions she could ask Edda without it sounding as if she were asking questions.

'That's an interesting shawl you have there,' Edda was saying to Egbert. 'Such an unusual shade . . .'

'It's . . . uh . . . a little stained,' Egbert said, clutching it protectively. 'Charcoal –'

'Ah yes,' Edda said. 'Quite a nasty stain, too. As someone who works with various oils and grease, I've seen my fair share of those. I have a special cleaning concoction I could try if you like?'

'Oh,' Egbert said, clutching the shawl more tightly. 'No, really –'

'I promise I won't damage it,' Edda said gently. 'Wouldn't it be wonderful to see it restored to its former glory?'

Milou set the clock face down a little too hard. It rolled off the edge and clattered to the floor. Everyone looked at her.

'Sorry –'

She bent down to pick it up, crawling under the workbench as it continued to roll away from her. When she finally managed to grab it, something sharp caught her finger. She stifled a hiss of pain as she plucked a splinter out. Then she saw what had caused it.

Four deep, long lines had been gouged into the wooden floorboards. Claw marks.

She looked a little further along the floor, noticing more of them. Along the skirting boards, up the workbench legs and poking out from beneath various clocks standing on the floor. They were everywhere.

As with the ones in the theatre, Milou was certain they were a match for the gouges on her coffin-basket. And much too big to have been made by Meneer Catticus. Which could only mean . . .

Milou swallowed hard and shuffled backwards out from under the workbench, crashing into a coat stand. It fell down beside her. Cheeks flaming in embarrassment, she scrambled to her feet and set the stand right, gathering Edda's coats and hanging them back up. She looked up at Edda, who met her gaze with a small frown.

'Are you all right?' the Polder Warden asked. 'You seem a little . . . flustered.'

Milou's heartbeat matched the *tick-tick-tock-tock-tick-tick-tock-tock* of the clocks around her. Edda was still staring. As were her friends.

Milou forced herself to hold the clock-maker's gaze.

Edda was connected to the Poppenmakers somehow. Milou's Sense prickled in agreement. She wasn't entirely certain what a werewolf would look like in human form, but Edda Finkelstein's gentle appearance was not what she would have expected.

'I feel sick,' Milou lied.

She turned and fled, down the stairs and out of the door. She was halfway to the oak tree when Fenna and Egbert caught up with her. She looked over her shoulder and saw that Lotta and Sem were still hovering on the doorstep, talking to Edda.

'Hurry up!' Milou yelled to them and Lotta's shoulders seemed to sag.

'What was that all about?' Sem whispered when they'd caught up. 'Are you really feeling ill?'

Milou hurried towards Poppenmill. 'Of course not –'

'Wait!' Edda called, suddenly just a few paces behind them, and Milou silently cursed those long, lamp-post legs of hers.

'Egg,' Edda said breathlessly. 'Your shawl . . .?'

Egbert blinked at her. Then hesitantly unwrapped it from around his neck and handed it over.

Edda smiled. 'I'll bring it back soon, I promise. And Lotta, I need an apprentice. I could do with a pair of hands as nimble as yours. Paid, of course.'

Lotta's grin nearly reached her pigtails. 'Oh, I'd love –'

'We'll have to ask our father,' Milou said, grabbing Lotta's hand and pulling her away. 'Goodbye, Mevrouw Finkelstein. Thank you again for the food.'

Dragging Lotta along with her, Milou sped towards the mill.

Milou's Book of Theories

Edda Finkelstein

- Approximate age: early thirties.
- The local Polder Warden – even though she's a woman.
- Lives alone and works – even though she's a woman.
- A clockmaker, but not a watchmaker.
- Unmarried and says she's never had children.
- Claw marks all over her workroom.
- Is far too curious about us. Probably spying on us, too.
- Is far too kind to us. What does she want?

She doesn't seem to like Bram much, despite what she says to the contrary. Every time his name comes up, there's a little twitch in the side of her nose. An almost-sneer that she never quite stops in time for me to notice.

She's connected to my family's disappearance. I just know it.

The claw marks and the clockwork – it's too much of a coincidence.

Perhaps they discovered she was the werewolf and she tried to kill them?

Perhaps it is her they are hiding from?

19

'What on earth were you thinking agreeing to work for her?' Milou growled, when they were safely through their front door. 'We should be keeping our distance!'

'She's nice,' Lotta snapped back. 'You're being paranoic.'

'No, I'm not. She knows more about my family's disappearance than she's letting on. I found claw marks *all* over her workroom floor.'

'You can't seriously be suggesting she's the *werewolf* from your Book of Theories –'

'What other explanation could there be? The claw marks were *huge*. There's no way that cat of hers could have made them.'

Lotta opened her mouth, then shut it again.

'We need food,' Egbert said. 'We can't survive forever on the small amount we took from the Little Tulip. If she's offering to pay Lotta . . .'

Milou growled inwardly. She should be focusing on finding her parents, not arguing with her friends. 'I'm trying to keep us safe.'

'It's a calculated risk,' Lotta said, softening slightly. 'And I'm sure there's a logical explanation for the claw marks, Milou. If I work for her, I could ask her –'

'No,' Milou said. 'You're definitely not asking her any questions. If she realizes we're on to her, we could be in even greater danger. And we already have a plan to make money. Sem and I are going to Amsterdam right now to sell the dolls. We don't need that woman's help.'

Before Lotta or Egbert could argue the matter any further, Milou marched into the kitchen towards the wardrobe, rifling through Liesel's dresses until she found something that no one would recognize her in: a lilac dress with an obscene amount of frills on the apron. She chose a matching bonnet, tucking her ebony hair into it, then covered the bottom of her face with a silk scarf, just as Sem walked into the room.

'Have you come to tell me off as well?' Milou asked. 'I'm only trying to keep us from harm.'

'No,' he said. 'I just came to say we should bring Puppet-Papa along. That way, no one will mistake us for orphans.'

Milou and Sem took a three-wheeled cargo bicycle that had been stashed at the back of the puppet theatre. It had a large crate at the front, perfect for carrying fake fathers.

'Do you know how to ride this thing?' Milou asked.

Sem shrugged. 'We've watched millions of people cycle,' he said. 'It can't be that difficult.'

It took Sem a few attempts to get the pedals going, but the extra wheel helped to keep the bike from toppling over. They sat Puppet-Papa in the front crate, his face swaddled in a thick scarf, with a hat that covered most of the rest of his head. They positioned him carefully, making it look like he was reading a book. Milou squeezed in in front of him.

It was far quicker, it turned out, to cycle to the city than it had been for them to walk from it. As it was, they only had to go as far as the outskirts, having discovered a market street full of shoppers and traders. They found a small space next to a cheese stall, in the shadow of a tall yew tree, that Milou felt was perfect. They parked the cargo bike under a branch and Milou covered Puppet-Papa with a blanket, right up to his hat, giving the impression of a sleeping figure. Then, arranging the dolls on a blanket on the ground, the two of them sat and waited, hoping to make their fortune.

But hours passed and they sold only one doll. The cold was seeping into every bit of Milou, making her irritable.

The crowds kept stepping over them, trampling their blanket and pushing them further back towards the oak tree.

'People just keep walking past,' Milou complained, wrapping her cloak more tightly round her shoulders. 'We need a table.'

'We can't very well carry a table all this way,' Sem replied. 'Perhaps we should ask Egg to make us a fancy advertising board or something.'

A small girl with a winged bonnet and cookie crumbs around her mouth suddenly appeared at Milou's feet, plopping down in a rumpled mass of skirts. She grinned up at Milou expectantly.

'What's her name?' the girl asked, pointing at a mouse doll. 'And why is she dressed like a pirate?'

'Her name is Theodora,' Milou said, smiling. 'And, actually, she's dressed like a werewolf hunter. See this sword? It's made of solid silver, forged in moonlight. All it takes is a single nip –' she slashed the doll mouse's sword at the girl's nose, eliciting a giggly shriek of surprise – 'and it will turn a werewolf's blood into solid stone.'

Milou picked up the werewolf doll, as two boys sat on the ground in front of her, their mittened hands cradling hot, oozing stroopwafels.

'What happened next?' asked one boy, licking a glob of syrup from his wrist. 'Did the werewolf eat her?'

Milou smiled, the cold suddenly gone as she made the two dolls face each other.

'Oh, he certainly tried to eat her,' Milou said softly and menacingly. 'But let me tell the story from the beginning.'

Clink-clunk-clink-clunk-clink-clunk.

Milou's unexpected audience, now twenty-something strong, began to throw coins into the bucket Sem had set out to collect their doll-selling earnings. Milou grinned as Sem carried it back to the bicycle.

'Puppet shows, Sem! That's how I could earn money for us,' she said. 'Did you see how I made them jump and squirm? I'm telling you, audiences love to be scared. I think I might add some decapitations next time ...'

'You did very well,' Sem said. Then he peered into the bucket and frowned. 'You made thirty-four cents, three buttons, a fingernail, a used handkerchief and a half-eaten cookie.'

Milou's smile faltered slightly. 'It's a start at least,' she said. 'I could come back tomorrow, and the day after. It'll soon add up.'

'I sold two more dolls while you were performing. It'll keep us going for a while. Maybe another good meal will raise everyone's spirits, so you, Lotta and Egg can make up. Here." He added some change from his pocket and then handed the bucket to Milou. "I just need to fix a spoke on the back wheel, then we'll go home.'

As Milou bent down to put the money-bucket in the crate next to Puppet-Papa, a familiar smell tickled the inside of her nostrils. An oily, smoky smell.

She stood, heart kicking against her ribcage, and scanned the market street. She'd made a half-turn when she spotted a familiar swirl of pipe smoke rising about the heads of the crowd. A gap appeared among the sea of people and Milou saw a grey wool suit and sealskin boots.

Rotman.

Milou froze, the back of her legs pressing tightly against the bicycle. She quickly pulled the scarf right over her nose and kept still as the sugar merchant ambled her way, smiling toothily at those he passed, and stopping to say '*hallo*' to a baby in a perambulator. Milou lowered her eyes, hoping she'd be invisible enough that he would walk straight past her.

She felt his gaze land on her a mere instant later. Instinctively, she looked up through her spider-leg lashes. He was still smiling that big, fake smile: all teeth and no soul. But, she realized, he did not appear to recognize her.

Heart galloping, she ducked her head in greeting. Rotman's smile remained fixed, then looked past her to Puppet-Papa. His eyes narrowed.

Then he dipped his head again. '*Goedemiddag*, Meneer.'

Milou's heart came to a shuddery stop – she watched in surprise as Puppet-Papa returned the nod, then a familiar, slightly squeaky, not-quite-baritone voice said, '*Goedemiddag.*'

Without a second glance, Rotman leaned on his cane and disappeared into the bustling crowd, a cloud of fishy pipe smoke trailing behind him. Sem appeared from behind Puppet-Papa, his expression grim.

'Let's go home.'

Dusk seemed to be creeping in from all directions by the time Sem peddled towards the bridge to Poppenmill. Edda Finkelstein was sitting on the wall of the flower garden, staring up at the oak tree with a frown. She started slightly as their bike squeaked past, her expression morphing into a forced smile. She waved as they passed. *Had she been spying again?* Milou wondered.

Milou mustered up a small smile, then lifted Puppet-Papa's arm to wave back.

Edda nodded once, then set off down her path towards her own gargoyle-gated canal bridge. Milou waited until the Polder Warden was walking down the road, her back to them, before stumbling wearily from the cargo crate. She helped Sem carry Puppet-Papa quickly into the mill.

Fenna was standing on the kitchen table, dangling a worm from her fingers, and her lips pursed.

Milou frowned. 'What are you –'

Fenna let out a sudden, sharp whistle in response to which there was a loud screech and a flash of white. Milou ducked as Mozart spiralled over her head, his wing flapping against her forehead. He swooshed down to Fenna's outstretched arm, took the worm, then landed on her shoulder and swallowed it in one gulp.

Standing at a safe distance by the walls, Egbert and Lotta clapped. 'Bravo!'

Fenna's responding giggle sent delighted shivers down Milou's spine.

They all turned to Milou and Sem, who set Puppet-Papa down in his rocking chair and then presented the basket of food they'd bought. Their smiles brightened.

'You did it,' Lotta said.

'It's not all good news,' Milou said as Sem set the food down on the table. 'Rotman's still in Amsterdam.'

Egbert frowned. 'But I thought you said he had a tight shipping schedule to keep to?'

'He has no *crew*,' Sem spat. 'And I don't suppose he's very happy about that, or the fact he's still limping after our last encounter.'

'Rotman's not our problem any more,' Egbert said. 'Not if we keep out of his way.'

Milou sighed, every part of her body filled with weariness. 'I'm sorry I was so awful earlier. I'm just scared that this will all be taken from us. And I'm scared Edda will be the one to do that.'

'We're all scared,' Lotta said softly. 'But look how far we've come already. It was a risk to leave the Little Tulip like we did. But we're making it work and we'll continue to do so.'

'You're right,' Milou said. 'I think I'm going to lie down before dinner. My head is spinning.'

She climbed into climbed into her cupboard bed, propping Puppet-Papa up beside her. She'd just settled in when there was a sharp rap at the front door. She heard footsteps, then the creaking of hinges, followed by four startled gasps.

Milou peered through the cupboard-bed doors and down the hallway. Sem was standing by the windmill's entrance and she could tell by the way his left leg was shaking that something was wrong. A woman stood on the threshold and Milou could tell right away that it wasn't Edda Finkelstein.

'*Goedeavond*,' Sem said over-brightly. 'How can I help you?'

Milou squinted at the visitor. She was tall, wearing a long red coat, and her blonde hair was pulled into a tight bun on top of her head. In her arms, she carried a large, leather book and seemed to be struggling under the weight of it.

'*Goedeavond*,' said the woman as she peered into the gloom of the windmill. 'I'm sorry for the late hour, but it took me a while to find this address.'

She didn't look like a farmer, Milou decided. She was far too neat and tidy, and Milou doubted that her clothes had ever got within sneezing distance of a cow. Additionally, she doubted that farmers were known for carrying unusually large books around with them. Milou tried to read the writing on the cover. It looked familiar.

'We are not really prepared to receive visitors *at this hour*,' Sem said, leaning over slightly in an attempt to block the woman's wandering gaze.

'I am here to speak to Meneer Poppenmaker,' she said. 'Is he in?'

'Might I ask what your business is with our father?' Sem asked curtly. 'He's not feeling very well at the moment.'

The woman tapped a gloved hand on the book. With the lettering no longer obscured, Milou's heart stuttered. The book *was* familiar. Egbert had written in it just a few days ago.

'My name is Rose Speelman,' the woman said. 'And I am here on behalf of the Kinderbureau.'

20

Milou shuffled forward and peered over the edge of the half-closed cupboard-bed door. Her friends were all frozen to the spot and Milou didn't need to see their faces to know they were as horrified as she was. Why was the Kinderbureau here? Had they made a mistake with the paperwork?

'Is Meneer Poppenmaker in?' the woman said, trying to peer over Sem's shoulder into the kitchen. 'It's awfully cold out here.'

She made an exaggerated *brrrr* noise to emphasize her point.

'I, um . . . you,' Sem stuttered. 'He . . . you . . . well . . .'

'Good evening, Mevrouw,' Lotta said, bumping Sem aside with her hip. 'I am Lotta Poppenmaker. How may I help you?'

'Ah yes,' Speelman said, peering down at a sheet of paper in her hand. 'Lotta. The clever one with more fingers than is usual. It's a pleasure to put faces to names. I don't usually get to see the faces. Yours is particularly pleasing. Now, if you wouldn't mind, I need to speak to your adoptive father urgently.'

'Father is asleep. How about you come back another –'

'Is that him there? Meneer Poppen–'

'Shh. You'll wake him.'

'I'm afraid I must insist on speaking with him.'

Rose Speelman pushed past Lotta and Sem. Milou reached out and pulled the corner of the curtain they'd hung above the cupboard bed, hiding Puppet-Papa fully behind it.

There was a sharp whistle, followed by a *Screeeeeeeeeeeeeeeeeeech!* Mozart flew from his nest, spiralled down to block Speelman's path and grabbed a piece of meat from Fenna's outstretched fingers before swooping back into the shadows.

'What is *that*?' shrieked Rose Speelman, clutching the record book tightly to her chest.

'*That* is Mozart,' Lotta said. 'It's his hunting time and he's very hungry.'

Speelman's eyes widened behind her glasses. She sidestepped cautiously over to the kitchen table and sank into a chair. 'How peculiar,' she said, eyeing Mozart's wardrobe-top nest warily. 'Does he bite?'

Fenna smiled sweetly and nodded, holding up a bloodied fingertip.

HooOOooOOooOO!

'I really must speak with your father,' Speelman said, keeping her gaze fixed firmly on Mozart's hiding place. She waved a hand in Puppet-Papa's direction. 'Please wake him.'

Milou groaned silently. The woman wanted to speak to Bram. There was clearly only one way to get rid of her. Quietly and carefully, Milou took Puppet-Papa's cross strings and lifted his head slightly.

'Lotta, *liefje*,' Milou croaked as deeply and huskily as she could. 'What is all the commotion about?'

She fake-coughed – heaving, wracking coughs that burned her throat. Peeking over the door, Milou saw Speelman hastily cover her nose and mouth with a handkerchief. The Kinderbureau agent shuffled her chair further away from Puppet-Papa.

'Meneer Poppenmaker,' Speelman said, her voice slightly muffled by the handkerchief. 'I'm awfully sorry to disturb you, but I am here on official orphan business.' She tapped the record book again. 'I was sent to audit the Little Tulip's adoption records and found an anomaly.'

'But the paperwork was perfect!' Egbert cried. He was sitting in the chair beside the cupboard bed.

Milou grimaced; Egbert did, too. Speelman gave him a curious look under her spectacles.

'I mean,' he spluttered, 'Matron Gassbeek always prides herself on perfect paperwork. She says it's ever so important.'

Milou let out another stream of coughing. She shook Puppet-Papa's strings, making his shoulders shake. 'And what – *cough* – anomaly – *cough, cough* – would that – *cough* – be?'

Over the top of the door, she watched Rose Speelman curl her lip.

'It seems you did not pay the adoption fees.'

Milou's blood turned to ice. In their haste to leave, they had forgotten all about the fees.

Balancing the record book on the table, Rose Speelman flipped it open, shook her head until her spectacles fell down her nose and then cleared her throat.

'The items payable are as follows. Five orphans at a rate of ten guilders each. Payable upon receipt of the goods, which was *several* days ago. That means the final outstanding sum is fifty guilders, sir.'

Rose Speelman snapped the record book closed again.

Fifty guilders.

That was more money than Milou had ever seen before. How on earth were they going to find that?

'I apologize you had to come all this way,' Milou said gruffly. 'However, the matron and I had an understanding –'

'Elinora Gassbeek is . . . um . . . no longer at the Little Tulip Orphanage,' Speelman said. 'I'm afraid that we really do need to settle this affair right here, right now. Perhaps one of your new children can go and fetch the money. I will wait a while to rest my feet.'

Milou's heart stuttered. Lotta looked up at her with wide eyes of panic. The others were trying their best not to look at anything.

'Um . . .' Milou said, clearing her throat. Her mind was racing, but she knew she had to keep talking. 'I'm afraid to say that I do not have the money just yet. This sickness, it has stopped me from –'

'With all due respect,' Speelman said sternly, 'you have taken five children without paying. Raising orphans is an expensive business; we must recoup the costs if we are to keep our orphanages running. Business is business, Meneer Poppenmaker, and our records must be updated and in perfect order or I wouldn't be doing my job properly, would I now? Regardless of your current condition, I must insist that you pay me today or I will have no choice but to take the children back with me.'

Lotta gasped. Fenna curled into a tight ball on her seat. Sem's left knee began to shake. Egbert shot Milou a panicked look. Careful not to jostle the puppet strings, she opened a small wedge of curtain so that only Egbert could see her. Then she pointed, with her nose, to the paper and quill beside him. Egbert looked confused.

Speelman leaned forward, squinting at the alcove. 'Did you hear what I said, Meneer Poppenmaker?'

Milou's stomach twisted painfully. She tried to speak but couldn't. This was it; there was no way out of it.

Lotta stepped in front of Speelman. 'Forgive my manners, Mevrouw Speelman, for I have not offered you refreshment. Can I get you a drink of water? Or perhaps some warm milk?'

'No thank you, dear,' Speelman said, waving her away. 'Not with this sickness around. Meneer Poppenmaker?'

Screeeeeeech!

Speelman shrieked in surprise, covering her head, and Milou used the distraction to whisper to Egbert.

'Write a letter from Gassbeek saying she gave us more time to pay,' she hissed. 'And sign it with her signature. Can you remember it?'

Egbert's eyes grew round and frightened, but he took the paper and turned his back to the rest of the room to do as Milou had asked. Milou took the puppet's strings again and lifted Puppet-Papa's left arm, just as Egbert shoved the paper on to Puppet-Papa's lap.

'Lotta,' Milou rasped. 'Be a dear and pass Mevrouw Speelman this letter, would you?'

Speelman stood. 'I can –'

'No, no, allow me,' Lotta said, pushing Speelman's shoulders down. The agent sat back down with an *oof*. 'Honestly, you do *not* want this sickness. Poor Papa, it's not been pleasant for him.'

Lotta hurried over, squeezed carefully past the curtain and took the note from Puppet-Papa's lap.

'Matron Gassbeek assured me that it was fine to settle the outstanding balance once I was convinced these orphans would actually be suitable adoptees,' Milou croaked. 'Matron Gassbeek said she was happy to wait for the money –'

'As I said, Elinora Gassbeek is ... uh ... no longer in charge.' Speelman said, eyeing Mozart warily. 'It's not at all usual to make such an arrangement with adoptions.'

'Yes, well, these children are anything but usual,' Milou said hoarsely. 'Matron Gassbeek was adamant that they were unadoptable. She said I would be doing the orphanage a favour by taking them off her hands. And, I have to say, they are very useful around the mill, despite their peculiarities.'

'I suppose they are a little peculiar,' Rose Speelman said, glancing at each one in turn.

Lotta met her eyes with a cold stare, Sem smiled unconvincingly, Fenna and Egbert dipped their chins and

Milou wanted to roar in the woman's face, but bit the inside of her cheek instead. Speelman drummed her fingers on Egbert's letter. There was a long pause. She stared at Puppet-Papa for so long that Milou was certain she'd realized something was amiss.

'Oh, I suppose I can just add this to the file for now,' Speelman said at last, tucking the letter into the record book. 'I should have finished my audit in a week or so's time, and as long as the fees are settled then – assuming you want to keep these peculiar children – then I see no harm in honouring Matron Gassbeek's offer.'

'That is most kind,' Milou croaked.

'It was a pleasure to meet you, Meneer Poppenmaker. I shall return in ten days for the fees.'

'Ten days it is,' Milou rasped. 'Have a pleasant journey back to Amsterdam.'

Speelman was only one step from the doorway when she turned, her brow furrowed. 'Where is the fifth orphan?'

Lotta flinched.

'Milou is fetching medicine for me,' Milou said gruffly.

'I see,' Speelman said. 'I'm sure you're taking as good care of her as she is of you. Anyway, I must be off. I have a long ride back with this beast.'

She heaved the record book on to her shoulder and slipped out into the night.

21

The front door closed behind the Kinder-bureau agent with a wind-slapped *thunk*. Milou dropped Puppet-Papa's strings and let out a long breath. She joined the others at the window above the table in the kitchen, and they watched as Speelman stuffed the record book into the front basket of her bicycle, then peddled off through the gates, over the bridge and off down the darkened road.

Edda Finkelstein was still sitting by the flower garden, pulling weeds from the low wall as she watched Poppenmill. The Polder Warden dipped her peaked cap as Speelman cycled past and, even from this distance, Milou could see the Eyebrow of Curiosity raised high and indomitable.

Milou growled. 'That woman just can't let us be, can she?'

Lotta let the curtain fall closed again. 'If Edda were on to us, Speelman would have had more suspicions about

Puppet-Papa. No, Milou, this is our fault. We were careless in forgetting about the fees.'

'Fifty guilders,' Sem said, his voice small and hollow.

Mozart let out a sharp *Screeeeech*.

'You could probably buy a small house for that,' said Lotta.

'Or some tickets to Asia,' said Egbert.

'Or five *peculiar* orphans,' Milou added.

No one spoke for several long minutes. Outside, the wind was picking up, howling and wailing, much like the despairing thoughts in Milou's head.

'We're going to have to buy our freedom then,' she said finally. 'We have ten days to work it out. We'll raise the money, pay her and be rid of the Kinderbureau once and for all.'

The others all looked at her as if she'd said something utterly stupid.

Milou's ears tingled softly. 'I realize it's an improbable feat, but –'

'No,' Lotta said, and Milou could almost see the cogs of her mind whirring round in search of a solution. But then she shook her head. 'It really is *impossible* this time.'

'But –'

'We should get some sleep,' Sem said. 'We must make the most of these warm beds in the few days we have left. We can talk about where to go next in the morning.'

Milou looked at each of them in turn, unwilling to believe that they could give up so easily. 'You want to *leave*?'

Egbert shook his head. 'We *have* to leave.'

One by one, they turned away and headed to bed, except for Sem and Milou.

They sat at the kitchen table, feet meeting in the middle, and stared out of the window, watching the frost glisten. Neither spoke.

Weariness gripped Milou. She couldn't let all this be taken from her. She *wouldn't*. She just had to be as brave and as clever as her parents and sister undoubtedly were, wherever they were. There had to be a way for the five of them to stay.

The others were soon asleep, thin plumes of breath-mist rising out of the blankets.

'That theatre ... it's the kind of thing you've always dreamed of, isn't it?' Sem said eventually.

'Almost,' Milou replied.

She didn't need to mention the fact that it was missing one vital thing: her family. Sem would know what she felt. He *always* seemed to know. They sat there for several long minutes, watching the dust motes swirl and the frost sparkle.

'Do you want to know what my dream was?' Sem said quietly.

Milou's head snapped towards him.

'Cirque de Lumière,' he said, smiling wistfully.

Milou frowned. Three years ago, a Parisian circus troupe had come to Amsterdam. The five of them had risked Gassbeek's cane by gathering on the street outside to watch the troupe parade down the street on their way to the park. They had each been given a poster for the show by a clown. The very same poster that was now one of her most treasured possessions: a keepsake of a moment of joy in an ocean of gloom. She still remembered the look on all their faces that day. It was the first time she had ever seen Fenna really smile.

'You want to be a clown?'

He rolled his eyes. 'Of course not. Though I'd probably make a good one.'

'Well? What then?'

'A few days after the parade, when I was cleaning the gutters out the front, a few of the acrobats were walking past. They had long cloaks over their outfits, but I recognized them right away. One of them, a woman with skin darker than Egbert's, caught the edge of her cloak on a railing. I ran over immediately and offered to stitch it up for her. We talked about the circus and she said their costumes were always getting ripped; that there didn't seem to be enough thread in the world to keep up with their costume-repair needs.'

Sem's voice trailed away. Milou waited quietly for him to continue, wondering why he had never told her any of this before. When he started speaking again, his expression had darkened.

'When I told her about some ideas I had for their costumes, she offered to take me on as an apprentice costume designer,' he said quietly. 'She wanted to go into the orphanage that very moment and arrange it with Gassbeek. The circus was due to leave for Denmark the following day.'

Milou tried to swallow, but found her mouth was completely dry. 'What happened?'

Sem gave a tight-lipped smile, but refused to meet her gaze. 'I told her I couldn't go, of course.'

'Sem! Why on earth did you tell her that?' But Milou realized she already knew why.

'I couldn't leave you four. I wanted to wait until each of you had a family before I left. And, well, I guess some things just aren't meant to be.' He gave her a rueful smile. 'You weren't the only one trying *not* to get adopted, you know. Although, to be honest, I didn't have to try very hard. These ears did most of the work for me.'

All Milou could do was stare at him. Sem had given up his dream for them?

'I'm telling you this because you need to decide what's most important to you,' Sem said. 'We followed you here because it was our only chance of getting out of that place. Now we all risk being sent back in ten days. Perhaps your family *will* come back for you one day, but the rest of us don't have that hope to cling on to. The freedom we have now is the only thing we've ever had that belongs to us.'

'My family –'

'Your family *abandoned* you, Milou.' Sem squeezed his eyes closed for a moment. When he opened them again, he looked nothing short of exhausted. 'I'm not sure I'll ever understand why it is you're so fixated on finding those people. I don't care what reason my birth family had for leaving me. The fact is they did leave me, in a wheat sack no less, to live in the most miserable orphanage imaginable. The last thing I'll ever do is set foot in that place again.'

'I won't let Speelman take you back there,' Milou said.

'Then you agree that we'll probably have to leave here?'

Milou looked from Sem to the flickering flames in the middle of the room, at the five pairs of boots Fenna had hung neatly beside the front door.

This was her home. It was *their* home.

Then she looked back at Sem: the boy who had given up his dream to stay with them and make sure they were looked after.

'I promise I'll do whatever I must to keep all five of us safe,' Milou said, wiping away a warm tear. 'Even if that means leaving.'

Milou's Book of Theories

Theory Reanalysis

The 'Werewolf Hunter' Theory
New clues: claw marks in the theatre and in Edda's workroom. A story, written by my sister, which includes a werewolf boy.
Theory viability: still possible.

The 'Secret Spy' Theory
New clues: no sign of my mother, unexplained desertion of the windmill, no photographs or personal documents. My family were reclusive and clearly very secretive.
Theory viability: <u>still possible.</u>

The 'Baby-phobia' Theory
New clues: no sign of a baby or any baby stuff.
Theory viability: <u>still possible.</u>

The 'Unthinkable' Theory
No dead bodies, no ghosts, no bloodstains.
New clues: none.
Theory viability: there is still no point thinking about this one until the others are disproven or further evidence comes to light.

Milou woke shivering. She was still lying on the kitchen table, cheek against the window frame, with a blanket that Sem must have wrapped round her now tangled about her ankles. She pulled it up to her shoulders and peeked through the curtain.

Despite the frosty morning, the fields, canals and main road were still bustling with activity. Her gaze settled on one particularly tall, long-legged figure that was weaving round the bonnet-clad farmwives, nodding to passing cyclists and looking all too officious.

Edda Finkelstein.

There was a shuffling noise from the next room, then Egbert appeared, his raven hair sticking up at all angles and his dark eyes squinting at the morning light.

'We should be packed and ready to run at a moment's

notice,' he said, rolling up his polder-map carefully and tucking it into his coal bucket.

'You're right,' Milou said glumly, turning her attention back to the Polder Warden, who seemed to be keeping within eyeshot of Poppenmill at all times.

Egbert continued to scour the kitchen for items to pack. 'I've been thinking – perhaps we could head south, to France or Spain. At least it'll be warmer down there.'

'Hmm-mmm.'

Edda had paused to talk to the same group of women who had stood at the gates of Poppenmill just a couple of days previously. They huddled together. Sly glances were cast at the mill and eyebrows were raised. Milou groaned and let the curtain fall closed.

'You're having second thoughts about leaving, aren't you?' Egbert asked flatly.

'Surely you understand why I can't just abandon my home with nothing, Egg,' she whispered. 'You've always wanted answers just as much as I have. You want to find your family, too, don't you?'

Egbert sighed. 'For me, it's never been about finding out who my parents are. It's about finding out who *I* am; it's hard to know for certain when I've never even met anyone else who looks like me.'

'I know who you are. You're Egbert Poppenmaker, a boy destined to be the greatest cartographer the world has ever known. What does it matter if you look a little different from the people around you?'

'It matters a great deal,' Egbert said. 'Because knowing where in the world I come from is just the first of the many answers *I* need.'

Milou swallowed, then nodded in understanding.

'Perhaps we could head east to Bavaria,' Egbert said, changing the subject. 'They have huge, ancient forests there we could hide in.'

'I don't suppose it matters much where we go,' Milou said dejectedly.

If they really were going to have to leave, it would mean she'd come all this way for nothing.

As they ate more potato stew for breakfast, the others discussed where they could go, how they might find food and shelter and when they should leave. Milou nodded and hmm-mmm'ed along to the discussion, but her ears were tingling and itching, her mind whirling with despair, and she didn't really hear them. After clearing the dishes, she slipped quietly away to the upper floors.

If they had to leave the windmill, then Milou was

determined to find something, anything, that might help her eventually locate her family.

She spent the afternoon scouring the place from top to bottom, then from bottom to top and back down again, certain that her mother or father or sister would have left a clue hidden for her somewhere; anything that would tell her where the three of them had disappeared to. But all she had to show for her efforts several hours later was hair full of cobwebs, three fingers full of splinters and a heart full of growing doubt.

Perhaps they didn't want to be found. Perhaps Gassbeek had been right all along. Perhaps her parents really hadn't wanted her.

That evening, despite the roaring hearth and warm blankets, Milou was shivering with unease, her ears prickling incessantly.

As the others settled down in front of the living room fire place, Milou curled up once more on the kitchen table, peering sneakily out of the window. The Polder Warden seemed to be continuing her campaign of scrutiny outside, undeterred by the gathering dusk or falling temperature. When she wasn't walking up and down the road talking to their neighbours, she was in her garden or tending to her pigs and chickens. Always within eyeshot and always looking as curious as ever.

'Here,' Egbert said, appearing on the table beside her. He put the Carnival of Nightmares notebook in Milou's hands. 'We should travel light, but I don't see why you couldn't take this.'

Milou flicked it open, her ears tingling as she ran a hand over the pencil drawing of the Night Tree. 'Thank you.'

He peeked through the other end of the curtain.

'Once we leave, you'll never have to worry about her again,' Egbert said, looking very worried. 'Though she . . . she still has my shawl. I can't leave without it.'

'If she doesn't return it tomorrow, I'll get it back for you,' Milou promised. 'Even if I have to knock her door down to get it.'

Egbert smiled. 'That won't draw attention to us in the slightest.'

They watched silently as Edda handed a basket of eggs to Arno, then waved him goodbye. She crossed the little bridge over the canal, her eyes never leaving the mill. Then halfway down her stone path she stopped, turned and walked up to the oak tree.

Milou pressed her face a little closer to the glass.

The Polder Warden stood in front of the tree, placing one hand against the trunk. Her shoulders seemed to sag slightly. Then, just as abruptly, she dropped her hand, straightened up and walked all the way to her house without a single glance back at the mill. Milou was still frowning in confusion long after Edda's front door had closed behind her.

'Hmm,' Egbert said.

'What?'

'I hadn't noticed before, but this tree –' he tapped Liesel's book – 'looks an awful lot like that tree.' Then he tapped the window and prickles spread from Milou's ears down her back.

Egbert was right. The oak tree *was* the Night Tree.

Milou waited until all the lights in Edda's house were out before slipping out of the front door and hurrying towards the tree. She didn't light the lantern she'd brought with her until she was safely hidden beneath the oak's skeletal canopy.

The tingling of her ears intensified the closer she got, spreading to the back of her neck as she reached out, just like Edda had, and touched it. Goosebumps erupted all up her arms.

This tree must have heard at least a century's worth of secrets. Maybe, just maybe, it had a secret only for her.

Lotta must have been right about the coordinates after all; Milou's parents wanted her to find this tree, she was certain of it. Her ears tingled as if in agreement.

Holding the lantern up to the gnarled bark, Milou circled the tree's trunk, running her fingers over it. Halfway round, she found her first clue. Claw marks.

They were hard to make out – moss had grown over them in places, meaning they must have been there for quite a long time – but Milou was certain they were the same as the ones on her coffin-basket and those in Edda's workshop. She spread her fingers out over them and their size confirmed her suspicions.

She glanced back at the Polder Warden's house, which was dark and still, her heart racing. Edda was *definitely* connected to all this somehow. Whatever role she'd played in the Poppenmakers' disappearance, Milou would find out.

Setting the lantern on a branch above her, Milou stepped onto the flower garden wall and hoisted herself up on to the first branch. In the glow of the lantern, she found herself staring at more marks gouged into the tree.

Names. Tens of them. Some covered over in moss, others – like Sanne and Arno's – carved more recently. Milou read them all. It wasn't until she got to the second branch that she found one that started a fresh wave of ear-tingles.

Edda

Milou stifled a growl and climbed higher. More names, none of which she knew.

She wasn't even halfway up yet, but already she could tell why the polder people liked to climb this tree. The only view that rivalled it was from the windmill's balcony.

Arms aching and chest heaving, Milou finally got to one of the topmost branches. It was a long drop to the ground below and, for a moment, she sat there, hugging the branch with her eyes closed, trying to stop the world from spinning. When the dizziness eased, she opened her eyes again.

There, right in front of her, were two names she recognized:

Thibault and Liesel

Her ear-tingling turned into a storm of tiny, ice-cold prickles and Milou rubbed at her ears frantically.

'Thibault,' she whispered, the foreign-sounding name feeling funny in her mouth. It was the same name she'd seen in Liesel's book. Milou felt an unfamiliar twist in her belly as if she'd eaten something too sour or too hot. It should have been her name there, not Thibault's. It should have been her sitting up here with her sister, sharing secrets and telling stories, gazing out across the polder and up at the stars, but this boy, Thibault, had been there instead.

Milou carefully clambered across to the next branch, using the glow of the moon to see by now. She had to climb across two more, then one higher before she found another carving etched just beside a small hollow.

Her fingers shook as she traced each small line.

Br m and An ese

Milou scratched at the moss, but the carving was so old that her scrubbing at it made little difference to its legibility. Still, Milou was certain it said Bram. And the name beside it must have been her mother's name. Her ear tips became a maelstrom of prickles.

Milou let her hand drop to her side, then her gaze settled on the hollow. Wedged inside was a small red bundle, half the size of her fist.

Milou pulled it out and held it in her open palm. Upon closer inspection, she realized it was a carefully folded handkerchief. Squeezing it, she could feel something small and hard inside. She turned it over and lifted one edge. Milou's stomach lurched and a small gasp left her lips. In the corner, embroidered in white silk thread, was a name:

A. Poppenmaker

Finally, she had proof of her mother. An initial, if not a whole name.

She carefully unrolled the yellowing handkerchief completely and two golden objects glinted up at her. Wedding rings.

Milou tilted one towards the moonlight. In the very same tiny font as on her pocket watch was an inscription:

Beneath the stars I found you.

Her ears tingling wildly, Milou looked up, at the bright constellations that twinkled above her, at the way the moon shone down, turning everything below it a silvery grey.

Her parents had climbed this tree to watch the night sky. And here she was, twelve years later, sitting in the same spot they had. From this height, she could see straight through the theatre's hole-pocked roof to the marionette on the stage, who stood, haloed by the moonlight, as if ready to begin her dance beneath the stars.

Milou gasped. The solution seemed so obvious now. It wasn't her who was meant to find *them*. They were supposed to find *her*.

They had lost her, but now Milou had everything she needed to let them know that she'd made it home.

And maybe, just maybe, it would also get her the money they needed to get Speelman off their backs at the same time.

The theatre still smelled mouldy, despite the fact that they had left the door open for days now. Dust motes floated in the columns of moonlight that streamed in through the holes in the roof, illuminating every cobweb and every bit of grime. The ballerina puppet was coated in a new layer of frost, its strings like stalactites. Milou sat her friends down on the front row of the theatre as she explained her money-making, parent-summoning plan.

'A puppet show?' Egbert asked, incredulous. 'In *here*?'

'Yes!' Milou beamed. 'It's such an obvious solution, isn't it?'

'Not really . . .'

'A grand reopening will be the talk of Amsterdam and the answer to *all* our problems. Not only will it make us the money we need, but, as soon as my parents hear about the show, they'll know I've returned and hurry home to me.'

<220>

Mozart, who was awake and sitting on Fenna's shoulder, let out a loud *Screeeeech*.

'It will be a huge task to get this place looking like it once was,' Lotta said. 'And it'll cost money, too.'

'On the contrary,' Milou said, feeling increasingly pleased with her idea. 'This place already looks fabulously horrendous.'

Sem shook his head. 'People will expect a certain kind of quality where this theatre is concerned. It looks like the scene of a horror show.'

'But that's my point, Sem Poppenmaker,' Milou grinned. 'Use those big ears of yours to listen properly. The mystery of the Poppenmakers' disappearance has been the source of gossip and intrigue for years. Everyone, except Edda, of course, is too scared to even set foot on this land.'

'You're not convincing us yet,' Egbert complained.

'Egg could paint a few monsters on that wall over there,' Milou said excitedly, think out loud. 'We could tear the velvet seats up a little bit more and add some dirt to the carpet. Oh! And we should do the show at night, when it's dark and cold like it is now.'

She realized her friends still looked unconvinced.

'Haven't my stories shown you that people *love* to be scared?' Milou said. 'We will *terrify* them, and they'll pay through the nose for the experience.'

Lotta's eyebrows began to relax. Fenna nodded. Even Mozart let out a *HooOOoooOOoo* of agreement. Sem's face broke into a huge, crooked grin.

'You truly are an evil genius, Milou Poppenmaker,' he said.

Milou grinned back. 'I know.'

'It'll still cost money to set up,' Lotta said, though her expression was more thoughtful than dubious. 'We'd need to make more puppets and add some lighting to the room. You can't operate more than one puppet on your own, but I could mechanize some of them. And perhaps we could install some speaking tubes, so your voice can be projected. We have some of the materials we need. I could ask Edda for some of the other bits – that way, it shouldn't be too expensive. I'm sure she won't mind lending it to us were I to accept her offer of an apprenticeship.'

Milou opened her mouth to protest, then shut it again. She gave Lotta a brief nod; they would need more money than they could make selling dolls if her idea were to work.

'We should be saving any money we earn for our escape plan,' Egbert said. 'Not throwing it away on something that has no guarantee of success.'

'I promise,' Milou said, 'that if my plan doesn't work we will have everything in place for running away. Please, Egg, give this a chance. We have the opportunity to not only get the Kinderbureau off our backs for good, but to really make something of ourselves.'

'We have *nine* days left, Milou.'

'Then we will hold our show in eight days and have one left over should it not work out the way we hope. It'll be tight, but *not* impossible.'

Egbert stared at her hard for a few moments, then nodded. 'Fine.'

Milou resisted the urge to hug him as his expression hinted that he was still apprehensive. She gave him a grateful smile instead.

'What show will we put on then?' Lotta asked. '*The Princess and the Werewolf* perhaps?'

'No,' Milou said, dropping her voice to a raspy growl. 'I'm thinking something *much* more terrifying than that.'

She climbed up on the stage and did a pirouette, her cloak flying around her.

'Welcome, ladies and gentlemen,' she said loudly and gruffly, 'to the Theatre of Terrors. Prepare to be spooked, prepare to tremble in your seats, prepare to be awed. I give you . . .'

She paused dramatically, then, in her best werewolf voice, said:

'. . . A *Carnival . . . of Nightmares*!'

*

February arrived the very next day, with a nose-numbing frost that drove most of the inhabitants of the polder indoors. Mist hung thick and low over the canals, refusing to lift. Milou hoped it would stay this gloriously gloomy until the night of the puppet show in seven days' time.

Lotta set off to Edda's house with her toolbox, a firm promise not to ask questions and a glint of delight in her eyes, as soon as the sun had risen. The others headed to the theatre, to begin the arduous task of preparing the stage for their show. By the afternoon, they had new curtains hanging from the rails, a huge Night Tree painted on the stage's back wall and rumbling stomachs all around.

That night, as Fenna and Sem prepared dinner from the last of the food they'd bought at the market, Liesel's book lay open on the table in front of Milou, a blank page staring up at her. She needed an ending for the tale, but, for the life of her, Milou had no idea how to finish Theodora's story. Every time she tried to think about what might lie beyond those carnival gates, her mind drifted to her family.

Would they come to the show?

Two days later, they had Theodora and Hendrik puppets, needle-pricked fingers and a flicker of excitement that they might actually pull this show off. Except for one irksome thing. Milou still couldn't think of an ending.

'My hands are going to fall off at this rate,' Egbert said, setting a poster aside to dry next to a teetering stack of them. 'And we need more ink . . . again.'

'Lotta will be back soon,' Milou said. 'She can give you money for ink.'

Fenna set a tray of steaming-hot stroopwafels out in front of them. Sem immediately put down his sewing and tucked in. Out of her apron, Fenna pulled a strip of dried meat. She held it up and whistled softly. Wings fluttered from the cupboard top and Mozart swooped down in a loose spiral, taking the meat from her fingers.

'He's getting better at flying,' Sem said, syrup dribbling down the side of his mouth.

Fenna's responding smile was bright enough to light up the dark side of the moon. Milou had even, that very morning, heard Fenna humming quietly as she baked. It seemed that this puppet show was working magic in more ways than she'd expected: it was making them happy.

The kitchen door opened with a howl of wind and Lotta stumbled in, stamping her clogs loose of snow. 'You need to come to the theatre,' she said. Her nose was bright pink from the cold. 'Right now.'

'It's too cold,' Egbert said, shuddering.

'Trust me,' Lotta said. She hurried over to the table and grabbed two stroopwafels. 'What Edda and I have done is worth a few frostbitten noses. Come on!'

'Edda?' Milou asked, frowning. 'What is Edda doing in the theatre?'

'Just come!' said Lotta.

It was no warmer inside the theatre than it was outside it. Edda Finkelstein was standing by the stage, holding a strange metal box. Milou bristled at the sight of her, the unease she felt around the clockmaker refusing to shift. Especially now the Kinderbureau was on to them.

'Aha!' Edda said, her voice muffled by her scarf. 'You're just in time. Watch this.'

She pressed a button on the top of the metal box. There was a low hum, then a crackle. Edda grinned at them as the stage erupted with the light of hundreds of little bulbs, twinkling like stars.

Milou couldn't help it: her jaw slackened. 'Is that . . .?'

'Electricity?' Lotta said. 'Yes. And Edda also thinks we should open the theatre with a firework display. Just imagine!'

'There's a firework stall in the city market,' Edda said, putting the metal box on the stage. 'Anyway, I should get back home now. Meneer Catticus needs feeding. Thank you for your help this morning, Lotta.'

'No, thank *you*,' Lotta said, beaming at Edda. 'Your help means the world to us.'

'You're most welcome,' Edda said, her eyes meeting Milou's. 'Do send my regards to Bram, won't you? I hope this weather isn't making him feel worse.'

Milou felt another twinge of unease. She nodded.

'Oh,' Edda said, reaching into her satchel. 'Egg, I almost forgot. Here's your shawl. I managed to get most of the charcoal off it, but not all, I'm afraid.'

She held out a folded bundle of bright red, orange and yellow silk. If it weren't for the familiar egg-shaped pattern and sooty patch, Milou wouldn't have believed it was the same shawl. Egbert just stared at it.

'It's Javanese batik, I believe,' Edda said, unfolding it and wrapping it carefully round his neck. 'Though I can't be a hundred per cent sure. If you could find someone who has travelled to that part of the world, they might be able to confirm it.'

'Thank you,' Egbert said, his voice choking with emotion. He rubbed at a tear. 'Thank you.'

Fenna shuffled up to him, wrapping an arm round his waist. Edda smiled kindly, then she gathered up her toolbox and left. Lotta trailed along, talking excitedly about the chemical compounds of fireworks. Milou followed them to the theatre door.

'Why are you scowling again?' Lotta asked when Edda had disappeared round the side of the building. 'You're not going to start on about Edda again, are you?'

'There's just something about her,' Milou said. 'Something that makes me feel like that woman will be our downfall.'

Lotta raised an Edda-like eyebrow. 'Are your magical danger-sensing ears telling you this?'

Milou flinched. 'No. Logic is. Nothing about her makes sense.'

Lotta was quiet for a moment. Milou avoided her gaze for as long as she could, worried she'd see smug satisfaction in Lotta's eyes at her admission, but, when she looked up, Lotta just looked thoughtful.

'I think Edda had a husband once,' Lotta said finally. 'I found a pair of men's boots by the back door. Far too big for her.'

'Maybe he died?'

Lotta shrugged. 'Maybe. There's a sadness about her that she doesn't let show very often. The kind of sadness I imagine someone might have when they miss someone dearly.' She looked at Milou. 'I honestly think she'll do us no harm, even if she did learn the truth about us. She's nothing like Gassbeek. She's good. I don't know how I know that, but I do. Deep down in the pit of my belly, I know it's true.'

'That sounds like a very unscientific hypothesis.'

Lotta smiled. 'Maybe I have magical goodness-sensing guts.'

'I'm still not convinced.'

'Will this convince you?'

Lotta grabbed Milou's hand and dropped a drawstring pouch into it. Milou squeezed it. It was filled with coins. Lots of coins.

'What's this?'

'An advance from Edda, for you to place an advertisement in the national paper.'

'An advertisement?'

'Your father isn't likely to be in Amsterdam, is he? If you want him to hear about the show, then you need the message to be spread further than just the city. It costs two guilders to place an advert for a week. Edda said I could borrow the money from her.'

Milou felt tears prickle in the corners of her eyes. 'Two guilders . . . don't you want it to go towards the adoption fees?'

Lotta shook her head. 'Not if it can help you, no.'

'Thank you,' whispered Milou.

'Tomorrow then,' Lotta said brightly.

'Tomorrow what?'

'Tomorrow we go to Amsterdam and let everyone know that, for one night only, the Poppenmaker theatre is open once more!'

Milou's Book of Theories

Beneath the stars they'll find me.

Here is the advertisement I plan on placing in the newspaper. I've even left a hidden message in the <u>underlined</u> words. My family are clever enough to work it out.

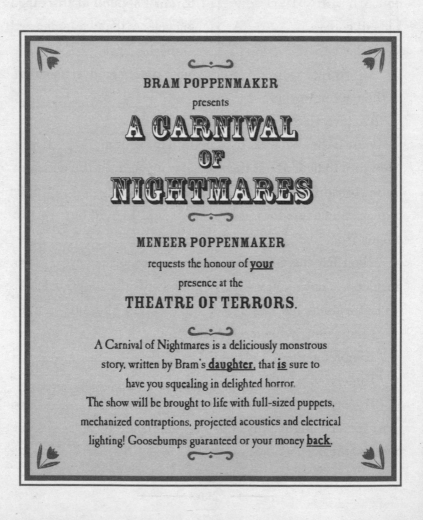

BRAM POPPENMAKER

presents

A CARNIVAL
OF
NIGHTMARES

MENEER POPPENMAKER

requests the honour of <u>**your**</u>

presence at the

THEATRE OF TERRORS.

A Carnival of Nightmares is a deliciously monstrous
story, written by Bram's <u>**daughter**</u>, that <u>**is**</u> sure to
have you squealing in delighted horror.
The show will be brought to life with full-sized puppets,
mechanized contraptions, projected acoustics and electrical
lighting! Goosebumps guaranteed or your money <u>**back**</u>.

They set off for Amsterdam at first light, all five of them on Bram Poppenmaker's cargo bicycle. Milou was squeezed into the back of the crate, clutching a bagful of posters and trying not to choke on Fenna's hair as the wind whipped it into her face. Behind her, Sem panted as he peddled at speed towards the city. The polder air tingled with the smallest promise that spring was on its way, and hope as she'd never felt it bloomed in Milou's chest. Today was the day that she would send the secret message to her parents. Soon they would know that she'd come home.

'The canals are thawing!' Lotta yelled from the front of the bicycle. 'Look!'

Milou pushed aside a handful of Fenna's red curls and peered over the edge of the crate. Sure enough, the ice was patchy. Grass was poking free from the blanket of frost on the banks, and the everlasting mist shimmered like spun gold.

'It won't be too much longer until the tulips are out,' Lotta said. 'That would be a sight worth painting, don't you think, Egg?'

Wedged near Milou's other knee, Egbert was staring silently down at his shawl, running his hand over the pattern.

'One day soon,' she said, more softly, 'when we're finally safe from Rotman and the Kinderbureau, we'll find someone who can tell us more about Java.'

Egbert frowned up at her. 'There's no reason I can't try to find someone today.'

'Yes, there is. We have an important mission. It'll have to wait, Egg. I'm sorry.'

Egbert gave her an odd look, then turned his face away.

Milou felt a sharp stab of regret in the pit of her stomach, recognizing his pained expression for what it was: a desperate hunger for answers. That same desperation gnawed at her, too. She'd help Egbert find his answers soon enough, in any way she could, but right now they all needed to focus on their mission. There was too much at stake to worry about anything else.

That's what she told herself, over and over, as Sem pedalled them onwards, and Egbert retreated further into himself, burying his face in his shawl.

Less than an hour later, they parked the bicycle on the outskirts of the city and tumbled, stiff-legged and aching, out of the crate as Sem propped the bicycle against a railing. Lotta had equipped them each with a bag of posters, a hammer, a pouch of nails and a hasty lesson on how not to squish their fingers. Two of Milou's fingers were still throbbing, but she barely noticed. Her stomach was full of jittery impatience.

'Milou and I will put posters up in the inner ring of the city,' Lotta said. 'Sem, you do all along the Prinsengracht canal. Egg and Fenna, you will do all along the Keizersgracht canal. One poster every ten metres. Avoid the Little Tulip and wear your scarves up high over your nose at all times, just in case. We will meet by the clock tower in Sophiaplein at four p.m. and then stop off at the newspaper on our way home.'

'Don't be late,' Milou added, her fingers seeking the reassuring presence of the coin pouch in her pocket. 'The newspaper closes at five p.m.'

Still refusing to meet her gaze, Egbert nodded, grabbed Fenna's hand and disappeared into the crowd. Sem dipped his cap, then set off with a jaunty lope in the direction of the nearest bridge. Hefting their bags over their shoulders, Milou and Lotta made for the busy market square on the other side of the canal. They rounded a corner and emerged among a rippling tide of walking canes, winged bonnets, clogs, boots, cloaks, wicker baskets and smiling faces. Milou had never seen so many people in one place before. It seemed that the whole of Amsterdam was out to enjoy the first snowless day in months.

The market stretched out in front of them, stalls lining both sides of the street. The air smelled of a thousand wonderful fragrances. Each fresh gust of wind carried a new scent: spices, smoke, caramel, fruit, fish, shoe polish. It wasn't just food and clothing on offer, though; there were Bavarian broom-sellers, an umbrella repairman from London, a man selling artificial limbs, children selling ribbons, carpet beaters and a woman with very few teeth offering moustache-trimming services. In the middle of it all was a huge street organ, decorated with a row of dancing wooden swans. A lively symphony burst from its pipes, and a smiley-faced man stood beside it, shaking a money tin to the rhythm.

'It's so noisy!' Lotta yelled, her smile gone as she dodged round a circle of dancing children. 'And cramped.'

Milou was too busy gawping to respond. Her eyes settled on a bell-shaped tent wedged between a clog stall and a tram stop. The tent's curtains, Milou noticed, were tightly closed. She had to squint to read the hand-painted sign attached to the side.

The UNADOPTABLES

Spiritualist from Bohemia – Seances and Fortune-telling

A shiver ran down the back of Milou's neck, and she found herself walking towards the tent – until six fingers closed on her forearm and pulled her back.

'Who in their right mind would buy rabbits' feet?' Lotta said, nodding towards a pedlar in a fur coat. She handed Milou the hammer and some nails, then uncurled a poster and held it up against a wooden signpost. 'People's silly superstitions can be so cruel.'

'I bet Gassbeek would have loved those,' Milou said, bringing the hammer down. 'She'd have probably worn them as earrings – ow!'

Lotta caught the hammer as it fell and rolled her eyes. 'How can you miss the nail so often?'

'*Uhh dunnuuh*,' Milou said, sucking a new lump on her thumb.

With three short *tack-tack-tacks*, Lotta drove a nail into the top of the poster. She added another at the bottom and then stepped back to examine her handiwork. 'Just another ninety-nine to go.'

They walked ten stretched-leg paces down the street and Lotta tacked another poster to some wooden scaffolding, and then another one over an advert for lace doilies. Milou's gaze kept drifting back to the spiritualist's tent, wondering

235

who was inside it. A sudden bell-tinkling made her jump. A tram was negotiating its way through the market and the bay-coloured horse pulling it snorted at Milou as she staggered out of its path. Milou turned to find Lotta watching the tram with pure mischief glinting in her eyes. She grabbed Milou's arm and they followed it to the tram stop.

'I'm going to nail a poster to the back of it,' Lotta whispered. 'That way, our advert will travel all over Amsterdam. Keep an eye out, would you?'

She disappeared round the side of the tram as people began climbing out of the carriage. Milou crossed her arms and tried to look inconspicuous, looking lazily up and down the market. Once again, her eyes were drawn to the strange tent right beside her. Then, before she knew what she was doing, she reached up to touch it, the curtains drew back and a girl emerged.

She wore a long green cloak, the hood pulled up over her head, long wisps of white-blonde hair spilling out of the sides of it. Her eyes were painted in a way that made them look almost catlike and her lips were stained blood-red. Milou's gaze dropped to just below the girl's chin, where a white, round object dangled from a chain. It was, Milou realized in horror, not a pendant but a human eyeball.

Milou staggered back a step.

The girl's eyes snapped to hers. Long fingers, covered in rings, reached up to touch the eyeball at her neck. Then a slow smile crept on to those blood-red lips.

'It's porcelain,' the girl said in a heavily accented voice. She held it up for Milou to see more clearly, then tapped with a long nail to show it was as hard as stone. 'See? An artificial eye. It belonged to a boy one hundred years ago. He lost his right eye in a sword fight with his little sister.'

'Oh,' Milou said. And then she frowned. 'How could you possibly know all that?'

The girl's smile twitched at both corners. 'Because his spirit told me.'

Milou felt a tiny pinch at her right earlobe. She gasped, but, before she could even reach up to her ear, the sensation was gone. The girl was squinting over Milou's shoulder, holding the eyeball to her right eye. Milou followed the girl's gaze, but there was no one behind her. She could just about hear the quiet *tap-tap-tap* of Lotta's hammer. When she turned back, the girl was staring intently at her. Milou wondered how old she was; certainly older than her and Lotta, but it couldn't be by much.

'Let me read your fortune,' the girl said, pulling the tent curtains open behind her. She lowered her voice. 'I could give you the answers you most crave.'

Milou opened her mouth to respond, but her ear tingled again. She looked up and found the girl squinting past her shoulder once more. Once again, Milou found nothing at all behind her.

'Thank you, but no,' Milou said. She touched the coin pouch. 'I already know what I need to know about my future.'

'But what about your past –'

The girl snapped her mouth closed, again looking past Milou. This time, Milou turned to find Lotta standing there, hammer in hand and scowling hard.

'We should get going, Milou,' Lotta said, taking her hand and pulling her away.

'Do your ears ever –' the girl whispered as Milou brushed past, but Lotta increased her pace and dragged her off before she could hear the rest.

'Try to keep away from the charlatans, would you?' Lotta said.

'She said she could read my fortune.'

'Honestly, Milou!' Lotta groaned, stopping at another signpost. 'Palmistry is such a sham. There is no scientific evidence whatsoever that the future can be predicted. You shouldn't waste your money on that nonsense.'

'She doesn't read palms. I think she uses the eyeball of a dead boy.'

Lotta stopped mid-hammer strike and gave her a disgusted look.

'Forget it,' Milou said, not wanting to start an argument. 'Let's just hurry up. I don't want to miss the newspaper. And you're right – I don't need to resort to silly superstitions to find my family.'

'Good,' Lotta said. 'Now let's get those fireworks, then we must hurry back to meet the others.'

Milou glanced over her shoulder. The tent curtains were closed again, the girl nowhere in sight.

Sem was already waiting at the rendezvous point when Milou and Lotta arrived just before 4 o'clock. He was sitting on a bench, covered in pigeons.

'I tripped over a bag of grain,' Sem said with a lopsided shrug. 'I managed to scoop most of it back into the bag, so they didn't charge me.'

Milou stifled a smile and wiped some grain from his hat into her hand. She held it up to a grey pigeon. Lotta dug a hand into her bag and pulled out a squashed bread roll. They watched the clock tower as they ate, swiping away greedy pigeons. At quarter past four, there was still no sign of Egbert and Fenna.

'What's taking them so long?' Milou said, her patience wearing thin with each tick of the grand clock.

'They probably just lost track of time,' Lotta said. 'They'll be here soon.'

Another five minutes ticked by achingly slowly.

'I'm not waiting any more.' Milou stood, brushing crumbs off her chest. 'You can stay here if you like. You can tell Egg I'm not happy. He knows how important this is.'

'He wouldn't do this on purpose,' Sem said.

'He's angry at me. Maybe he's trying to make a point.'

Sem shook his head, looking up and down the square with worried eyes. 'No, something's not right.'

Milou opened her mouth to respond, but then caught a glimpse of a figure running across the other side of the square. An embroidered silk cap bobbed through the crowd and then Fenna emerged just ahead of them, panting and panic-stricken, tears streaming down each cheek. Sem was on his feet and bounding towards her in an instant. Milou and Lotta hurried after him.

'What's wrong?' Lotta asked at the same time as Sem asked, 'Where's Egg?'

Fenna's fists were balled up and she was gasping and gulping. Lotta took Fenna's hands in her own and rubbed them. 'Take a deep breath,' she said.

Fenna shook her head. She pointed behind her.

'Did he get lost?' Milou asked.

Fenna groaned and shook her head again.

'Is he hurt?' Sem asked. 'Did something happen to him?'

Fenna squeezed her eyes closed and took a few steadying breaths.

'What happened?' Lotta asked. 'Where is he?'

Fresh tears spilled out of Fenna's eyes. Milou reached up and wiped them away with shaky fingers. Then, in a quiet voice, Fenna spoke:

'Rotman.'

The clock tower struck the quarter-hour, but it was Fenna's raspy voice that rang as loud and clear as church bells in Milou's ears. It took a few stunned moments before the significance of what she'd said finally sank in.

'Did Rotman snatch him?' Sem asked at last.

Fenna opened her mouth as if to speak again, then bit her lip and shook her head instead. Tears streamed down her cheeks.

'But you saw Rotman?' Lotta asked.

Fenna nodded.

'Did Egg go up to him?'

Fenna nodded again.

'You must have seen where they went.'

Fenna waved at the crowds, miming a frantic search and a hopeless defeat.

'So you don't know where they went?'

'No.'

Her voice was no more than a whisper and Milou wasn't sure if she'd imagined it or not. Fenna collapsed on to the bench and buried her face in her hands.

Sem pinched his brow. 'I'll go and ask around, see if anyone knows where we can find Rotman.'

He was loping off into the crowds before any of them had a chance to respond. Milou's fingers clutched the coin pouch in her pocket tightly. She and Lotta sat either side of Fenna on the bench. The three of them huddled together, silent and morose, minds racing. What was Egbert thinking?

Sem appeared in front of them, grim-faced and panting. 'No one has heard of Rotman,' he said breathlessly. 'Nor his ship. I asked in all the shops along the square. We're going to have to search every dock, one at a time.'

'The port of Amsterdam is roughly twenty-five kilometres long,' Lotta said. 'Roughly six square kilometres of waterway and twenty square kilometres of land mass. There will be hundreds of ships across eleven major docks.' When they all stared in amazement at her, Lotta added softly: 'It took me and Egg over a week to estimate that.'

'That would take us hours to search,' Milou said, her stomach twisting with worry and regret.

This was her fault. She should have known it would be too tempting for Egbert to follow the clue Edda had given him.

He'd been waiting over twelve years for something, anything, after all. And Milou had selfishly insisted he wait even *longer*.

'We don't have hours,' Sem said. 'Anything could happen to Egg in that time. We need to find him quickly.'

'Perhaps we should split up,' Lotta said. 'Cover more ground.'

'No,' Sem said. 'No more splitting up. If we'd stuck together earlier, perhaps we could have stopped him going in the first place.'

Fenna stiffened. Milou wrapped an arm round her. 'It's not your fault, Fen. You couldn't have stopped him.'

The clock tower chimed the half-hour. Milou got to her feet and took the coin pouch out of her pocket. 'Let's go,' she said. 'We've wasted enough time.'

'Milou,' Lotta said crossly. 'You can't really be thinking about the newspaper –'

'No. We're going to use this money to get Egg back. There's only one person I can think of who might be able to find out where he is.'

The market was almost deserted when they arrived; half the stalls had been packed away as a dreary dusk settled over the city. Milou sprinted over the cobbles, the cold air burning her lungs. The others followed. Milou noticed with relief that the bell-shaped tent was still there. She slowed to a jog, a stitch beginning under her ribs, elbowing her way past a few pedlars and round wagons to get to it. The tent's curtains were closed, but a thin strip of light spilled out in a ring around the bottom.

'Milou,' Lotta said, her voice full of protest.

'Have you got any better ideas?'

Lotta fell silent, but her expression remained fixed. Beside her, Fenna eyed the tent with obvious apprehension. Sem's face was shadowed beneath the brim of his hat, but Milou could just about make out the tight line of his mouth.

'I just don't like this,' Lotta grunted.

'I can go in alone,' Milou said. 'I won't be long.'

'No,' Sem said sternly. 'I'm coming in with you.'

There was a rustle and then the tent's curtains opened. The girl stood there, smiling pleasantly, her catlike eyes glinting in the lamplight. 'Ah, there you are!' she said. 'I'd almost given up waiting for you to come back.'

Goosebumps rose all over Milou's neck. In the distance, the clock tower struck the fifth hour and Milou tried to ignore the knotted lump of disappointment that sat heavy in her stomach. All that mattered was finding Egbert.

'Are you all here for a reading?' the girl asked. 'Four fortunes might be a little more than I can manage at this hour. Perhaps –'

'No,' Milou cut in. 'We don't want our fortunes told.' She tried to keep her voice strong, but it came out all rough around the edges. 'We've lost someone. Can you . . . can you find people?'

The girl stopped smiling. 'Is this person alive or dead?'

'Alive,' Sem said. 'He went missing about an hour ago. Not far from here.'

'I can pay you,' Milou added. She held up the pouch. 'Please. It's urgent.'

'I'm much better at finding the dead than the living.'

Sem let out an angry breath. 'Can you tell us where he is or not?'

The girl was silent for a moment, then nodded. 'Probably.'

'Good.' Milou grabbed her hand, shoved the coin pouch into it, then pushed past into the tent.

The inside was just big enough for a table and three chairs. There were animal skulls hanging from the frame above their heads. Candlelight flickered and incense burned, creating a hazy effect that left Milou feeling somewhat dizzy. She collapsed into one of the chairs and took off her gloves. Sem followed. He removed his hat and stared open-mouthed round the room. Milou fidgeted nervously. How many more minutes had it been now? Would Egbert be locked away somewhere dark and cold? Was he alone and frightened? Was he hurt?

The girl sat opposite them and dropped the coin pouch on the table. 'It's mostly for show,' she said as Sem continued to gawk. 'People only seem to believe me if I add all this theatre and pomp.'

Milou sucked in an angry breath. 'Is this all just an act then?'

'I think you *know* it's real or you wouldn't be here.'

'I don't *know* anything about any of this,' Milou spat, her voice cracking.

The girl looked pointedly over Milou's shoulder, as she'd done earlier that day, and cocked her head. 'Don't you?'

Milou glowered, her ears tingling unpleasantly, but she didn't look behind her this time. She knew there wouldn't be anyone there. Doubt gnawed at her. Had she just handed over their money to a charlatan? Was she wasting precious time that Egbert didn't have? Milou didn't know what to believe any more. Had it been any other time, she would have wanted to ask this girl a thousand questions about ghosts and fortune-telling and that long-dead boy's eyeball. She'd have marvelled at the theatre and pomp, filled with curiosity and intrigue. But, in that moment, Milou didn't feel curious or intrigued. She felt scared and desperate because Rotman had Egbert and this strange, unsettling girl might be the only hope Milou had of getting him back again. The air seemed to chill as the two girls stared at each other.

'What's your name?' Sem said nervously. 'We never introduced ourselves properly.'

The girl reached up and pulled her hood down, shaking her long, spider-silk hair loose. 'My name,' she said, 'is Emiliana.'

Sem's nose turned bright red. 'I'm S . . . Sem Poppenmaker. This is my . . . uh . . . this is Milou.'

'The puppet-makers. Yes, I saw the posters you put up. Everyone seems very excited about it. If I weren't leaving Amsterdam tomorrow, I would have loved to have seen your show. It sounds like just my kind of thing.'

'I'm sorry, but we really are in a hurry,' Milou said gruffly. 'How does this work? How can we find Egg?'

'Have you got anything that belongs to him?' Emiliana asked. 'It might help me to locate him.'

Milou reached into her cloak, to where her Book of Theories was nestled. She rifled through it until she came to a page with a charcoal sketch of two people fighting a werewolf.

'He drew this for me,' Milou said. 'Will that work?'

Emiliana took the book from Milou, raising her eyebrows as she looked at the picture, then at the scribbled notes of Milou's werewolf-hunter theory. 'I guess we'll find out,' she said finally. Then, reaching into her collar, she pulled out the eyeball necklace and held it over her left eye.

Sem let out a cry of surprise. Milou covered his mouth with her hand and shook her head at him. Emiliana began to speak again, but in no language that Milou recognized. Her words were hurried and clipped; she kept pausing for a few moments, then starting again. It was almost as if she were talking to someone. An *invisible* someone.

The hairs on Milou's forearms stood on end. She snuck a subtle glance around her, but, other than the three of them, there was no one else in the room. Sem began to fidget, scrunching his hat up in his fists.

'Just sit still, would you?' Milou whispered. 'You're making me nervous.'

Sem looked taken aback. '*I'm* making you nervous? She's speaking in tongues!'

'*Shh!*'

They watched Emiliana for several long minutes. A draught whistled in through the gaps in the tent's fabric, making the skulls rattle. One candle was blown out, its smoke curling upward.

'He's on a ship,' Emiliana said at last. 'A big one.' She squinted behind the eyeball. 'But also . . . old and battered. Sorry, the image I see is somewhat blurry. It's . . . eighth . . . no . . . *ninth* along the dock.'

'Which dock?' Milou asked.

Emiliana spoke a quick burst of that foreign tongue again, then smiled. 'There are locomotives nearby. Lots of them. Cargo trains, too.'

'The eastern docklands.'

Milou started. It hadn't been Sem or Emiliana that had spoken, but Lotta. She and Fenna were standing in the tent's entrance.

'The eastern docklands are a short distance from Amsterdam Centraal Station,' Lotta said. 'It's not that far. Let's go. Now.'

Milou grabbed her Book of Theories from the table and tucked it back in her breast pocket. Its familiar weight felt reassuring. 'Thank you, Emiliana,' she said. 'Truly.'

She and Sem stood. Lotta and Fenna were already outside, waiting. Emiliana picked up Milou's coin pouch and followed them to the doorway, grabbing Milou's arm just as Sem stepped outside.

'A shadow follows you, Milou,' Emiliana whispered, her face grave and those catlike eyes deadly serious.

'What kind of shadow?'

'The dead kind.'

Milou's breathing stopped and her pulse roared in her ears. She tried to shake her arm free, but the girl held it firmly.

'I hope you find all that you are looking for, Milou. Not just your brother.'

Emiliana let go of her elbow and Milou noticed the coin pouch was no longer in her hand. Most likely she had stashed it in the folds of that strange green cloak. Still, if Emiliana's directions really did lead them to Egbert and, even if it meant she had to wait longer to get that message to her parents, it would have been worth the sacrifice.

Milou hurried out into the darkening dusk, trying not to think of dead things lurking in the many shadows that surrounded her. It was only when she and the others were halfway down the road that she realized Emiliana had called Egbert her *brother*.

The thought of what Rotman might do to him sent a fresh wave of despair coursing through her. It was more terrifying that anything Milou could have imagined. Worse than anything the matron had ever inflicted upon her. As bad, even, as not knowing where her own family was.

Was this what it felt like to love a *brother*? Perhaps. But, right then, the only thing Milou knew for certain was that she would set the world on fire if that's what it took to get Egbert back.

Her fear mingled with something new, something both fiery and sharp, something like fury. Fury at Rotman for taking someone so precious to her.

And fury at herself for letting it happen.

26

They arrived at the eastern docklands just as the sun had finally dipped below the watery horizon. Steam billowed from huge smokestacks, giving the impression that the dusk-reddened sky was melting into the vast expanse of the North Sea Canal. Milou's eyes darted in every direction as she tried to take in the sight of it all. Men in woollen coats and flat caps carried sacks up and down planks and walkways. Horses and mules pulled carts piled high with crates. Cargo was hoisted up by steam-powered cranes on to ships' decks. Dogs barked, horns blew, and the smog-thickened air reeked of burnt oil and smoked fish.

'Holy Gouda,' Lotta breathed, her wide eyes reflecting the fiery red glow. 'Those are paddle-wheel steamships. Edda told me they were big, but . . . wow.'

'That smaller ship,' Milou said, extending a gloved finger

towards a more shadowy area further down the dockyard. 'The one with all the sails and the questionable mast.' She counted its position. 'It's the ninth one along.'

Compared to its neighbours, *De Zeehond* really was the runt of the litter. And, apart from the canal barges, it was the only vessel made of wood rather than steel. It looked, Milou decided, like a pirate ship that had been hauled up from the bottom of the ocean floor.

'A clipper, I believe,' Lotta said, squinting. 'It must be at least a hundred years old and been battered by a thousand storms. If Rotman really is a wealthy sugar merchant, then I'm a three-legged peacock. The witch-girl was right then.'

'*Milou* was right,' Sem said darkly. 'Everything Rotman told us really was a lie.' He flexed his fingers. 'The ship looks unguarded. Let's get this over with.'

He went to step out of their hiding spot beside a warehouse, but Milou grabbed his arm. 'No,' she said. 'We need to be careful.'

'But there's no one anywhere near the ship!'

He and Fenna looked ready to burn a path through anything that stood in their way.

'I want Egg back, too,' she said softly. 'But we can't help him if we get caught, and we can't walk along the dock without being seen.'

Lotta frowned. 'Perhaps we could wait until there's fewer people –'

'Egg could be hurt,' Sem seethed. 'It's already been over an hour. We need to get him now.'

Milou studied the shipyard again. Each ship had a warehouse at the end of its dock, but the gap between each warehouse was wide open and well lit. The only cover they would have was the odd crate or wagon. They'd have to be very quick and very careful.

'We're cold and tired,' Milou said. 'If Rotman sees us and gives chase, we won't make it far. Stealth is the key. We need to be long gone before Rotman even realizes we've taken Egg.' She pointed towards a ramshackle building that was within spitting distance of Rotman's ship. 'We need to get to that warehouse and assess the situation from closer up.'

Fenna led the way, crawling under wagons, leaping over fences and slipping through uncomfortably tight spaces between stacks of crates. They paused behind a pile of burlap sacks filled with spices, waiting for a nearby dockworker to finish smoking. Milou tucked her face into her scarf to still her ragged breathing. They had reached the last of the sprawling warehouses and needed to cross an almost empty patch of ground to make it to the rundown warehouse opposite *De Zeehond*'s mooring. After what felt like an age, the dockworker flicked his cigarillo into the shadows, where it soared over Lotta's head and landed in the dirt.

'Go!' Milou whispered as soon as he disappeared round the corner.

Fenna was on her feet in an instant. Like a circus acrobat, she rolled three times the length of a low wall, sprang up again and was across the empty clearing within seconds. Lotta went next, crawling like a panic-stricken spider. Milou copied Lotta's approach. Then, from the shadows behind the warehouse, they waited nervously for Sem to follow. Milou half expected him to trip and knock over one of the teetering sacks, but, within a few long-legged, determined strides, he had made it across the wall and into the cover of darkness beside her.

Rotman's warehouse was larger than it had appeared from a distance, with a window that not even Sem could reach. It glowed dimly from within and, as they tiptoed underneath it, muffled voices drifted out.

'I think Rotman's in there,' Milou whispered, looking up at the window. 'With any luck, that's where he'll stay.'

She and Fenna were about to carry on, but Lotta tugged them both back.

'Wait. We should listen to what they're saying.'

'We don't have time,' Milou whispered.

'Lotta's right,' Sem sighed, then crouched down beside Milou and patted his shoulders. 'We need to know what we're up against. Come on, hop up.'

'Why do I have to climb up there?'

'Lotta's too short and Fenna can't tell us what she hears. Just hurry, would you?'

Milou clambered up, managing to get a firm hold of the window ledge with her other hand and heave herself up enough to look inside. The window was practically opaque from a coating of grease, but Milou found a small hole through which to peer. She pressed her eye against it.

A single oil lamp hung from the middle of the ceiling, illuminating a room that was stacked full of crates. In the middle was a small space in which there was a desk, two chairs and two men. Rotman sat behind the desk, his forehead wrinkled in a frown. He was wearing an expression of utter disdain, as if his nostrils were under attack from an unpleasant smell. His eyes were as cold and hard as black ice. Opposite him, with his back to Milou, sat his apprentice, Pieter.

Milou put her ear to the glass.

'Has the boy spoken yet?' Rotman said.

'No, sir,' replied Pieter, in a voice so quiet Milou could barely hear it. 'He won't give them up.'

'We'll see if he still feels that way in the morning. A cold night in the hold under the watchful eye of Dolly should convince him how serious I am.'

'Yessir.'

'Don't give him any food or water, either.'

'No, sir.'

'Is he securely tied up?'

'Yes sir.'

'Good. I want to be out of this stinking city by the week's end, and I intend to leave with the crew that woman promised me. One way or another I'll find them.'

There was a brief pause, then Pieter gave another quiet, 'Yessir.'

'I have these blasted logs to finish,' Rotman said. 'Get my cabin ready for me. I'll be aboard shortly. Maybe I'll have a word with the boy myself . . .'

A chair scraped noisily across the floor. Milou quickly put her eye to the peephole, just in time to see Pieter leaving through the warehouse door, and Rotman returning to his paperwork. Milou tapped Sem's shoulder and he bent to let her down.

'Egg is tied up. He's in the hold,' she whispered. She turned to Lotta. 'What does that mean?'

'Below decks,' Lotta replied quietly. 'It's where they store the cargo.'

Milou told them what she had heard. The children looked at each other in quiet despair.

'We'll just have to be clever about this,' Lotta said. 'First of all, getting on to the ship will be tricky. We can't go up the main gangplank without the entire dockyard seeing us, so we'll have to see if we can climb up the mooring ropes on the other side. There are portholes all along the hull. Perhaps one of us can draw this Dolly person away from the hold so that another one of us can free Egg.'

'And at least one of us will have to stay here and keep watch,' Sem added. 'We should have a signal in case Rotman leaves this warehouse and some way of causing a distraction to give us time to get off the ship again.'

Lotta smiled suddenly and rummaged in her bag, pulling out one of the fireworks she'd bought earlier that day. 'Will this work? A signal *and* a distraction all in one.'

'Perfect,' Milou said. 'OK. Sem and I will go aboard and get Egg. Lotta, you'll be on lookout and distraction duty. Fenna, you'll draw Dolly away. Everyone agreed?'

They all gave a curt nod, then crept along the side of the warehouse, into the waiting shadows.

27

There was only one rope tied to the rear walkway of *De Zeehond*, and it was as thick as Milou's arm. Sem went up it first, like an upside-down squirrel. She watched as he reached the side of the deck, then turned and gave her a thumbs up. Milou peered down at the black water lapping just a few centimetres below. She could feel the iciness radiating off it. It held her there, like a statue, unable to move.

Fenna gave her a little nudge and a small, sympathetic smile. 'Egg,' she rasped gruffly.

And that was all it took for Milou to grab the rope, with her hands and then her legs, and start shimmying. Hanging upside down, she found herself watching the cloudless, star-bright sky instead of the water. And then Sem's strong hands were hauling her over the side of the deck. They crouched behind a barrel and peered round it.

The ship's sails were rolled up tightly, and the masts looked like giant crosses. The deck reminded Milou of a graveyard. Cold, dark, windy, haunting. Every shadow seemed as if it might contain a monster. Every ghostly creak and groan of wood sent uncomfortable shivers up her spine. And the way the ship swayed gently from side to side made Milou feel as if the world was shifting. There were lights on inside the cabin under the poop deck and the occasional thin silhouette of Pieter as he prepared Rotman's abode. Other than that, the deck was clear.

'There's a hatch there,' Milou whispered, pointing towards the bow of the ship. 'That should take us below decks.'

Milou and Sem made their way over to it. Hinges squeaked as Milou lifted the hatch, but the sound blended in with the whistling wind. She looked in and, seeing nothing in the gloom, stepped on to the ladder, which groaned loudly under her weight. She descended as quickly as she could. Sem followed, the hatch squeaking shut above his head and plunging them into complete darkness.

The air was thick with the smell of oil and salt, which clung to Milou's skin and throat. Her pulse roared loudly in her ears and her breath stuttered. She reached out to steady herself on the wall, only to find it was sticky with grime.

'Light,' Milou whispered.

Sem struck a match and held it up.

They were in a big, long room. Two rows of hammocks hung on either side. In the centre of the room was a large, horizontal wheel, with five poles sticking out of it. It reminded Milou of the cogs that Lotta has shown her in the windmill mechanism room, but there was no other cog connected to it, so Milou assumed it was turned by hand. Empty crates were piled everywhere, secured by rope. There were mops and brooms, buckets and barrels. Having spent most of her life doing hard chores, Milou recognized this as a room in which knuckles were rubbed raw and backs were bent.

Sem's match fizzled out, so he struck another one while Milou found a candle for him to light. There was a knock on one of the porthole windows. Fenna's face appeared at the glass, hanging over the side of the ship by one of the guide ropes. She was waving frantically at them. Milou hurried over and opened the window, taking in a deep lungful of the fresh air as it rushed in.

'Have you seen Egg?' she whispered.

Fenna gave a quick nod, her chest heaving. She reached in through the window and pointed excitedly to a door at the far end of the room.

'He's in there?' Milou asked.

Fenna nodded again, smiling brightly.

'Did you see the guard? Dolly?'

Fenna shook her head, her smile widening.

'So Egg's alone?'

Fenna nodded again.

Milou turned to Sem, who was frowning. 'Rotman said Dolly was in there. I heard him.'

'Maybe she's gone on a break?' Sem whispered, eyeing every shadow around them. 'Or perhaps she's gone to bed already. We should just count ourselves lucky. Come on.'

Milou turned back to Fenna. 'Wait by the nearest window, OK?'

Fenna gave an eager nod and disappeared.

Milou left the window slightly ajar and turned back to Sem who was holding the candle high over his head, peering round with a look of concern.

'Dolly might come back at any moment,' he whispered, grabbing a broomstick with his free hand. 'Be ready.'

Milou nodded and seized a mop. Not the most impressive of weapons, but they would have to do. As they crept forward, Milou's pulse was so loud in her ears, she could no longer hear the groaning of wood or the slapping of water on the hull.

The door Fenna had pointed at was firmly shut. Milou pressed her ear to it. Beyond the whooshing of her pulse, she was certain she could hear the rattling of chains. Sem raised the broom higher, and Milou moved her shaking fingers to the door handle . . . and pushed it open. The door emitted a creaking groan, and Milou and Sem found themselves staring into another long room filled with even more crates. It was almost pitch-dark, except for the thin columns of moonlight that spilled in through the portholes.

Two round, frightened, familiar eyes stared at them from the end of the room. Egbert was huddled between two beams, ropes bound tightly around his wrists and waist, and his mouth stuffed with cloth. He blinked up at them and his eyes grew wider and more panicked. He groaned, shaking his head vigorously. He didn't look happy to see them. In fact, he looked horrified at the sight of them.

Confused, Milou took a step into the room, the floorboards creaking beneath her. A low growl made her stop.

It had been so quiet she'd barely heard it. She peered into a gap between several crates, but saw nothing at all. To her other side was a dark storeroom. Egbert gave a loud, muffled moan, shifting his eyes to where Milou had just looked. He shook his head again. Milou took another tentative step forward.

Another growl. Both Sem and Milou stopped in their tracks. This time, as she squinted into the storeroom and Sem held the candle higher, Milou thought she saw two glowing eyes.

The eyes blinked. Another growl.

Like the first roll of thunder in a storm, it started off quietly and got louder, deeper, more menacing. The tip of a snout appeared from the darkness. Its lips were pulled back as the monster growled once more, revealing two rows of deadly, razor-sharp fangs.

28

Milou staggered backwards, bumping into Sem, fear stabbing at her stomach. The monster stepped fully out from the shadows, snapping at the air. Its claws scraped across the hardwood floor, its pointed ears pinned back. A hand landed heavily on Milou's shoulder and yanked her backwards.

'Dolly,' Sem said, pushing Milou behind him.

The dog stalked towards them on its huge paws, looking for all the world as if it might tear Sem and Milou to pieces with just one bite of its slavering jaws.

Holding the broomstick out in front of him with one hand, Sem wedged the candle on top of a crate with the other.

'Free him,' Sem rasped, nodding at Egbert. 'Quickly.'

He raised his broom and lowered his brow. Milou had never seen him look so determined.

'But –'

'Now!' Sem cried, just as Dolly launched herself forward.

Milou watched in horror as the dog's jaws latched on to the broom handle, sending Sem crashing to the floor.

'Quick!' he groaned, twisting the broom every time Dolly tried to snap at him. 'I won't be able to hold her off for long!'

Milou staggered to the end of the room and sank to the floor beside Egbert, yanking the cloth from his mouth.

'Are you crazy?' Egbert cried, his voice quivering. 'Why did you come here? It's too dangerous.'

Milou reached for the rope that bound his wrists. Her hands were trembling.

'Why wouldn't we have come?' She tugged at the knot, her fingers slipping, and growled in frustration. 'Why aren't my hands working properly?'

She didn't dare look behind her, to where she could hear Sem still wrestling with Dolly. The beast was growling and Sem was grunting with exertion, but there had been no cries of agony yet.

'Just take a deep breath,' Egbert said softly. 'You can do it, Milou.'

She shook her hands and tried again, managing to wriggle one end of the rope out of the knot. Egbert wriggled his wrists out of their binding and smiled gratefully at her.

As Milou reached for the rope around Egbert's waist, Sem yelped in pain. She scrambled to her feet, the hammer clutched tightly in her hand, and darted across the room to him. Dolly had snapped the broom in half and was gnawing on one piece as Sem stood, wobbling, clutching at a gash on his leg.

'Sem!' Milou skidded to a stop. Dolly blocked her way. 'Are you all right?'

'Stay back!' Sem cried, his voice full of pain. 'I'm OK, it's just a scratch –'

'No, it's not!' Milou cried, anger brimming. 'Leave him alone!'

She whacked the hammer against the wall to get the dog's attention. Dolly's giant head turned towards her, lips pulled back in a vicious snarl. Huge claws scraped the floor as the dog now stalked towards Milou, fangs so sharp they could likely tear through her skin as if it were paper.

'Hey!' Sem cried, banging the mop on the floor. Milou could see his leg was causing him pain, but he held the mop firmly and his fierce expression even more so. 'Leave her alone!'

Dolly ignored him entirely, snapping her teeth just centimetres from Milou's stomach.

'*Hey!*' Sem called again.

Dolly turned to him, her growl trebling in volume. She barked, loud enough to wake the dead and certainly loud enough to be heard above deck. Milou watched in frozen terror as Dolly's back legs braced to jump. Sem took a wobbly step forward, but his injured leg buckled beneath him. He fell, defenceless, as Dolly launched herself into the air. Milou could only watch in horror, a scream building in her throat.

Sem twisted on the ground, swinging his good leg round. Dolly soared over him, straight through an open doorway, landing with a thud in the empty storeroom she had come out of. Sem was quicker than Milou had ever seen him move. He scrambled to the door and slammed it shut. There was a muffled growl, then a loud bang as the dog threw herself against it. More barking. Another bang. But the door held firm.

Milou ran over and helped Sem to slide a crate across the door to hold it closed. He grinned lopsidedly at her.

'Well, that was –'

His words died away as a strange whistling sounded just outside the porthole window. Sem hopped over to it, Milou holding on to his elbow. The sky exploded with colour.

Lotta's warning firework.

'Milou!' Egbert called urgently. 'Sem!'

Egbert was still struggling to free himself, staring across the room with a look of pure panic on his face. Milou followed his gaze. A figure emerged from the darkness. Pieter stepped into the room, wielding a large wooden mallet above his head.

'What are you doing?' he yelled, eyes darting between the three of them.

Sem bristled beside her. He reached for a nearby cargo hook, but fell, clutching his leg again. Milou stood over him and grabbed the broken broomstick.

'What does it look like?' she said, holding the sharp point out towards Pieter. 'We're taking Egg home.'

Pieter frowned, lowering his mallet slightly. 'Where's –'

Dolly chose that moment to bash against the storeroom door again, right next to Pieter. He shrieked in surprise and staggered across the room.

'She's in there?' he shrieked, his face pale. 'How did you –'

Milou watched his hands shake. She realized he was younger than she'd first thought. Young and terrified of the consequences he'd face if he let them leave. She lowered her weapon.

'Help us,' she said softly. 'You don't have to do his bidding, you know.'

Pieter shook his head.

'Please,' Milou said. 'We don't deserve this any more than you do.'

Pieter's nostrils flared.

'Help us. Please.'

'He'll kill me.'

'Then leave with us.'

Pieter shook his head again. 'I can't. You don't know what he's like. He'd find me. He'll find you, too, even if I did let you go.'

There was another whistle, another crackle, and a colourful glow flickered across the room. Lotta had set off another firework. Which could only mean that Rotman was now on the ship. Milou realized she couldn't wait any longer for Pieter to change his mind. She needed a new tactic. A quicker one.

In three quick steps, she was next to the storeroom door. 'I'll open this and let her out,' Milou said. 'She's not happy.'

Pieter paled. 'Don't.'

'Please,' Sem said. He was standing now, but only barely. Sweat glistened on his face. 'Just give us the keys so we can free Egg. You can come with us. We'll be safe together, I promise.'

Pieter made one more indecisive noise, then dropped the mallet. With trembling fingers, he reached for the keyring on his belt. Milou's heart leaped up to her throat in relief. She took a few steps towards Egbert, but then stopped as her left ear prickled painfully. Pieter stared at her as she took slow, silent steps backwards. There was the unmistakable creak of a floorboard coming from the hallway. The smell of oil and smoke drifted in through the doorway, then the tips of two sealskin boots appeared.

'Well, isn't this a delightful surprise?'

Meneer Rotman emerged fully from the gloom, all cruel-eyed and stony-faced, aiming a pearl-handled pistol at Milou's chest.

29

Milou stared at the pistol, hardly daring to breathe. Her ear now prickled so much it felt like it was on fire.

'My darling little *kindjes*,' Rotman crooned, cocking the pistol's hammer with his thumb. 'I've been so worried. Papa is so pleased to see you.'

Milou couldn't speak. Out the corner of her eye, she saw Sem slump to the floor and Fenna's frightened face disappear from the other side of the porthole. Pieter was whimpering, pressing himself against the storeroom door, despite Dolly still scratching at it from the other side.

'And Pieter!' Rotman said. 'I am surprised. You saw what these brats did to that poor old matron of theirs. Do you think they care about anyone but themselves?'

Milou looked down. Her shadow pooled at her feet, thicker and darker than any shadow ought to be. Instinctively, she took a step backwards, the floor groaning in protest beneath her boots.

'Do. Not. Move. Girl.'

Milou froze. The merchant's cruel grin was replaced with a look of pure menace. His mustachios twitched. Dolly barked, slamming into the door. Rotman's eyebrows rose.

'My, my. You lot really are full of surprises. Pieter, I've half a mind to put you in there with Dolly, to remind you of where your loyalties lie.'

'Please, no. I'm sorry. I didn't mean —'

Rotman limped forward and elbowed his apprentice in the face, sending him staggering backwards. Blood spurted from the boy's nose. He fell to the floor beside her, curled up and whimpering.

'We should have left this port over a week ago!' Rotman roared. 'Do you have any idea how much money you've cost me! Not to mention the medical bills for my foot, you little —'

'That's not our problem,' Milou seethed.

Rotman scoffed. 'Oh, it very much is your problem, child.' He limped towards her. 'And you are very much going to repay what you owe me.'

'Our father is waiting for us nearby,' Milou said. 'He'll come looking for us if we don't return soon. He is not a man you'd wish to anger.'

'Father?' Rotman's smile slipped momentarily, but then he shook his head. 'Never mind that – we can be on our way within minutes.'

'You don't have the paperwork to take us.'

'I'll risk sneaking you out of this harbour in these crates if I have to –'

'Hey, cheese-face!' cried a shrill voice from the porthole.

Lotta had half crawled through the window and in her hand was a long tube, sparks spewing out of the end of it. Rotman swivelled his gun towards her, but Lotta was quicker. The firework shot from her hand, hitting the floor by his sealskin boots. The room exploded with light.

Milou threw herself to the ground, covering Pieter with one arm, as the firework ricocheted, whistling and screeching, from wall to wall. It knocked the candle over, then bounced from every surface, fiery sparks flying in its wake. Smoke plumed, filling the room. When Milou waved it from her face, she saw fire erupting in patches all over the hold. Rotman was lying in the doorway, coughing and spluttering as flames licked at his boots.

As Milou pushed herself up, her hand connected with something cold and metal on the floor. The pearl-handled pistol. She locked eyes with the merchant. Rotman took one look at the pistol by Milou's hand and staggered, hand over his mouth, out of the hold door, slamming it shut behind him and leaving them trapped with the smoke and fire.

'Milou!' Lotta yelled. She and Fenna were holding Sem between them, trying to get him out through the window. 'Hurry!'

Milou shook Pieter, rolling him on to his back. He had stopped crying, but looked stupefied. 'Give me the keys!' She tugged at the keyring gripped in his hand and he didn't resist. 'You're going to help my friends get Sem to the dock,' she said, pulling him to his feet and pushing him towards the porthole. 'And then we'll help you get far away from him, I promise.'

He nodded dumbly.

'We're not going without you,' Sem said to Milou, then began to choke.

'I'm going to free Egg, and then we'll be right behind you.'

She didn't wait for Sem to argue, but merely turned away, coughing as smoke crawled up her nose and down her throat. She staggered across the hold to Egbert, who was still desperately tugging at the knot behind him.

'I'm coming, hang on.'

There was a creak and a crash behind her as a wooden beam broke from the ceiling, blocking their route to the window through which Sem and the others had just left.

Milou cursed, but her hands were surprisingly still as she untied the rope. The moment he was fully free, he wrapped his arms round her, squeezing the last of the air from her lungs. She pushed him gently away. There wasn't time.

They heard a crash and a long howl from the storeroom. Dolly was still trapped.

'Wait here a moment,' Milou said. 'Put your shawl over your mouth.'

She skirted round a burning crate. She opened the hold door, then, using the tip of the broom, pushed it through the flames and hooked it under the storeroom door handle. With a flick of her wrist, the door opened and a dark shape shot out. Dolly yelped at the flames, then turned and bounded out of the door. Milou made her way quickly back to Egbert, who was staring at her in disbelief.

'I couldn't let her perish,' Milou explained. 'Fenna would never have forgiven me, even if that beast did try to eat Sem. Right, let's get out of here.'

She pushed a porthole window open and peered out, sucking in a lungful of fresh air. They were on the opposite side of the ship to the walkway. Milou couldn't see past the smoke to tell how far away the dock was. Looking the other way, all she could see was a long stretch of endless water.

'Come on,' she said, climbing out and pulling Egbert with her.

They clung to the porthole ledge, nothing but black water beneath them.

'We're trapped,' Egbert gasped.

Milou's grip on the ledge nearly slipped. She cast her gaze around in panic. There were shouts and barking from the dock. The wind was stoking the fire and thick black smoke curled round the ship. The flames had reached the deck, spreading up to the folded sails at sickening speed.

'Our choices are *up*,' Milou choked, 'or *down*.'

'We can't swim,' Egbert replied grimly. 'And we're not fireproof.'

'How about sideways then?'

One of the crossbeams of the mast groaned, snapped and plummeted down past them. It hit the river with a hiss of steam, and a spume of icy water slapped at their legs. Milou and Egbert pressed themselves against the side of the swaying, burning ship. Egbert clasped her hand, looking resigned and defeated.

'Milou, I am so sorry –'

'Egbert Poppenmaker. Now is *not* the time for apologies, of which I have plenty of my own to make. Now is the time to *not die*.'

Egbert nodded. Milou turned her attention back to the ship's side, looking for an escape route. Suddenly the image of Lotta sliding down the bucket-winch rope from the laundry-room window came to her. If she and Egbert were going to survive, they would have to start thinking like Lotta. There were plenty of loose ropes dangling from the side of the ship. Milou grabbed the nearest one with both hands.

'Here,' she said. 'Hold on tightly to this rope with me. We're going to have to swing ourselves over to the next rope over there. If we can make it to the front of the ship, maybe we can climb that anchor line down to the dock. Ready?'

Egbert nodded once, his expression grim. Pushing their feet against the hull, they swung themselves sideways, hitting the next porthole hard. Milou only just managed to clasp her hand around the next rope and haul herself and Egbert onto it.

They hung there for a moment, panting heavily.

Another piece of flaming debris fell past them. The fire was roaring so loudly now that Milou could barely hear the dockworkers' shouts. A bell began to chime: a fire cart had arrived.

'Seven more portholes to get past,' Egbert said with a forced smile.

They swung twice more, with faltering success. Milou's hands were beginning to burn; her shins and ankles were battered. Milou hoped that the others had got to safety. Her eyes were streaming and she couldn't stop coughing. Beside her, Egbert was struggling, too. If they didn't hurry, they'd suffocate.

'Come on,' Milou rasped. 'We can do this.' They made for the next rope only for it to suddenly fall away before Milou could reach it. She and Egbert swung back the way they'd come, hitting the side of the ship with such force most of the air left her lungs. Her ears gave a sudden, agonizing pinch.

'Up!' Egbert gasped.

Wheezing in pain, Milou looked up. Above them, leaning over the side of the ship, haloed by the firelight, was a large figure. Despite the cloth that covered his face, Milou recognized that hard, cold gaze.

Rotman.

Their eyes met, and his murderous expression made her heart stop. Dizziness skewed her vision and she blinked furiously to see what he was doing. Rotman held a sandbag over the railings, right above Milou's head. He smiled cruelly before launching it off the side.

Milou's stomach dropped to her knees, but, before the sandbag made contact with her upturned face, she was pushed sideways. She watched in horror as the sandbag hit Egbert square in the chest, knocking him away from her. She reached out with one hand, her fingertips grazing his shawl as he flew backwards.

Egbert landed in the water with a heavy splash, his limbs splayed out around him and his eyes and mouth open wide in shock. The water seemed to hollow out around him, then the waves changed direction and swallowed him whole.

He was gone so quickly, Milou scarcely had time to process what had happened.

Egbert had pushed her out of the way and taken the hit himself.

Smoke clung to her hair and her face and Milou was growing dizzier. She looked up, but Rotman was gone. She looked down again, but Egbert didn't reappear. Bubbles erupted from where he had sunk; his shawl bobbed on the surface of the water.

Egbert couldn't swim. But neither could Milou.

Something pinched at her ear and a shadow wrapped round her hand. As she readied herself to jump, a voice, made only of the breeze, spoke to her in a desperate plea.

NO!

It was so quiet and insubstantial she would probably never have heard it had it not spoken right into her tingling ear. The shadow around her hand swelled.

'I have to,' she rasped.

And then her fingers uncurled from the rope. A heartbeat later, her feet hit the canal and the icy water closed over her head, sucking her down into the darkness.

30

Milou didn't notice the cold straight away. It struck a few heartbeats later, constricting her body from head to toe. She thrashed and kicked, but that just seemed to make her sink faster. The darkness left her blind; she couldn't tell which way was up. Bubbles rushed in her ears. Again she thrashed and kicked, praying for the surface, but the icy water held her firm. She was going to drown, she realized. Then, in her left ear, that insubstantial voice once more said: *NO!*

A hand clasped round Milou's leg and she stifled a scream of surprise. Egbert. He pulled her towards him and they held each other tightly. She'd taken a deep breath of air when she'd jumped, but already her chest was burning to let it out. She kicked her legs with what little energy she had left. The voice returned, quiet but insistent.

STOP.

A bubble of air left her lips, tickling her cheek.

STOP.

Milou stopped kicking.

GOOD.

Beside her, Egbert was thrashing just as wildly. She squeezed his hand until he calmed. Her chest was on fire now. Another bubble escaped, ticking along her cheek to her ear. They were sideways, she realized. Using weak arms, she pushed at the water until the next bubble tickled up round her nose, to her hairline. Towards the surface.

YES.

Milou began to kick her legs again in small, controlled movements. Her head was spinning and the pressure in her lungs building into agony. Still she kicked. Slowly, painfully slowly, she and Egbert began to rise.

She broke the surface. The cold winter air felt blissfully warm as she sucked in a lungful. Beside her, Egbert was doing the same. His hair was plastered down his cheeks, and his eyes were barely open. He looked as ill as she felt.

They floated on their backs, clasping each other's hands tightly, looking up at the smouldering wreckage of *De Zeehond*, listening to the clamour of the panicked dockworkers. Milou's vision was blurred and her eyelids felt heavy. The burning in her chest faded as her consciousness started to drift. She was only vaguely aware of Egbert's grip on her hand loosening. Even less aware of the water that slowly lapped over her face.

She was sinking again.

NO!

Water sloshed up her nose, then up over her eyes. This time, however, she didn't have the strength to fight it. All she could think was that now her family would never find her. It wouldn't occur to them to look at the bottom of the North Sea Canal for her. Perhaps she'd wash ashore, but no one would know who she was.

NO!

She'd die a nameless orphan.

MILOU!

Egbert's hand disappeared from hers completely, leaving her entirely alone as the water swallowed her once more.

MILOU!

It was warm now. Gloriously so. Milou's eyes were only open in thin slits, but the water seemed clearer this time.

MILOU!

There, just out of reach on the canal bed but growing steadily closer, was a gate. Just like the one in Liesel's story. Milou sank towards it.

NO!

The water began to darken, until once again she was completely blind.

MILOU!

Milou's arm was suddenly yanked hard, nearly wrenched from its socket. The water over her face disappeared and then she was sucking in air. Her vision was little more than a speckled haze in which she could make out the shape of a round head with slightly wonky ears.

Her back collided with something hard and water erupted from her lips. It burned her throat. Someone was coughing loudly, as if their lungs were trying to escape through their throat. She realized it was her.

'Milou?' The voice seemed both familiar and new, raspy and quiet.

'Milou?' The next voice was more recognizable, sweet and soft.

'Milou?' The last voice was like home.

The voices merged as they called her name again. They intermingled until Milou couldn't tell where one started and another ended. The only thing she knew was that the combination sounded like a lullaby. Her eyes closed and she fell into a troubled, restless sleep.

Milou woke to the world swaying and rocking. The first thing she noticed as her eyes blinked open was that there was a bright night sky above her, a smattering of stars twinkling in the glow of the not-quite-full moon. The next thing she became aware of was the moving silhouettes of trees in her peripheral vision. She blinked. Like floating wraiths, they continued to glide past.

Her heart stuttered. Her body remained frozen and heavy. Had she entered Theodora's nightmare?

A pale face loomed over her with a wonky frown, dishevelled blond hair and crooked ears.

'Milou?' Sem asked, his frown easing as he smiled down at her in relief. 'Oh, thank goodness you're awake.'

Milou let out a groan as a shiver convulsed her shoulders. She was still wet and cold. Lotta's woollen coat was draped over her, shielding her from the wind, but it wasn't quite enough to remove the chill in her bones. With Sem's help, Milou sat up. They were in a paddle boat. Lotta and Fenna were each holding on to a notched axle, rotating it in synchronization to power the two paddle wheels on their side of the boat, propelling them down the canal at a steady speed. At the front of the boat, wrapped in Sem's velvet jacket, Egbert slept fitfully. Beside him, drying on the boat's edge, was his soggy shawl.

'What –'

'Pieter showed us to a lifeboat,' Sem said quietly. 'I thought we'd lost you both.'

Milou blinked. 'Where is Pieter?'

'We dropped him off halfway out of the city,' Lotta said. 'He climbed on to a barge heading south. He said his family is in Rotterdam.'

'Where are we?' Milou asked weakly.

'Look,' Sem responded with a tiny smile.

Milou rubbed her eyes. She realized they were passing Edda's house. Just ahead was their windmill. They had made it home.

Her gaze flicked back to Egbert. The reflection of moonlight from the water sent a rippling glow over his sleeping face.

They had *all* made it home.

31

Milou spent the next day in her cupboard bed, being force-fed herbal concoctions by Fenna. Her wracking cough eventually abated, but her chest was still sore. In the cupboard bed in the living room, Egbert was in a similar state. He'd only woken a few times since they'd returned. Every now and then, she could hear him mutter her name, apologizing and weeping, reliving the trauma of *De Zeehond* in his fever-laced dreams.

Milou had the same problem. Whenever she drifted off to sleep, without fail, she dreamed of smoke and darkness, of sea creatures trying to pull her to the dark, murky depths of the ocean, and towards those ghastly iron gates. And, no matter how much she kicked her feet, she could never find the surface. It was an Ocean of Nightmares. And so Milou tried her best not to sleep, instead staring at the blank pages of Liesel's still-unfinished story. If she didn't find an ending soon, and they couldn't begin rehearsing it, their entire plan would crumble – opening night was in just three days' time.

The kitchen door opened with a creak and Lotta and Fenna walked in. They each held a mug of steaming liquid in their hands, and Milou could smell the nauseating herbal mixture from the other side of the room.

'It smells like old socks and cheese,' Milou groaned, pushing herself as far away from Fenna's mug as she could get.

'Drink,' Fenna said in a quiet, raspy voice that nevertheless sounded like music to Milou's ears.

Fenna reached forward, pinched Milou's nose and pushed the mug to her lips. Milou's mouth opened in protest, which gave Fenna the chance to pour the warm liquid in.

'Ugh,' Milou groaned, coughing and gagging. 'It *tastes* like old socks and cheese, too.'

Fenna smiled, then took Lotta's mug and left to turn her attention to Egbert.

Lotta looked grave. 'At least you're both alive.'

'I guess Emiliana earned all that money I handed over . . .'

Lotta frowned. 'You didn't give her all your money.'

'Yes, I did. And I don't regret it.'

Lotta shook her head. 'No, you didn't. I found the coin pouch in your pocket. Sem used it to place your advert this morning.'

Milou opened her mouth, then closed it again. Emiliana must have slipped the money back into her pocket when she'd given her that strange warning about shadows and spirits.

There was a spluttering noise from the living room.

'That's disgusting,' Egbert groaned.

Milou slowly got to her feet. The ground no longer wobbled quite so much underneath her, but her head still felt a little dizzy as she hobbled over to Egbert's room with Lotta holding her arm.

'I've had enough of this,' Egbert said, scrambling out of his own cupboard bed, only for his legs to fold beneath him the moment he tried to stand.

Lotta and Fenna each grabbed an arm, hoisting him up. Egbert shrugged them off and pitched forward again, but this time his arms went right round Milou's neck and he pulled her into a fierce hug.

'Gah!' she spluttered round a mouthful of his hair. 'You're surprisingly strong for a nearly drowned person.'

'Oh, Milou,' he said, squeezing her tighter. 'I'm sorry I almost got us all killed.'

Milou tried not to wheeze as she squeezed him back. 'And I'm sorry I made you feel like your quest wasn't as important as mine. All four of you have helped me so much, I should've been there to help you. You have just as much right as I do to find answers about your family.'

'I know, but it was reckless to go straight to Rotman. I wish I'd made a proper plan.'

'Why *did* you go to Rotman?' Lotta asked.

Egbert leaned against the bed and grimaced. 'He was the only person I knew who had travelled widely. I just wanted to know for certain if Edda's theory was right . . . if my shawl really did come from Java. I thought I could pretend to want to go with him, ask him about my shawl and then run away again.'

'I probably would have done the same thing,' Milou admitted. 'Or something equally as reckless no doubt.'

'I was desperate,' Egbert said, reaching into his cupboard bed for his shawl. He wrapped it round his neck and looked down at it. 'And I still have no idea where to start.'

Milou's heart twisted painfully. 'As soon as Speelman is off our backs, we'll sit down and work it out. Together. If we have to knock on every door in Amsterdam to find someone who can tell us more about your shawl, we will. I swear it.'

'Together,' Egbert repeated with a small smile. Then he swayed.

Lotta looked at him sternly. 'You should go back into bed.'

'I want to get up for a bit.'

He cast a nervous glance at the wooden walls of the cupboard bed and Milou knew it reminded him of the ship's hold.

'Why don't we get some fresh air?' she suggested.

Lotta and Fenna narrowed their eyes. Then Lotta sighed.

'If you two are determined to ignore all medical advice, then you might as well come and see what we've been doing while you've slept.'

The sun was so bright, Milou and Egbert were temporarily dazzled as they hobbled out of the front door. Lotta led Milou by the hand, and Milou led Egbert, and they walked down the gravel path to the barn. The theatre door opened with a delightful creak. It sent shivers up Milou's spine and made Egbert shudder beside her. Lotta grinned wickedly.

'I degreased the hinges a little more,' she beamed, leading them inside. 'For atmosphere.'

Milou stood on the threshold and gaped. Sem, Lotta and Fenna had transformed the interior. There were ghosts, made from thin white gauze, suspended from the rafters on rotating wires, floating across against the night-sky backdrop in a whisper of fabric. The stage was hidden behind two new curtains, made of black Amsterdam velvet with the words A CARNIVAL OF NIGHTMARES written in elegant swirls across it. Fenna was dangling from the roof of a wheeled booth at the far end, painting the words WARM STROOPWAFELS in bright red across the roof.

What made Milou's skin tingle the most, however, was the large skeletal Night Tree that sprouted from the left side of the stage, its black branches creeping along the floor and ceiling to wrap round the stage like a frightening frame. Sem was halfway up the trunk, attaching claws and bones. His hair was sticking up and bits of grey cobweb dangled from his left ear.

'What do you think, Papa?' Lotta asked Puppet-Father, who was currently reclining in a seat at the back of the theatre, watching them work. 'Splendid, isn't it?'

'It's amazing,' Egbert said. Milou was speechless.

'Come and sit in the front row,' Lotta said. 'The best is yet to come.'

They followed her down the aisle and sat, quietly dumbfounded, in front of the stage. Lotta disappeared through the curtains. Sem and Fenna came to sit beside them.

'You'll like this –' Sem started, but his voice was drowned out by a sudden loud voice that made Milou jump out of her skin.

'WELCOME, FIENDS AND GHOULS!'

Lotta's voice blasted through the room, tinny and impossibly loud. The curtains opened and Milou found herself staring at the giant fangs of a monstrously large puppet-spider. Its legs twitched and its pincers snapped. There was a creaking sound and then the puppet-spider started walking off the stage and over Milou's head. She ducked and squealed as the beast went sailing over her head and over the rows of seating, suspended from a cable she hadn't seen until just then. The spider wriggled to the back of the barn, then reversed all the way back to the stage, the curtains closing behind it.

A moment later, Lotta reappeared from the side of the stage, grinning maniacally. 'Well?'

Milou and Egbert shared a look of awe.

'It's perfect,' Milou said finally, her cheeks aching with the smile that wouldn't leave her lips. 'Absolutely perfect.'

'I found a barrel organ, too!' Lotta said, pulling back a smaller curtain at the side of the stage. 'It was under all that junk at the back of the barn.'

The organ was the size of a handcart, with lots of brass tubes sprouting from the top. A pile of concertinaed paper was stacked on a ledge next to the ivory keys, one end protruding from a postbox-type slot. Lotta turned a crank on the side and organ music filled the room. As soon as she stopped turning the crank, the music disappeared.

'Have you finished the story?' Sem asked.

Milou's smile faltered. She'd spent all the previous day wracking her brains for ideas, but had been too consumed with thoughts of her underwater nightmares. Each time she drifted off to sleep, the nightmare returned and Milou felt as if she were dying. It was hard to concentrate on writing stories when you were scared of falling asleep and never waking up.

'Well –' she started, wondering whether they'd be disappointed in her, and fearful that she would spoil the mood. All their efforts would go to waste if she didn't do her share of the work. 'I –'

'It looks just like how I imagined Theodora's nightmare world,' Egbert said suddenly. Then his voice turned quiet. 'It's quite a bit like the nightmares I have, as well.'

Milou snapped her attention to him. He was right. Theodora's nightmare world had dragged her in every time she fell asleep, too, as Milou's had. Theodora had been scared to fall asleep. Perhaps Theodora's nightmares had been about her fear of –

'Milou?' Sem asked.

Milou looked up at the ghosts and the cobwebs. Like Lotta's talk of cogwheels, the answer to her problem was slotting perfectly into place.

'Milou?' Sem repeated.

'Yes,' said Milou, her heart fluttering like the wings of a bat. 'Yes. I know how the story will end.'

The others smiled at her.

'Then the Poppenmakers are truly all set to go,' Lotta said, smiling gleefully. 'The Theatre of Terrors will be ready.'

Milou smiled. 'And our *own* nightmare will end.'

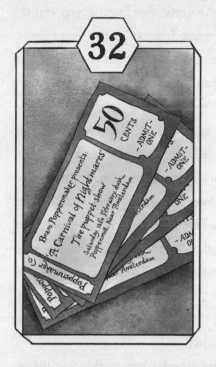

32

Two days later, the night of the show arrived. It was heavy with a low-lying mist that curled up the canal banks and wrapped round ankles. The full moon hung like a giant opal in the star-dappled dusk, and the sky had turned a ghostly shade of purple. Halfway up one of the windmill's sails, Milou drew the frigid air in through her nostrils to try and calm her nerves, but her heart refused to slow to anything less than a gallop. She watched, breathless, as a procession of swaying lanterns wove its way towards Poppenmill. The neighing of horses and scraping of carriage wheels mingled with the hum of voices. Behind the iron gates, a crowd was swelling.

Their audience had arrived.

Milou wondered which one of those flickering lanterns belonged to her parents. Just thinking about being reunited with them made her hands shake so much she nearly fell from the sail twice. She gave the moon one last nervous smile and then hurried down to join her friends at the front door. They all wore matching blue cloaks, spattered with silver paint, and identical expressions of panic-stricken excitement.

'It's time,' Milou said. 'Let's open the gates.'

Lotta's eyes widened in eagerness above the top of her scarf and she nodded. They all put their hoods over their heads, their faces disappearing into shadow, and hurried to the gated bridge. Milou heard several gasps of surprise from beyond the iron bars; then a few more as the five of them heaved the protesting iron gates open. Metal groaned and scraped and the crowd surged forward, a sea of curious faces and red-tipped noses.

'Milou,' Lotta whispered. 'Meet me at the theatre in no more than five minutes, all right?'

Milou barely registered her words, but nodded anyway. Lotta and Fenna disappeared, leaving the boys and Milou to sell tickets. The first couple stepped up to Milou and smiled. They were smartly dressed and bright-eyed. The man had a tidy moustache under his long nose and the woman had dark curly hair, tied up elegantly on top of her head. They were, however, far too young to be her parents.

'Fifty cents each, please,' Milou said impatiently, trying not to snatch the silver coin they offered her. She gave them two tickets and a forced smile. 'Follow the lantern trail to that tree over there.' She pointed to the oak tree, which was twinkling prettily with lanterns hung from every branch. 'You'll be able to buy warm stroopwafels while you wait. The theatre will open shortly.'

'Thank y–'

But Milou had already nudged them along, eager to see who was waiting behind them. She snuck a glance at Sem's customers, but they looked nothing like her. Neither did the small family that were buying tickets from Egbert.

The queue slowly made its way in through the gates, ticket after ticket leaving Milou's hands. Her money pouch began to grow heavier and heavier. There were more people arriving than she'd have dared dream. Young families, old couples, ladies wearing silk bonnets, men in tall top hats, children with nervous smiles. Milou's smile slipped slightly with each person who did not have midnight-dark hair or eyes that were almost black. Her ears tingled slightly, but she ignored it. Her family would be here somewhere. She'd find them.

'You should go and help Lotta,' Sem whispered after a few minutes. 'Egbert and I can handle this.'

'Just one more minute,' Milou replied as another figure stepped towards her.

It was a tall cowled figure in a bright green cloak and a face just as hidden in shadows as her own.

'Fifty cents, please,' Milou said, holding her palm up.

There was a pregnant pause. Milou had the feeling she was being stared hard at, but it was too dark to see even the faintest outline of the person's face. Then a white glove emerged from the green cloak and dropped a guilder into her hand.

'Follow the lanterns to that tree,' she said, rummaging through her coin purse for change. 'The theatre will open in just –'

She looked up to find the cowled figure had swept past her and disappeared into the crowd. Lotta emerged, scowling hard.

'It's been twelve minutes,' she said crossly. 'We're behind schedule. Fenna's nearly run out of waffles and everyone's cold and growing impatient.'

Milou looked back to the queue, which still meandered out of the gate and on to the main road. Lotta tugged at her arm.

'I'll keep an eye out for them,' Sem whispered. 'I promise.'

Milou let out a shaky breath and nodded, following Lotta down the crowded gravel path to the theatre, which stood tall and black and empty-looking in the distance.

It was too dark to see people's faces clearly and Lotta tugged Milou too quickly for her to get a closer look. They snuck round the side of the theatre to where Lotta had installed a smaller side door. Next to the door, on the wall, was a brass mouthpiece. One of Edda's speaking tubes. Lotta pushed Milou towards it.

'We need them sitting in their seats in four minutes,' she said. 'It will only work if we time things perfectly.' She tapped Milou's pocket watch pointedly. 'Four minutes *exactly*. Be ready.'

Lotta slipped off round the back of the theatre barn. Milou stood there, trembling in the cold, trying to quell her growing panic. Her parents would come. Wouldn't they?

She checked the time; a minute had passed already. She was going to ruin the entire show if she didn't pull herself together. All these people would demand their money back and all their hard work would have been for nothing. They'd have to leave the windmill.

Milou cleared her throat. Sem would find them and it would all be fine, she told herself. She pressed her lips to the mouthpiece and, in the deepest, boomiest voice she could summon, she addressed her audience.

'LADIES AND GENTLEMEN!'

Her voice projected outwards in a tinny crackle. Out of the corner of her eye, she saw the shadowed mass of people straighten.

'BOYSSSSS AND GIRRRRLS.'

The hum of voices dropped completely.

'IT IS MY DELIGHT TO WELCOME YOU TO THE GREATEST, MOST GHOULISH EVENT OF THE CENTURY.'

Milou heard a small child whimper.

'WELCOME, FIENDS, TO THE *THEATRE OF TERRORS!*'

There was an ear-splitting screech of hinges as the theatre doors slid open. The sound stretched upward in pitch. Milou saw hands reach up to cover ears and several people clung to each other. A thrill ran through her.

'STEP INSIDE . . . IF YOU DARE.'

No one moved. Milou could picture what they were seeing because it was exactly as she and the others had planned it: a large open doorway that appeared to lead into nothing but foreboding darkness.

A sudden, dramatic discord sounded from the barrel organ inside the barn. Egbert had clearly taken his place. Milou checked her watch. She had one minute to get into her own position and yet the crowd was still staring at the theatre in apprehension.

'TICK-TOCK. YOUR DOOM AWAITS YOU.'

A giggle rose. Then another. And another.

Milou was about to speak again when the crowd surged forward into the theatre. Counting down the seconds in her head, Milou allowed herself a small smile, then slipped in through the side door, emerging in the space behind the stage. The curtains were tightly closed, and the area was drenched in darkness. She felt her way to the ladder that led up to the puppeteering platform above the stage, still counting down.

Thirty seconds left.

She heard the side door open and close, then Sem appeared on the platform next to her. They each shuffled on their bellies to take the cross-sticks of their puppets.

'Ten seconds,' Sem whispered.

Through the small grille next to their faces, which looked out into the main theatre seating area, they could just about make out the shadowed lumps of people settling in.

'Well?' Milou asked, her voice full of pleading. 'Did you see them?'

She couldn't see Sem's face, but she heard him sigh softly and her heart dropped to her boots.

'No –'

A long whistling sound came through the large hole in the barn roof, then the theatre exploded with colour and light. Lotta's fireworks lit up the night sky in bright bursts and wriggling lines. The audience all gaped upward, their faces glowing red, yellow, blue, green. Milou pressed against the grille, searching each illuminated face. She spotted Edda by the door, and that strange cowled figure that still had its hood up and white gloved hands folded neatly in its lap.

No midnight-dark hair, though. And no eyes that were almost black.

A lump climbed up her throat and lodged at the back of her mouth.

The audience cheered as the firework display came to a loud, dramatic end. Then Egbert's harsh, discordant organ music began again, as pleasing as nails on a blackboard. Milou felt like she might be sick, but for a very different reason. Why hadn't she seen her family? Why hadn't Sem?

Lotta's mechanical ghosts began to swirl across the ceiling, trailing ripped cloth over the heads of the startled and delighted crowd. They circled the room once and then came to a stop. Below her, Milou felt the clunking of cogs being turned. The stage curtains squealed open and several electrical lights popped into life on the stage roof, illuminating a life-sized girl puppet. In her arms was a rusted cage, a blood-red heart suspended in the middle of it.

A particularly loud chord sounded, Milou's cue to start, and the sound echoed. The crowd's cheers died away, and they all looked on expectantly, waiting for the show to begin. In the light that spilled up from the stage, she saw Sem smile encouragingly at her.

Egbert repeated his cue chord and Milou put her lips to the speaking tube set up beside her.

All that came out of her mouth, however, was a deep, strangled croak.

33

Milou squeezed her eyes closed. The deathly silence crackled in her ears. Panic clung to her skin with tiny, ice-like needles. She'd never frozen like this before, not once. And yet, despite the urgency of the situation, there was nothing she could do to get the words to leave her lips. She just couldn't do it.

'Milou?'

Sem's voice was quiet, but enough to make Milou's eyes snap open again. Lotta's head had appeared at the end of the puppeteering platform. They both looked at her in panic.

Another discord rang out.

More awkward silence followed, winding its way round Milou's throat and squeezing tight. Someone in the crowd booed. Again Milou tried to speak into the speaking tube, but couldn't form the words.

Where were her parents?

Somebody stood up to leave and Sem gave her a little shake.

'Milou,' he urged. His face was lined with worry. 'Please –'

Milou felt a hot, sticky tear slide down her cheek. Her chest was too heavy.

Then a whistle sounded, high and melodic, like birdsong. Through the gaps in the platform, Milou saw Fenna standing on the stage, one hand held up in the air.

Milou's breath hitched at the sight. She didn't have to look at the audience to know that all eyes were fixed on Fenna, who just weeks ago would more likely have jumped into a pit of hungry snakes than stand on a stage in front of over a hundred strangers.

She could tell by the stiffness of Fenna's shoulders that her friend was anything but comfortable. And yet there she stood, as brave as a warrior, with the sole purpose, no doubt, of giving Milou a moment to gather herself before their entire plan crumbled to dust.

Fenna whistled again, the opening two bars of *Eine Kleine Nachtmusik*. Where her new voice was rough and wavering, her whistling was smooth and assured, as if she were part songbird herself. She whistled the tune once more and, as soon as the last note tapered off, a *Screeeeeeeeech* responded from the theatre-barn's worm-eaten rafters.

A collective gasp sounded round the audience and then Milou heard the rustle of wings. Mozart emerged against the night sky, spiralling down into the theatre. He screeched as he flew, making his way to Fenna's outstretched hand.

Mozart *hooOOooOOed* from the stage and the crowd clapped. Fenna cast a glance upward and, even though Milou knew she couldn't see her, she nodded down to her friend and pressed her lips to the speaking tube once more.

She banished all thoughts of her parents and sister, holding the faces of her friends in her mind's eye. They were counting on her and she refused to let them down.

'EVERY NIGHT, THE NIGHTMARES COME.'

Her voice was raspy and dry, but steady. She kept her eyes locked on Sem, who smiled in encouragement.

'THERE IS NO STOPPING THEM. NOT WHEN THEY SINK THEIR CLAWS INTO YOU, ONCE THEY'VE DRUNK FROM YOUR SOUL AND TASTED YOUR FEAR.'

Milou tilted the puppet's head so that Theodora looked out across the audience. Egbert had painted her face in eternal sadness; her long red hair hung limply down her cheeks and her knees were drawn up to her chin.

A soft tinkling of music emanated from the barrel organ and the ghosts dropped on invisible strings to glide in circles over the audience once more. Under Milou's deft control,

Theodora walked to the front of the stage, her limbs moving oddly but somehow elegantly, matching the beat of the sad symphony that filled the barn.

'MY NAME IS THEODORA TENDERHEART AND TONIGHT THE NIGHTMARES WILL COME FOR ME ONCE MORE.'

The plain backdrop fell, revealing the gnarled and twisting Night Tree on the back wall.

'THEODORA TENDERHEART,' the Night Tree said in Milou's raspy voice. 'IT IS TIME.'

'LEAVE ME BE, HENDRIK LONGTOOTH!'

Sem's werewolf puppet walked onstage, lunged forward and grabbed Theodora. Milou howled into the speaking tube.

'*ARROOOOOOOOOOOOOOOOOOOOOOOOOOOOOOO!*'

The audience's gasps turned into strangled yelps.

Milou and Sem guided the puppets on their journey through the nightmare realm. Even though she didn't look at the audience, Milou could hear their gasps and cries. As the carnival's ghastly gates slammed down on to the stage, Milou couldn't help herself; she leaned forward to get a peek at the crowd. Their eyes were wide and unblinking. Milou smiled, puppet sticks dancing in her hands.

'YOU MUST GO THROUGH THE GATES!'

Egbert's music started again. This time it was a livelier, though still tuneless, as if someone were dancing on the keys. More puppets appeared onstage, behind the iron gate. Monstrous ones. Mechanical, like the ghosts. They called Theodora's name again and again as Milou dragged the puppet towards the gate, seemingly against its will. Theodora was just one step away when the curtains whipped closed and the oil lamps extinguished simultaneously, throwing the theatre into sudden darkness. But, before the audience had a chance to respond, the curtains squealed open again and a single electric light bulb lit the stage.

It was time for Milou's ending to Liesel's story.

It was time for Theodora Tenderheart to die.

That, Milou had realized, was what the nightmares represented: Theodora's fear of dying. It was why she had had nightmares herself, about drowning beneath Rotman's burning ship. Milou had not stepped through those ghastly gates, but Theodora *had*. She had entered the carnival, but that didn't mean she had to suffer. Milou knew there was only one antidote to nightmares.

Theodora was back in her bed, her head in her hands and her shoulders heaving with every sob. Slowly, she climbed out and walked to the edge of the stage.

'I CANNOT REFUSE THE CARNIVAL MUCH LONGER.' Milou paused for a long moment, keeping the audience waiting and wanting. 'NEXT TIME I FALL ASLEEP, THE NIGHTMARES WILL HAVE ME.

I WILL BECOME ONE OF THEM: A SPIRIT BOUND TO THE SHADOWS. I WILL BE LOST . . . FOREVER MORE.'

The crowd was silent, except for the creaking of seats as they leaned forward. Milou adjusted the puppet's strings. A steady *thud-thud-thud* filled the room as Milou tapped the speaking tube's mouthpiece.

Theodora's heart beat slowed.

Thud.   Thud.   Thud.

And slowed.

Thud.   Thud.   Thud.

And slowed.

Thud.   Thud.   Thud.

'I AM DYING,' Theodora said quietly, 'AND I AM SCARED.'

There were sniffs from the front row and a wail from the middle of the audience. Milou heard the distant clunking of a crank being turned. The curtains closed once more, then opened again to reveal Theodora standing in front of the carnival's gates. Hendriks emerged from stage left; a cotton wolf's head on cotton boy's body. The audience gasped as Sem guided the puppet in a creeping walk towards Theodora.

'THEODORA,' Hendrik said, stalking ever closer. 'THE CARNIVAL AWAITS.'

The monsters danced to the wailing organ, their grotesque shadows swaying behind them. Their faces were terrifying: blood-red eyes, long teeth emerging from hideous snarls. And the music . . . it was the type of music that sets teeth on edge; each clashing discord was like listening to the screaming brakes of a steam train. Then it came to an abrupt halt.

'IT IS TIME,' Hendrik Longtooth said, holding out a cotton hand to Theodora. 'THERE IS NO NEED TO BE SCARED.'

'NO NEED!' Theodora cried. 'THOSE MONSTERS WILL EAT ME! THEY'LL TEAR MY FLESH FROM MY BONES. THEY'LL SLURP MY EYEBALLS. THEY'LL –'

'MONSTERS?' Hendrik said quizzically. 'WHAT MONSTERS?'

An unpleasant, high-pitched minor chord punctuated his sentence.

'THOSE MONSTERS,' Theodora said, nodding towards the gate.

'WHAT MONSTERS?' Hendrik repeated, looking behind him and then back at Theodora.

Milou smiled at Sem. She moved her mouth away from the mouthpiece. 'Any moment now,' she whispered to him.

'Behind you!' someone shouted.

Milou's grin widened and she nodded to Sem. It was just as they'd rehearsed.

Sem twisted Hendrik Longtooth's head to face the audience.

'WHAT DID YOU SAY?' Hendrik said, cocking his cotton head.

Someone giggled. 'The monsters are behind you!' a girl cried out.

'Behind the gates!' shouted another.

More shouts and laughter erupted from the crowd. The music rose with it. Hendrik Longtooth leaped to the front of the stage in one huge jump and snapped his teeth. The shouts and laughter stopped, so did the music.

'MONSTERS, YOU SAY?' He turned and approached the gate. It swung open and the monsters behind it stopped dancing. 'YOU THINK THERE ARE MONSTERS IN THERE?'

'I CAN *SEE* MONSTERS IN THERE!' Theodora shouted. 'AND I WON'T LET YOU FEED ME TO THEM!'

'FEED YOU?' Hendrik said. 'TO MONSTERS?' He shook his cotton head. 'THEY ARE NOT MONSTERS, THEODORA.'

'LIES!'

'COME NOW, I'LL SHOW YOU.'

He held out a hand. Theodora clutched her heart-cage to her chest.

'NO!' she cried out.

Members of the audience began to repeat her cries. Theodora Tenderheart took a wobbly step towards the gate. She moved forward, her limbs moving in a disjointed way.

'No!' someone called out again.

Theodora stepped inside the gate and the shadow monsters lunged for her.

The lights blinked out and the stage was swathed in utter darkness. The organ fell silent. The shadows were so deep that no amount of squinting or leaning forward would help the crowd see what was on the stage.

And then a *screeeeeech* sounded at the back of the barn. Milou saw the audience twist in their seats. Standing atop a crate was Fenna, red curls spilling out from the shadow of her hood. Mozart was perched on her outstretched arm.

The owl's head turned mechanically round the room. Milou whistled, just as Fenna had taught her. Mozart flapped his wings frantically for a few moments and then launched into the air, a piece of string dangling from his claw. The bottom of the string was sparking, tiny little flames shooting out of it. As Mozart spiralled towards the stage, small sparks sprayed over the crowd. He flew over the stage and dropped the string. It fell like a feather, but, as soon as it hit the stage floor, more silvery sparks erupted and then what seemed like a thousand tiny oil lamps erupted into light. The stage shimmered brightly, revealing that the monsters were gone. Mozart settled on the platform beside Milou, chewing happily at the piece of meat she'd just handed him.

'WHERE ARE THEY?' Theodora Tenderheart asked, performing a shaky pirouette.

'SHH,' Hendrik said. His head had twisted around in a half-rotation, revealing an entirely plain-looking face. 'LISTEN.'

There was a squeak from the side of the stage, and then music began to tinkle into the room as the barrel organ emitted light, flighty notes.

'BUT ... THE NIGHTMARES ...'

Hendrik shook his head. 'THERE ARE NO NIGHTMARES HERE.'

More stars appeared, lowered down from the stage ceiling, and twinkled merrily.

'AM I DREAMING?' Theodora asked.

'YES,' Hendrik replied. He caught a star and held it out to her. 'A DREAM WHICH WILL NEVER END. NO MORE FEAR, NO MORE PAIN. A DREAM IN WHICH YOU CAN BE HAPPY AND AT PEACE. FOREVER.'

Theodora took the star from him and held it to her chest, where her heart-cage had been. Then the curtains closed.

Silence settled like a blanket over the crowd.

Nervously, Milou peered through the grate to see their reaction. A woman three rows from the front was on the verge of bawling, snot bubbling from her left nostril. Edda's cheeks looked damp. The cowled figure sat more rigidly, gloved fingers tightly entwined. A man in a bright blue tailcoat stood and began to clap. Another did the same. Then another. Milou felt the lump in her throat loosen as the entire audience got to their feet to clap and cheer.

She did not notice the cowled figure slip quietly away.

The Poppenmaker children peered through the closed curtains as the crowd slowly made its way out of the theatre, some of them still clapping, many of them still wiping tears from their cheeks.

'Isn't that the Fortuyns over there, the ones who adopted little Jan?' Egbert said. 'And there's the doctor who set Sem's broken arm last year.'

'Where's Edda?' Lotta asked. 'I wanted to ask her what she thought of it all.'

Milou was searching the crowd, too, still desperately hoping to spot a trio with hair as dark as midnight and eyes that were almost black. She saw no one who matched that description, though. The glee she'd felt when performing was gone, snuffed out by overwhelming despair. Milou looked for the cowled figure she'd seen earlier, too, but that person seemed long gone, as well. There was no one lingering in the theatre. No one making their way to the stage to find her. Where was her family?

'Are you all right?' Sem asked quietly.

Milou couldn't speak; she couldn't even shake her head. She took a deep breath and closed her eyes for a moment. All was not lost. It was just a setback. If they weren't here, then they obviously hadn't seen her advertisement. Milou would just have to wait until they did the next show – she'd send adverts out to France, Belgium and Germany, too.

'Milou?' Sem repeated.

'I'm OK,' Milou said, trying to believe her own words. 'They'll come one day. I just need to wait a bit longer.'

There was a tinkling behind her and Milou turned to find Lotta now sitting on the stage, running her fingers through a basket full of coins.

'How did we do?' Egbert asked.

The others all crowded round Lotta, but Milou couldn't make herself let go of the curtain. Perhaps, when she looked round again, she'd see her family waiting.

Lotta grabbed a handful of silver coins. 'It will take a little while to count it all to be certain, but –' she let the money slip through her fingers and tinkle into the basket again – 'this looks like more than double what we'd hoped for.'

Milou smiled, thoughts of her family momentarily forgotten beneath a deep sense of achievement. 'We did it,' she said breathlessly. 'We're fr–'

There was a sharp pinch at her ear and a screeching of curtain rails above her. The curtain was wrenched from Milou's fingers and someone grabbed her hair. She was pushed forward, her neck pulled backwards, and found herself looking up a large nose, thick mustachios sprouting out from underneath it. Her blood turned cold.

Rotman.

Milou caught a glimmer of metal in her peripheral vision. A cold, sharp point pressed against her collarbone. Sem straightened to his full height, his gangly limbs poised to move. Lotta staggered to her feet, clasping Fenna and Egbert tightly. Milou's scalp was burning from where Rotman held her hair in his fist and she was certain her neck would snap if he pulled it any further back.

'Nice show,' Rotman growled. 'It seems I underestimated just how profitable you lot could be,' he continued, eyeing their money basket. 'I suppose that might cover *some* of the damage you did to my ship.'

'Go!' Milou cried to the others, struggling to free herself. If she could hold Rotman off for just a few moments, the others would have time to flee. 'Run!'

The others remained unmoving.

'Leave!' Milou repeated.

Sem shook his head. 'No.'

Egbert coughed, his face pale. He shook his head, too. 'We're not leaving you.'

'How sweet,' Rotman growled in Milou's ear. 'I have some delightful plans for the five of you.'

Sem took a step towards Milou, his fists clenched.

'Uh-uh!' Rotman said, bringing the tip of his knife closer to her neck. 'I'll have no nonsense. Especially not when I have such a lovely surprise for you. There's someone I'm very keen for you to meet again.'

Milou's first thought was Dolly. The image of those sharp fangs and Sem's still healing wound flashed in her mind. Was he going to feed them to that beastly dog?

'She should be here any moment now,' Rotman said. 'As for the rest of you, behave yourselves or little Milou here will no longer have a head attached to her neck.'

Click-clack.

Milou's heart seemed to stop.

Click-clack-click-clack.

'It can't be,' Lotta said, her eyes turning to the curtains.

Rotman smiled gleefully. 'She's been *ever* so keen to see you again.'

Click-clack-click-clack.

Milou's mind conjured the image of blank, staring eyes.

'No,' Egbert choked.

Click-clack-click-clack.

Milou knew that sound as well as she knew the faces of the four terrified children in front of her, but her mind still refused to believe it.

Click.

Clack.

Click.

Milou was just contemplating whether Rotman was playing a cruel joke on them when the curtains were wrenched open. A large, rotund silhouette stood on the edge of the stage, face hidden in shadows. The five of them stared up at it.

Clack.

Click.

Two steps in and the small lantern behind the stage illuminated the figure's hawk-like face and furious, beady eyes. Milou's legs went completely limp and she sagged against Rotman.

Gassbeek was back from the dead.

35

The matron's face looked pale and sickly, but her expression was just as brutal as it had always been. Her chest heaved up and down as she glared at the orphans, fury radiating from every pore. Milou felt bile climb up her throat. What she was seeing couldn't be true; and yet . . . it was.

Gassbeek was *alive*, and Milou was certain she'd die herself, right there and then, from the horror of it.

'*Hallo, kindjes.*'

Sem shook his head. 'You're dead.'

The matron clucked her tongue. 'You really should have checked more carefully. I was no deader than you are right now.'

'How?' Lotta asked.

'An acute episode of terror-induced catatonia. That's what the doctors in the asylum called it. I spent twelve days in a lumpy bed, staring at a grey wall, unable to talk or move. I did, however, have a lot of time to think about how much I'd like to rip each one of your limbs off.'

Her friends fell silent. Milou was starting to lose the feeling in her legs.

'Pleasant reunions aside,' Rotman said, addressing the matron, 'is she here yet?'

She? Who else could there be?

Gassbeek nodded. 'You keep a firm hold of that one.' She reached out and grabbed Lotta by one pigtail. 'I'll take this one. The other three can carry our money between them.'

She twisted her fingers and Lotta whimpered in pain. Fenna let out a deep growl, right from the chest. Gassbeek paused, cocked her head, then laughed. Fenna launched herself at Gassbeek, grabbed her arm and shoved her away from Lotta. From the stage roof, Mozart let out a shrill, angry shriek.

Gassbeek gaped up at the owl, then down at Fenna.

'These children aren't very bright, are they?' Rotman growled. He pressed the blade closer to Milou's throat and she gasped as a sharp sting bit just below her chin. 'If you don't do as we say, I will spill more than just a droplet of this one's blood. Four orphans would be enough for my ship. I'd just have to work you all a little harder to make up for losing the fifth is all.'

Fenna lowered her gaze and stepped away from Gassbeek.

'Let's get this over with,' Rotman said, dragging Milou to the steps beside the stage.

She staggered along with him, her feet barely touching the floor. What did he mean by 'get it over with'? Was he going to kill them? How had they found them? And who else were they waiting for?

The air was bitingly cold as they made their way back to the windmill. The crowds were gone and Milou could see a trail of swaying lanterns meandering down the road back to the city.

As they rounded the corner, Milou saw a horse and carriage pulled up outside the front door with Rose Speelman stepping out of it. She was, of course, carrying the enormous Little Tulip record book in her arms and wearing an impatient frown. It was the second figure at the doorway, however, that made Milou bite back a scream of fury.

Edda Finkelstein was standing there, arms crossed, and wearing her Polder Warden uniform.

She'd betrayed them.

'*Goedeavond!*' Rotman said cheerfully. Milou's hair was suddenly released and the knife disappeared from her throat. Rotman put a heavy hand on her shoulder. 'I was just retrieving the little darlings – so sorry to keep you waiting.'

'I'm still not sure why you asked me here,' Speelman said. 'And I am entirely confuddled as to why this couldn't have waited until morning.'

'Let's get inside so we can explain,' Gassbeek cawed. 'The children can get us each a nice mug of warm milk while we talk.'

'My father is still not well,' Milou said hastily. 'He'll be upset if we disturb him.'

Speelman shifted the record book on to her other hip.

'Yes,' Edda said, to Milou's surprise. 'Perhaps it's a little late in the day –'

'Nonsense!' Gassbeek squawked, elbowing her way to the door. 'Meneer Poppenmaker doesn't mind at all.'

Before Milou could think of anything else to forestall the inevitable, Gassbeek shouldered the door open and they were all marched inside. Edda closed the door behind them.

'Matron Gassbeek,' Speelman sputtered, staggering in behind them. 'It is polite to knock first –'

Gassbeek whirled from her spot in the middle of the kitchen, a delighted smirk on her face.

'Mevrouw Speelman,' she said. 'I have already checked with Meneer Poppenmaker here –' she nodded towards the chair in the corner where Puppet-Papa sat – 'and he really doesn't mind us intruding. Isn't that so, Meneer?'

'Stop!' Milou shouted, but Gassbeek *click-clacked* across the room and stood next to Puppet-Papa. 'Just stop, please.'

'Stop what, Milou?' the matron said, feigning innocence.

Milou squeezed her lips together and scowled. This shouldn't be happening. They had been free just a few minutes ago. And now Gassbeek was going to take everything from them, like she always had done. Milou realized she had no fight left in her. Beside her, she saw her friends' shoulders droop in resignation.

Their escape, the ship, the show. It had all been for nothing. Edda Finkelstein had lived up to Milou's suspicions. And, on top of it all, her parents hadn't come home to her.

'Matron Gassbeek,' Speelman said, looking between Milou and the matron with a look of confusion. 'What is going on here?'

'Let me show you,' Gassbeek cawed, patting Puppet-Papa on the shoulder. 'These little orphans have woven quite the deception for you and, quite frankly, it needs exposing.'

Then, with a smirk aimed straight at Milou, Gassbeek wrenched Puppet-Papa's cotton head from his grass-filled body.

36

Speelman's shriek ricocheted off the walls. She dropped the record book and held her hands over her mouth in horror. Milou sank into a chair by the table, too distraught to cry. She barely listened as the matron began to explain to the Kinderbureau agent that the children had left her for dead, stolen from her, forged documents and run away like petty criminals. Instead, Milou glanced at Edda, who was showing no signs of shock at seeing Puppet-Papa for what he really was. In fact, her face was completely blank, except for the tiniest crease of her brow.

'Why would you do this to us?' Milou stared at Edda. 'You've ruined everything.'

Both Edda's eyebrows rose. 'I didn't –'

'You knew all along, didn't you? It was you at the window that first night, wasn't it?'

Edda nodded. 'I knew, but —'

Gassbeek's voice reached a crescendo. 'They are charlatans!'

'I don't believe it,' Speelman said. She was holding Puppet-Papa's head and frowning. 'How can five little *orphans* manage all this?'

'These five are nothing but trouble!' Gassbeek shrieked. 'Trust me, I've had the unpleasant misfortune of knowing them all their pathetic little lives. You have no idea how pleased I was when I heard the doctors at the asylum talking about the show. Bram Poppenmaker indeed. The very name on that stupid little cat puppet of yours, Milou. It seems that was enough to rouse me from my stupor.'

Milou swallowed, casting a guilty glance at Edda, who was glowering at Gassbeek and clasping her locket.

'I just . . .' Speelman said. 'I'm not sure what I should do about this. I'll have to consider the legalities —'

'There's nothing to consider,' Gassbeek cut her off. 'These children lied. They are still *my* property and need to be brought back to the Little Tulip immediately. Meneer Rotman here has already agreed to purchase them.'

'We are not property!' Milou said. 'And we're not coming back with you!'

'Girl, be quiet and let the grown-ups talk,' Gassbeek said with a wave of her hand. 'Now Meneer Rotman and I will be taking them back to Amsterdam. You need not bother yourself with these delinquents, Mevrouw Speelman. I will make sure that they are suitably punished.'

'We have the money to buy our adoption,' Milou said, nodding at the basket of coins by Rotman's feet. 'Take it and leave us be. We don't need Rotman to adopt us – we're fine as we are.'

'That is my money,' Gassbeek said. 'They stole it from me.'

'No,' Fenna croaked.

Gassbeek shot Fenna a dangerous look, one that promised repercussions. Milou watched in amazement as Fenna – shy, timid Fenna – stared right back at the matron, unblinking and fierce.

'You can't do this!' Sem cried. 'We earned that money!'

'They are lying,' Gassbeek snapped. 'It's mine and I shall be taking it back right this instant.'

'She made a deal with Rotman,' Lotta cut in. 'She was going to sell us and keep the money for herself. And Rotman is nothing more than a charlatan. He plans to work us until we drop dead. We had to rescue Egg from his ship; he was *chained* below decks.'

'Oh my,' Rotman chuckled. 'These five little darlings have such delightfully fertile imaginations. Dolly and I cannot wait for them to join our seafaring family.'

'You tried to kill us!' Egbert cried. 'You nearly did, in fact . . .'

Rotman's eyes glimmered with mirth. Gassbeek's smile was – as ever – all teeth but no soul.

'And Gassbeek,' said Lotta, 'is not only a miserable witch, but she also takes money that should be spent on the orphans –'

Gassbeek grabbed Lotta's pigtail. 'Liar!'

'Mevrouw Gassbeek,' Speelman said. 'The Kinderbureau does not tolerate the manhandling of children –'

'Nonsense,' Gassbeek said. 'I've manhandled plenty of orph–' She cut herself off with a shake of her head and let go of Lotta's hair. 'Fine,' she spat out. 'But you will be silent, Lotta, unless you want to incur more of my wrath.'

'It's true,' Milou said. 'What Lotta's saying. I heard them strike a deal. He even laughed when he said he could bury our bodies at sea. And this Dolly he claims will be our mother is a *dog*.'

'Don't be so rude!' Speelman cried. 'I will not abide name-calling.'

'It's true!' Milou yelled back. 'She's a real dog, not a woman.'

Rose Speelman pinched the bridge of her nose in frustration. Milou glanced at Edda, whose expression had hardened.

'This is ridiculous,' Gassbeek squawked. 'These children are proven liars. They are simply trying to weasel out of the trouble they've got themselves into.'

'That's not true!' Lotta cried.

'Enough!' Speelman slammed her fist on the table, making everyone jump. 'You five have not only broken the law by forging official records, you have intruded on private property,' she said. 'I will not listen to any more of your nonsense.'

Gassbeek grinned triumphantly. Milou balled her fingers into tight fists. From Fenna's shoulder, Mozart let out a shrill screech.

'This ends now,' Speelman continued, picking up the record book and placing it with a *thunk* on the table. 'These records *must* be put right. The five of you *must* have legal guardians and the fees *must* be settled immediately or you *must* return to the orphanage.'

'Perhaps you should leave the children in my care and investigate their claims further,' Edda said.

Everyone turned to stare at the Polder Warden.

'Absolutely not,' Speelman spluttered. 'This is being settled this very instant.'

'But –' Milou started.

'No!' Speelman cried, her cheeks flushed. 'The rules are the rules and I will not abide them being broken any further.' She opened the record book. 'From this day forward, you will be charges of Meneer Rotman. And that is my final decision.'

37

The tears Milou had been holding back finally began to trickle down her cheeks. Sem slumped into the chair beside her and squeezed her hand. Edda pulled Lotta and Fenna into a hug and Egbert was staring at the record book as if he might make it disintegrate with nothing but his mind.

They had fought so hard for their freedom. And they had lost.

'Hurry along and fetch your belongings then, little *liefjes*,' sang Rotman. 'Dolly will be keen to get you settled in for the night, and it's terribly late already.'

Reluctantly, Milou got to her feet and looked to where Puppet-Papa's limp body lay crumpled and broken.

'I need a quill,' Speelman was saying, patting down her cloak. 'And an inkpot.'

'Wait,' interrupted Egbert. 'I can prove they're lying.'

He was still staring at the record book. Then his eyes flicked to Milou's.

'She never recorded the Fortuyns' adoption,' Egbert said. 'Do you remember? There was nothing in the book when we wrote our own adoption record.'

Milou frowned, the memory tickling the edges of her mind.

'*That's* how she did it,' Egbert said, more loudly this time. 'She removed all record of those orphans whose adoption fees she kept for herself.'

The kitchen fell so silent, they could have heard an eyelash drop.

'My records are, and always have been, utterly flawless,' Gassbeek said indignantly. 'Each orphan in that book is accounted for. There is no evidence whatsoever to back such a ridiculous claim.'

'There is *always* evidence,' Edda said coldly. 'You just need to –'

'Look closely enough,' Lotta finished. 'Mevrouw Speelman, may I please see that record book?'

'No, girl!' screeched Gassbeek. 'You may not!'

A charge of invisible energy seemed to pass between Lotta and Gassbeek; Milou could almost feel it. They both stood, shoulders stiffened and backs straight, glaring at each other and then at the record book that lay open on the table.

Gassbeek sucked in a sharp breath. 'Don't you dare –'

Lotta sprang towards the table, but Gassbeek was closer. The matron scooped up the book and clutched it tightly to her chest as Lotta clawed at it.

'Give it to me!' Lotta yelled.

With her free hand, Gassbeek struck Lotta hard across the face. Redness blooming on her cheek, Lotta dived again at the matron. They both fell to the floor. It had happened within mere seconds, before Milou could remember how to move her limbs. In the corner, by Mozart's wardrobe, she noticed Rotman grinning wildly at the display.

Sem staggered towards the fight, but stopped when Edda let out a yell of anger. The clockmaker had a broom handle in her hands, which she held over her head as she strode purposefully towards the fighting duo. A carefully aimed kick sent Gassbeek sprawling on to her back. This was followed by swift jab of the broom handle that dislodged the record book from the matron's grasp. Milou gawped in astonishment.

It was over within a few heartbeats. Edda held the matron in a headlock and Gassbeek cawed and squawked incoherently, her face growing redder and redder. Still lying on the floor, Lotta's twelve fingers clutched the record book to her heaving chest.

'I'll find the evidence!' Lotta yelled, her lip bloodied and her eyes ablaze. 'And you can't stop me from revealing it, you spiteful old crow!'

'This is absurd!' Speelman cried. 'Never in all my life have I seen such appalling behaviour!'

'I told you they were brats!' Gassbeek choked out.

'I'm talking about *your* vile actions, Matron!' Speelman said. 'You should know better than anyone that striking children is against the rules!'

'She struck me, too!' Gassbeek squawked, six thin red lines dribbling blood down her cheeks where Lotta had clawed her.

'You struck her *first*!' Edda said, her tone so furious that Milou barely recognized it. 'And it is perfectly within my power to arrest you for such an action. Now –' she glared at Speelman – 'sit down and let Lotta speak freely.'

Speelman opened her mouth to protest again, but Edda cut her off.

'You will hear these children out or so help me I will put in a complaint about your conduct. I have contacts in high enough places.'

Speelman slumped into a chair with groan and waved a hand at Lotta. 'You have two minutes.'

Rotman's mirthful smile had become forced. Standing beside him, Fenna clutched a startled Mozart in her arms.

'Egg,' Lotta said. 'Show me what you noticed.'

'The little boy that the Fortuyns adopted, Jan,' said Egbert, kneeling beside her. 'When Milou and I were forging our own document, we saw that the matron hadn't recorded the adoption at all.'

'Nonsense!' Gassbeek shrieked. 'There was no boy called Jan. They're trying to cover up the fact they tried to kill me –'

'Continue, please,' Speelman said, raising a hand to silence Gassbeek.

Lotta was staring at the matron and Milou could almost hear the cogs of her mind clunking away, working out the puzzle.

'There *was* a little boy called Jan; he was even at our show tonight,' Lotta said, narrowing her eyes. Then she smiled. 'He arrived at the Little Tulip in October, didn't he? Which means he'll be listed in the abandonment records.'

She rifled through the pages, paused, rifled some more and frowned.

'He's not in there because he never existed,' Gassbeek squawked, smiling cruelly. 'Now unhand me.'

'No,' Lotta said. 'This doesn't make sense.' She ran her finger along the inside crease of the book and then pulled it quickly away. 'Ow!'

Her fingertip was bleeding.

'She's cut the page out,' Egbert gasped.

Speelman leaned over the book, scanned the page, then shot Gassbeek a furious glare. 'They're right. You've sliced a page out.'

'And if you look closely,' Lotta said, pressing her nose right to the page, 'you can see the imprint of Jan's name . . . *here*.'

Gassbeek paled and began squirming again, but Edda held her tight. Rotman, meanwhile, was leaning against the sink next to Fenna, tapping his chin.

'I bet there's others,' Lotta said. Sucking her finger, she flicked through more pages. 'Here's another page missing. And another.'

'I've been set up!' Gassbeek cried.

'Matron Gassbeek,' Speelman said sternly. 'Fraud on this scale is punishable by imprisonment. That money was meant to go to the Kinderbureau, to be shared out among *all* our orphanages.'

Gassbeek opened her mouth, but then snapped it closed again.

'I have to say,' Rotman said, 'I am very shocked that the matron has been so duplicitous. Mevrouw Speelman, I think I shall just take these orphans and go. I have a ship to repair!'

'Duplicitous?' Gassbeek squawked. 'You're a fine one to talk!'

Rotman's smile widened and his mustachios twitched in double time. 'I have no idea what you're talking about –'

'Matron Gassbeek,' Speelman interrupted, ignoring Rotman completely, 'I will be reporting this to the police at once.'

'You can't do that!' Gassbeek cried. 'I can't go to prison! Please!'

'Come now, orphans,' Rotman crooned. 'Let's get you settled into your new home, shall we? My ship is much more luxurious that this rickety old windmill. You'll love it, I just know you will.'

Milou glared at him. Fenna and Sem took a step backwards. Egbert glowered and Lotta snorted. Gassbeek began thrashing wildly in Edda's grip.

'I'll make a deal!' the matron squawked, her face as terrified as those of the orphans she had tormented. 'I have information on a larger, much more sinister orphan trade –'

'Come now!' Rotman repeated, more loudly this time, reaching out and grabbing Fenna's arm.

'Rotman's entire trade is off the backs of helpless orphans!' Gassbeek cawed. 'He threatened me. I had no choice –'

'The matron is clearly still insane,' Rotman growled, pulling Fenna towards him, who immediately began to struggle in his grip. 'Perhaps she needs to go back to the lunatic asylum.'

'Let Fenna go!' Milou cried.

'No,' Rotman growled. 'I don't think I will.'

In a flash of metal, his blade came out again. This time, it was pointed at Fenna's throat, pressed right against her thumping pulse.

Mozart let out a screech, claws and beak aimed at Rotman's face, but the merchant slapped the bird away. With a flutter of ruffled feathers, Mozart spiralled up to the cupboard top. Milou picked up a candlestick from the kitchen worktop. The sight of Fenna helpless in Rotman's grip was enough to make her recklessly angry. She would not let him hurt her.

'Meneer Rotman!' Speelman cried, eyeing his knife in horror. 'What are you doing?'

'I am taking what belongs to me,' Rotman said, his mustachios trembling. 'Five orphans, just as Matron Gassbeek promised me.' With his free hand, he picked up the basket of coins. 'And the money these little brats owe me after setting fire to my ship.'

Sem, Egbert and Lotta came to stand next to Milou. Edda wrestled to keep Gassbeek contained, as the matron wriggled and mumbled round the tea towel that now protruded from her mouth.

'Let Fenna go,' Edda said. 'These children are not going anywhere with you.'

Rotman chuckled. 'And who, exactly, is going to stop me?'

No one spoke. No one dared. The knife point was too close to Fenna's jugular. A single twist of his wrist would kill her.

'Well?' Rotman boomed. 'Which one of you pathetic idiots is going to stop me?'

'I am,' said a deep voice.

It had come from near the stairwell, on the opposite side of the room from every single person in the kitchen. Startled gasps sounded as everyone spun to peer into the shadows of the understairs, to where Puppet-Papa's headless body was slumped over the side of the rocking chair, just as Gassbeek had left him. Slowly, his right arm raised up to grab the side of the chair. Then his left one. He pulled himself upright, his back to them, then slowly turned.

'Let the child go,' Puppet-Papa said in a voice like grinding bones.

38

There was a thud and Milou spun round to find Rose Speelman had fainted head first on to the table where she'd been sitting.

'*I* will stop you,' Puppet-Papa said in a ghoulish grumble, rasping and ominous. Milou could practically hear the hairs rising on everyone's arms. 'Let her go now, and I'll let you live.'

Milou caught a tiny glimpse of a white glove above the stairwell door. The same white gloves, she thought, that had handed her coins at the gate earlier that evening.

Who was it?

She peeked at the others.

Rotman was gawping at the puppet. 'How –'

'Surely you must have heard the rumours?' Milou said, her voice dropping to a menacing whisper. 'This windmill is haunted. Did you not read the sign at the gate?'

Rotman blinked in disbelief. Gassbeek was now clutching Edda in terror and the clockmaker's Eyebrow of Curiosity was halfway up her forehead. Speelman was still face down on the table, muttering incoherently to herself as she slowly came to.

'Heed my warning,' Puppet-Papa growled. He raised his hands up in front of him, as if he were ready to throttle Rotman. 'Or I will crush your skull and pull your brains out through your nose.'

Milou watched Rotman's hand twitch. She would have laughed were it not for the fact that Fenna was still trapped beneath that cruel blade of his.

'I'll cut you open before you have a chance,' Rotman said, but his voice trembled as much as his mustachios.

Milou kept her eyes fixed on the blade, noticing with silent glee that Rotman was lowering his hand. She shared a pointed look with the others. With the adults no longer looking her way, she used her eyes to indicate that they should move to free Fenna.

'Who . . . who are you?' Rotman whispered, squinting at Puppet-Papa.

'Your greatest nightmare . . .'

The blade lowered a fraction more and Milou felt a gentle tingling in her ears. It ran down the back of her shoulders and gave her a nudge of encouragement.

'*Now*,' Milou mouthed to the others.

Sem swung his leg; it connected with the back of Rotman's knee and the merchant tipped forward. At the same moment, Fenna twisted at an impossible angle, sliding out of his loosened grip as if she were made of water. She tucked and rolled out of reach. Lotta staggered over and threw the contents of a mug into Rotman's face, just as Milou brought the candlestick down on Rotman's knife-wielding hand, sending the blade clattering to the ground.

She kicked the knife under the table as Rotman swayed and rubbed at his eyes. When his gaze met hers, he roared in fury and strode towards her with deadly intent. He had made it only two steps when Egbert appeared on the table behind the merchant and brought the record book down hard on his head.

Rotman crumpled, landing on his stomach. It was over within a few hammering heartbeats.

'Did I kill him?' Egbert squeaked. Rotman let out a muffled groan in response.

Edda pushed Gassbeek into a chair. The matron squawked in indignation, but remained seated as the clockmaker grabbed some puppet string from the table and began tying the merchant's hands behind his back.

'You didn't kill him,' Edda said, 'but he'll wish he was dead when he wakes up. I intend to make sure he's locked in the darkest cell in all of Amsterdam, with nothing but rats and fleas to keep him company.'

Speelman sat up, blinking furiously. 'What's happening?' she asked. She looked down at Rotman and gasped. 'How –'

Gassbeek gave a muffled squawk behind her tea-towel gag, her expression pained and defeated.

Milou, however, was staring at Puppet-Papa, who was now slumped once more in his chair. Two white gloves appeared round the edge of the stairwell door, pushing it open. The cowled figure Milou had seen earlier stepped into the room, face still hidden in deep shadow.

The white gloves reached up and lowered the hood.

Milou's heart stopped dead. It was a man she had never seen before, yet she knew him immediately. He looked . . . like Liesel's portrait.

He had a potato-shaped face and one eye slightly larger than the other. Two plum-sized ears stuck out of the side of his head. And his hair . . .

His hair was the colour of a sky-burnt sunset.

Milou couldn't speak. Her mouth was as dry as grave dirt; her chest felt as if it were being crushed.

'Bram Poppenmaker?' Sem gasped.

The man was silent for what seemed like an age, his eyes boring into Milou's and his cheek twitching in annoyance. And then, with a low and disconcerting voice, he spoke.

'Indeed.'

Milou realized she was biting the inside of her lip when the coppery taste of blood curled round her tongue. Her father was standing right there in front of her. He'd seen her message and come back.

She took a step towards him, wanting to wrap her arms round him, but stopping as she felt a sharp pinch on her left ear.

Why was he not overjoyed to see her? Why was he . . . glowering?

'Excuse me,' Speelman said, pushing through the five of them to get to Bram. 'Meneer Poppenmaker. On behalf of the Kinderbureau, I apologize that these orphans have intruded on your property, stolen your identity, created a cotton copy of you and caused general pandemonium. I shall see to it that they are suitably reprimanded, once I work out what to do with them –'

Bram Poppenmaker turned the full force of his glower on the Kinderbureau agent, silencing her instantly.

'I want to hear from this pandemonium of Poppenmakers myself,' he said. 'I want to know why they saw fit to use my name, and my *daughter's*, to drag me back here.'

Milou noticed his voice crack slightly. There was sadness leaking from beneath that angry glare, she could see it clearly, even though he was trying to keep it hidden.

'Bram,' Edda said. 'Perhaps we could all sit down and discuss this calmly.'

'Is this your doing, Finkelstein?' Poppenmaker said, his words biting the air between them. 'You seem to be in on it all. Why doesn't that surprise me?'

'It had nothing to do with Edda,' Milou found herself saying. 'It was all me.'

Bram's gaze bored through her. 'And who, exactly, are you?'

'My name is Milou Po–' she stopped, trying to swallow the lump in her throat, but it wouldn't budge. A gentle tingle tickled her neck. 'I am Milou Poppenmaker,' she said with a confidence she didn't truly feel. '*That* is who I am.'

Bram cocked his head slightly. 'Is that so?'

This was it. The moment she had been hoping for. The answers she craved, needed, were just a few heartbeats away. And yet Bram Poppenmaker barely even acknowledged her.

'Milou,' she repeated slowly, waiting for him to show any sign of recognition. 'It's me, *Milou.*'

'And what are you doing in my windmill, Milou *Poppenmaker*?'

The bite to his words made Milou flinch. Why was he pretending not to know who she was?

'It's a long story –'

'It seems you're rather good at telling stories.' He set Puppet-Papa aside and sat down on the rocking chair, crossing his arms and legs. 'So why don't you tell me exactly how you came to be in my windmill.'

'I grew up in the Little Tulip Orphanage in Amsterdam,' she began. 'I was left on the roof . . .'

His gaze remained cold and fixed on her. If he now realized who she was, he was doing a very good job of not showing it. A tiny flutter of doubt settled in her, but her ears tingled softly, urging her to continue.

'That was twelve years ago . . .'

Still no response.

'In my basket was a cat puppet, made by you.'

The tiniest frown creased his brow, but still he didn't speak or acknowledge that it was he who had left her there.

Anger surged through Milou. Her ears prickled in warning, but she ignored it.

'I followed the coordinates you left for me. They led me right to that tree of yours.'

He blinked. That was all.

'I found your name, and my mother's, carved up on the highest branch. I found the handkerchief with the rings ... Why are you pretending you don't know me? You know full well who I am, seeing as you abandoned me and never returned!'

Milou didn't realize she was shouting until she saw him flinch.

'I waited twelve years for you,' she said, quieter this time but just as resentful. 'I spent every single morning staring out of the window, wondering if today would be the day you came back for me. And then, when you didn't, I thought perhaps you needed me to find you. I dreamed of you. I wrote down every little detail, every little clue, hoping to work out how I could find you. And here I am –'

Her voice caught. Tears burned a path down her cheeks.

'You had another daughter,' she whispered. 'Did you love Liesel more? Is that why you left me?'

She didn't know what else it could be. This was not how she expected her reunion with her father to go. All these years of waiting, wondering, wishing – she had never considered she'd be met with this cold, hard look he wore, and his insistence on pretending he had no idea who she was.

'Do you even realize what it was *like* in that orphanage?' she continued when he still didn't respond. It infuriated her. 'The matron was cruel. We were worked until our fingers cracked. We slept in cold rooms, in beds barely big enough for one, let alone two or three. She was going to *sell* us. Do you not care about any of that?'

Bram Poppenmaker blinked again. He opened his mouth to respond, but Milou cut him off.

'Please don't pretend you don't know who I am. All I want . . . all I've ever wanted . . . is answers.'

'Milou . . .' Bram sighed, and now, finally, he looked sorry. 'I'm not your father.'

Milou blinked.

'You're lying. You're . . . you must be . . . My baby blanket,' she mumbled. 'It's velvet, just like your cloak. You stitched my name on to it – I know you did. And . . . and my puppet. You made it. I must be your daughter!'

She looked at him, searching his face for any hint of dishonesty, but she couldn't see any. His glower had softened, replaced with a new emotion that turned Milou's insides into a maelstrom of anguish. He pitied her.

'But –'

Her words clogged her throat as she studied his features again. If she squinted, which she did just then, she thought that maybe, just maybe, their noses had the same rounded tip, but his was much longer. And his eyes were the brightest blue, not nearly black. And that red hair . . .

He looked *nothing* like her.

'I'm not your father, Milou,' he repeated softly. 'I'm sorry, but that is the simple truth of it. My wife, Annaliese, died many years before you were born. When Liesel was not much younger than you, in fact.'

His words echoed round her head, and it felt as if she'd fallen down a well. Even though her mind was insisting it was just a cruel lie – it *had* to be – her heart could see the truth of it in his eyes. He wasn't lying.

Bram Poppenmaker was not her father.

'I had only one child,' Bram said quietly. 'And I loved her very much. I would never have given her up. Liesel was everything to me.'

Milou's trembling stopped, her ear tips turned to ice. 'Liesel *was* –?'

Bram's face crumpled. 'Liesel is dead.'

Milou's heart didn't break, it shattered. The tingling of her ears fell deathly still. An anguished cry filled the room; Milou turned to find Edda had slumped into the chair beside Gassbeek, her face completely pale and her eyes squeezed closed.

'Liesel . . . she's . . .?' The Polder Warden's voice cracked at the edges. 'She's *dead*?'

'Yes.' Bram's expression hardened again. 'No thanks to that cousin of yours.'

Edda's eyes snapped open, and they were filled with both pain and fury. 'He loved her!'

'He killed her!'

The room fell silent. Eyebrows either furrowed or were raised high and it seemed like everyone had sucked in a startled, collective breath as Bram's words settled over them.

'No.' The Polder Warden scowled. 'He would never harm her. How did she die?'

'Consumption,' Bram sighed. 'The very same illness that took her mother.'

Edda's scowl deepened. 'How on earth can you blame that on –'

'She was supposed to be in bed, resting. I came back from Amsterdam late one night only to see that unscrupulous cousin of yours hurrying away from the mill – even though I had forbidden his visits. I found Liesel slumped on the doorstep, paler than a ghost and shaking like a frightened mouse. A fever set in . . . It didn't get any better, no matter how much I tried –' He stared down at his gloved hands. 'She died a week later, the day before her nineteenth birthday, in my arms.'

Milou felt heartbroken. It didn't matter that Liesel wasn't actually her sister, as she'd believed. Not when she'd spent the last few weeks dreaming of what it would be like to meet her, to love her and be loved by her. They'd had so much in common after all. Milou felt as if she had known Liesel, had already *loved* her.

'She's really gone?' Edda asked, her voice ragged. 'She's been dead for twelve years – and you never thought to *tell* me? You let me think she'd just . . . left me.'

Edda was shaking, tears spilling down her cheeks.

'Where is she?' she asked Bram. 'Where did you bury her?'

Bram was silent for a moment, looking beyond the polder warden. He let out a long breath. 'She's with her mother of course.'

Edda paled, her head snapping towards the window. Milou followed their gaze, to where the oak tree was framed perfectly in the centre of the window.

'The flower garden,' she whispered, understanding dawning on her. 'You were tending to Mevrouw Poppenmaker's grave in Liesel's absence. That's why you were always under the tree.'

Edda wiped a tear. 'Liesel always said a flower garden was much more apt than a cold headstone. I just . . . I didn't want her to come back to find it overgrown or worse, barren. Little did I realise that I've spent the last twelve years tending to *her* grave too –'

Milou realized she'd been very, very wrong about the Polder Warden. She hadn't hated Liesel. She'd *loved* her. It was written plainly over every part of her anguished expression.

'You were friends with Liesel?' Milou asked Edda. 'Was that why you've been loitering around here? Were you trying to find out what happened to her?'

Edda nodded. 'She was the best friend I've ever had. The only one really. When my family first moved here from Strasbourg, she didn't stare at us like we didn't belong. She didn't care that we were different. But then she just *vanished*.

I was hurt and angry that she would leave without explanation, as if I meant nothing to her – not even a postcard. When months, then years passed, I bolted the mill's gates and refused to even look at it. And then the five of you turned up and brought it all back. And now I know –'

Silence fell heavily once more. Milou's head was spinning.

'Liesel was stronger-willed than even you and I put together,' Edda said finally, staring hard at Bram. 'If she left her sickbed, she'd have done it of her own volition. I realize losing her must have broken your heart, but there's no use blaming someone whose only crime was to love your daughter. And then punishing me for it, too.'

'Theodora Tenderheart,' Lotta said suddenly. 'Was Liesel writing about herself? Did she know she was going to die?'

Bram nodded.

'She would have liked your ending,' Bram said, smiling ruefully. 'And she loved the puppet theatre. Oh, how she loved it! Your show would have delighted her.'

'Yes,' Edda said, smiling slightly. 'It really would have.'

Fresh tears spilled from the Polder Warden's eyes. After another tense few heartbeats, she got to her feet. It looked like she was trying very hard to stop crying.

'Come on,' she said, pulling Gassbeek up to her feet and nodding disdainfully at Rotman's still prone figure. With all that had just happened, Milou had nearly forgotten about them. 'Let's get these two reprobates into Speelman's carriage, shall we?' She turned to the Kinderbureau agent. 'The jailhouse is on your way back to the city, I'm sure you don't mind delivering them there, do you?' Then, before Speelman could protest, she faced the other children, her expression softening. 'Let's give Bram and Milou a few minutes to talk in peace, shall we?'

Gassbeek made indignant protests, muffled by the tea towel, as Edda dragged her to her feet. Rotman was still unconscious. It took all four children to lift him, one limb each, and carry him out of the door. Speelman tutted once, shot a sympathetic look in Milou's direction, then followed them outside.

The kitchen door was slammed shut by the wind and Bram and Milou were alone.

Milou sat on the chair opposite him, tucked her knees under her chin and clutched them tightly. She didn't know what to say. Her ears tingled softly but constantly.

None of this felt right. She couldn't have come all this way for nothing. But, if Bram wasn't her father, who was?

Who left her the watch, and the coordinates, and the puppet? And why did they lead her here of all places?

'Liesel –' Bram began, then took a deep breath and let out a sigh. 'Do you know, I haven't said her name aloud since she –'

A hot tear rolled into the corner of Milou's mouth partly for Bram's sad story, partly for the fact that everything she had ever believed in had just been torn from her. Even the sister she'd spent the last few weeks pining for.

Bram lifted one of Puppet-Papa's limp arms and smiled. 'This is just the kind of madcap ruse Liesel would have come up with. You've got a fine imagination, I'll give you that. It was her dying wish that I fill that theatre with her stories, so that she could live on through them.'

'You promised her you wouldn't stop the puppet shows?' Milou asked, glowering at the puppet-maker. 'So why did you leave?'

'Because my heart cannot bear to be here,' Bram said. 'This place . . . there are too many memories of her – and her mother. Every item in this mill is a memory that hurts too much to hold on to. I left with nothing except the clothes on my back and a few boxes of work documents. Just sitting here I feel like my heart is shattering all over again.'

Milou's ears tingled again, more insistently this time. There had to be something she'd missed. Something to make sense of it all. A thought was trying to push its way to the forefront of her mind, but she couldn't quite grasp at it. She was so very, very tired. And so very, very confused.

Bram Poppenmaker was now looking at Liesel's portrait of him. He seemed to have forgotten Milou was there entirely, lost to his memories.

She untucked the pocket watch from under her collar and held it out to him. 'Do you really not recognize this?'

Bram shook his head. 'Sorry, I don't.'

Milou hurried to the back door and got her coffin-basket. 'This?'

Again Bram shook his head. Again Milou's ears prodded her on.

She set the coffin-basket on the floor and began to unpack it, setting her clothes then the cat puppet aside. She unwrapped the handkerchief and held the rings out to him. 'These?'

Bram jumped to his feet, his expression transforming instantly. But it was not the rings he was looking at, it was her puppet.

Carefully, he picked it up. 'This is Liesel's. How did you –'

The door opened and the Kinderbureau agent marched in, looking pleased with herself.

'Milou,' Speelman said. 'It's time to go.'

Behind Speelman, Milou's friends wandered back in, all looking resigned.

'Wait,' Milou said.

Bram was turning the cat puppet over in his hands, looking grief-stricken once more.

'I've waited long enough. I really must get you back.' Speelman turned round, only to walk into Edda, who had just appeared from outside.

The Polder Warden was staring at Milou's coffin in wide-eyed horror, looking as if she'd seen a ghost.

'That coffin . . .'

'It's all right,' Lotta said. 'It doesn't have a body in it. It's just –'

'No!' Edda cried. 'I *made* that coffin.'

41

Milou's ears prickled sharply at their tips and her heart shuddered almost to a stop. She looked at the basket, then back to Edda. A sliver of hope began to beat in her chest.

Edda shook her head. 'I made it for my previous cat, Madame Meowkins. Those clasps ... the weave ... Look, it even has the claw marks from that pesky hound ... I thought she'd chewed up the whole thing. How on earth did you –'

'My parents abandoned me inside it,' Milou said, hardly able to breathe. 'When I was about a week old, according to Gassbeek.'

A heavy silence settled on the room. Bram sat down heavily in the rocking chair again, frowning at Milou and Edda, clutching the cat puppet tightly. A chill crawled up the back of Milou's neck and her ears prickled wildly, but, when she tried to speak, no sound came out.

'It was December 1880,' Egbert said. 'On an orphanage rooftop, under a full moon.'

'It must have been the same night that Liesel died,' Sem added. 'Milou said you were seen leaving Poppenmill under a full moon that month.'

Bram paled. Edda gave a small croak and her eyes widened as she turned back to Milou. 'But –'

'There's more,' Lotta said officially, reaching into Milou's sleeve and pulling out the Book of Theories. 'A velvet blanket that looks like it could have come straight out of the Poppenmakers' workroom. The cat puppet which certainly *did* come out of his workroom – it belonged to Liesel. A pocket watch with the coordinates of the tree just outside Poppenmill. Two wedding bands wrapped in a handkerchief embroidered with the name A. Poppenmaker –'

Lotta kept talking, but Milou's ears were now tingling so insistently her friend's voice sounded muffled and distant. She rubbed at them as she watched Edda's expression change from confusion to utter shock and Bram's face get impossibly paler.

'It can't be,' Edda whispered, clutching her locket with both hands.

The clockmaker took Milou's pocket watch, her face paling. 'This is his.' She looked up at Milou, eyes glistening with tears. 'Oh, sweet cheese, do you think –'

She and the puppet-maker shared a look.

'No. It can't be,' Bram rasped. 'I would have known.'

Milou looked up at Lotta, who was frowning thoughtfully. Fenna and Egbert were casting nervous glances between Milou and Edda. Sem inched closer towards her, his eyes never leaving Edda.

Neither Bram nor Edda moved or spoke for several long moments. They were both too busy staring at Milou.

Then, letting go of the pocket watch, Edda reached up and gently tilted Milou's face this way and that, examining every detail. The tingling on Milou's ears intensified, running down the sides of her neck and back up again.

'How did I not notice?'

Sem squeezed in closer. 'Notice what?'

Edda shook her head again, staring deeply into Milou's eyes. Milou's breath seemed to be stuck in her chest. Finally, Edda's shaking fingers let go of her chin and the clockmaker took a step back.

'You look just like him.'

The world seemed to tilt around Milou. Sem's hand clasped her elbow and held her tight.

'But you have *her* nose,' Edda continued.

Milou felt rivulets of thick, hot tears sliding down her cheeks. Yet still her lips seemed unable to form words.

'Whose nose?' Egbert asked.

'Liesel's,' Lotta whispered. 'She was named Anna*liese*, after her mother. That's why her handkerchief had the initial A on it. Is that right?'

'Yes,' Bram said softly, getting slowly to his feet. He took Milou's chin in one gloved hand and studied her. 'Dear God, Finkelstein, you're right. She's Liesel's – but . . . but how could she have hidden this from me?'

'The dresses,' Sem said. 'The aprons around the middle. Perhaps Liesel made them to hide her growing stomach?'

Bram seemed not to hear him, but Milou's ears were ringing with his words.

'But Bram would have noticed her having the baby!' Edda said, sending a questioning glare at the puppet-maker. 'You must have known.'

Bram let go of Milou's chin and closed his eyes. 'I did not.'

'Maybe Milou was born elsewhere,' Lotta said. 'Somewhere close –'

'The theatre!' Egbert said. 'That *might* explain the blankets we found on the stage. It *would* explain why she left the mill that night, even though she was so ill.'

Her friends' voices were getting louder, but the tightness in Milou's chest and throat was getting worse. She tried to answer, but she couldn't even nod. Edda and Bram seemed just as much at a loss for words.

'And the wedding rings,' Lotta said. 'Perhaps they were planning to marry, as soon as you were born. But Liesel was already too sick. Oh! He must have been heartbroken when he learned Liesel had –'

'Who is he?'

Milou's voice was barely audible, but it silenced the room nonetheless.

Edda wiped a tear from her cheek and shook herself. When she spoke again, her voice cracked on almost every word. 'Thirteen years ago, my cousin came to live with me. He and Liesel, they were ... well, they were very close, although – oh, Milou, I never suspected they had – and then he left so suddenly, just after Liesel did, without any explanation. I simply assumed he ... your *father* ... had gone to find her, wherever she had gone.'

Father.

The word shot through Milou's heart like an arrow. It broke her apart and then pieced her together again, slightly more whole than before, but still achingly hollow in places.

'The people around here –' Edda wiped at a tear. 'Let's just say they didn't think much of a scruffy boy with a wild look about him and a large dog that ate everything she could get her jaws round. They didn't know the kind-hearted, slightly awkward boy I knew. Only Liesel saw it because, like with me, she was the only one willing to *look*.'

Milou's throat clogged again. The tears seemed to thicken, curling over her chin and down her neck. The ear-tingling became a gentle, soothing caress.

'Here,' Edda said, clasping her locket again. 'I have him here.'

With shaking fingers, she reached up and pulled it up over her head. Milou took the locket from Edda and looked down at it, her hands shaking so much she thought she might drop it. A six-fingered hand appeared and helped her unclip the small clasp. But, as her friends gathered more closely round her, Milou's fingers closed round the locket. She looked up helplessly at them, then took a shaky breath and opened it.

Inside was a photograph of a young man with a wolfish grin. His unruly hair was as dark as midnight and his eyes were almost black. At his feet lay a large grey hound – its paws the size of breakfast plates. And on the corner of the photogram, etched in neat handwriting, was a name:

Thibault.

42

Milou stared at the picture of her father.

The claw marks.

The pocket watch.

The wildness of her very own features.

It had all come from him.

Milou clasped a hand round the pocket watch.

Beneath the stars I
found you.
52.284040, 4.784040
Under the moon I lost you.

Her parents had fallen in love, sitting in the oak tree, watching the stars. Then her mother had died, on the night of a full moon.

The inscription hadn't been for Milou at all. It had been for Liesel.

'I don't know why he left you the way he did,' Edda said. 'But I do know he always did what he felt was right.'

Milou snapped the locket closed and handed it back to Edda. She had wanted answers and now she had them.

Her mother was dead. Her father was gone. Her heart felt hollow.

'Sorry to interrupt,' Speelman said, without sounding sorry in the slightest. 'But I need to get the orphans back to the Little Tulip tonight.' She gave Bram a big, toothy smile, then nodded her head at Milou. 'I suppose you'd like to keep this one, yes?'

Bram blinked.

'Excellent.' Speelman dropped the record book on his lap and handed him a quill. 'Please sign here – that's it, thank you. Now the rest of you, let's go.'

'No,' Milou said. 'You can't take them back there.'

'Rules are rules, dear child,' Speelman said, heaving the record book up.

Milou looked at Bram pleadingly. 'Can you –'

Her grandfather sighed. 'Milou, until a few moments ago I was a childless widower. Now I have a surprise granddaughter to take care of. I can't take on five . . .'

'Well then,' Speelman said brightly, 'that's that. *Kindjes*, gather your things, say goodbye. Do it quickly.'

Milou blocked the doorway, her mind whirling. 'Please don't –'

'Wait,' Edda said.

They all turned to her expectantly. She was holding Lotta protectively. Speelman frowned at her.

'These children are perfectly adept at caring for themselves,' Edda said. 'They've certainly proven that. Their tenacity is quite astonishing. Surely there must be some way round all this?'

The Kinderbureau agent sighed. 'Firstly, I would require a legal guardian to be named for any minor without a biological parent or relative. Secondly, tenacity does not impress the Kinderbureau nearly as much as accurate records do. And thirdly the children have nowhere to live.'

'They can live here, of course,' Bram said matter-of-factly. 'Edda, would you still be interested in buying this place?'

Edda looked stunned for a moment, then nodded. 'Yes, but –'

'Excellent,' Bram said. 'I'll take the fox-shaped clock as first payment if you still have it?'

The Eyebrow rose. 'I do. But –'

'Liesel loved that clock,' Bram said with a small smile. 'And this place will only crumble into the canal if it's left uninhabited. These children, no doubt, will make good use of it. Liesel would have liked that.'

'The *children* need a *guardian*,' Speelman cried in exasperation. 'The records –'

'If it's merely a question of silly paperwork,' Edda said, 'I will sign as their guardian.'

Milou heard her friends each suck in a surprised breath. Lotta clung to Edda. The others stared at her.

'It would be my honour to adopt them,' Edda said. 'If they'll have *me*, that is.'

Four sets of arms tangled themselves round the Polder Warden's waist. Milou wrapped her own arms round herself.

'Oh, very well,' Speelman said, clucking her tongue. 'That's the matter settled then. I honestly can't cope with any more surprises, so I think I shall just take the fees and leave you to it. I still have two criminals to deliver to the jailhouse before I can go to bed.'

Lotta counted out fifty guilders, put it in a hessian onion bag and handed it to the Kinderbureau agent while Edda signed her name. Rose Speelman took one last look at Puppet-Papa, then at the children, and shook her head in disbelief, disappearing once more into the cold night.

Bram stood, running a hand through his hair. 'Come on then, Milou,' he said. 'Let's go home.'

'But . . . this is our home, surely?' she asked. 'Why are you selling it? Why would we leave? Where would we go?'

'I have a houseboat in Antwerp. That's where I've been the past twelve years. I can't live here. The memories are too painful. I'm sorry, but we're leaving. Tonight.'

The resulting silence was louder than a winter storm.

Milou watched as several emotions played out on her friends' faces. Fenna looked confused, Lotta seemed shocked and Egbert shook his head, as if he hadn't heard Bram properly. It was Sem's expression, however, that twisted her insides.

He looked nothing short of heartbroken.

'Say your goodbyes,' Bram said. 'I'll gather our belongings.'

Milou shuffled, uncomfortable beneath their bewildered stares. She realized she had no idea how to say goodbye to them. Neither, it seemed, did they.

A moment later, Bram appeared beside her again. 'Ready?'

He nodded courteously to Edda, then took Milou's hand and guided her to the door, her coffin-basket under his arm. Milou's feet moved with him, but her gaze remained fixed on the four shocked faces behind her. Sem tried to muster an encouraging smile for her, but it wobbled too much to be even slightly convincing.

This is what happened with orphans. They found a family and then they left. There was no reason why it shouldn't be any different for Milou.

And, just like that, she was out of Poppenmill. The four faces she'd come to know better than even her own were gone.

Milou walked mechanically towards a carriage parked beyond the front gate. Bram heaved her coffinbasket on to the back of it and, hands shaking, Milou unfastened the clasps and opened the coffin lid to put her cat puppet inside.

On top of her clothes, in the same spot as always, were her treasures: a lock of red curly hair tied with an emerald-green ribbon, a charcoal portrait of her, the poster for Cirque de Lumière and, of course, her Book of Theories. The journey to Antwerp would be long. Plenty of time for her to begin filling the blank pages with new theories about where her father might be. Milou opened it. The book had been a comforting presence throughout her time at the Little Tulip, but now, for some reason, that comforting feeling seemed to have gone.

She turned to the first page, her eyes falling on one particular line:

My family would never leave me –

Sem had refused to leave them, even if that meant giving up his dream.

They'd all followed her from the Little Tulip to Poppenmill. They'd all stayed, despite the risks, to raise the adoption fees. They'd pulled her from that frozen canal and carried her home. And, when Rotman had her by the hair onstage, all four of them had refused to leave her behind. And yet here she was, leaving *them*.

'Hop up then,' Bram said, patting the front bench. 'It's a long journey –'

'Wait,' she said.

Milou rubbed at her ears, hoping for a tingle or a prickle to guide her. But her Sense was silent. She rubbed at them again.

Bram looked down at her in bewilderment. 'What's wrong with your ears?'

Milou gave up rubbing them and sighed. Emiliana's words came back to her.

A shadow follows you . . . the dead kind.

Could it have been her mother all this time? If so, why

wasn't Liesel helping her now, when she needed guidance the most?

But Milou knew the answer already. This was a decision only she, and she alone, could make.

She looked up at Bram, who was waiting for her to speak.

'We could stay here,' Milou said. 'Together, we could make the theatre everything Liesel dreamed it would be.'

'Milou –'

'You've been hiding from this place for twelve years. You've all but forgotten her.'

Bram's gaze flicked towards the oak tree and the flower garden graves below it. Then he closed his eyes for a moment. 'Forgetting is easier than remembering. It's far less painful.'

'I belong here,' Milou said. 'I never knew her, but I want to honour her memory nonetheless. And I belong with *them*.' She turned and pointed to the four faces pressed nose first against the kitchen window. 'I always have.'

Bram nodded grimly and sighed. 'Then you should stay here.'

'And you?'

She saw his answer in the pained frown that creased his brow. Milou could tell that looking at her reminded him of the daughter he'd lost, and the young man he felt had stolen her from him; that it wasn't just being back at the windmill that threatened to break his heart all over again each day – and that he couldn't survive doing anything less than forgetting it all.

Bram Poppenmaker wasn't ready to remember. Perhaps he never would be.

Milou reached up and took her coffin-basket into her arms. 'Goodbye, *Opa.*'

Bram ran the back of a gloved hand down her cheek.

'Goodbye, Miloutje. For now.'

She gave him a small nod, then turned towards the mill.

Her friends were already outside, their faces agog with disbelief.

Egbert shook his head. 'Are you –'

Lotta blinked. 'Aren't you –'

Sem opened his mouth to speak, then hiccuped once.

Milou placed her coffin on the ground. 'I couldn't leave. This is my home. And you're my –'

Her words were cut off as the four of them leaped forward and smothered her in a crushing embrace.

'Family,' Fenna said, somewhere beyond the tufts of hair in Milou's face.

Milou extracted herself from the huddle and smiled at them, pleased to find her stomach was no longer twisting and churning. She'd made the right choice, she knew.

'Yes – family.'

Peering behind her, she saw Bram staring at the five of them. He gave her a small smile and an even smaller nod, then clucked his tongue at his horse. In a rattle of wheels and a clatter of hoofbeats, the carriage pulled slowly away from the gates of Poppenmill.

Bram Poppenmaker was gone.

Again.

44

M ilou sat on the lowest branch of the oak tree and watched as Bram Poppenmaker's carriage rattled down the canal road. Her friends sat beside her, the tips of their noses glowing in the lantern light that still dotted each branch. As the carriage finally merged into the night-time gloom and disappeared from sight entirely, Milou let out a long, shaky breath. She clutched her cat puppet to her chest, right over the pocket watch, until she could just about feel its heartbeat *tick-tocking* in tandem with hers.

'What now?' she whispered, looking up to the constellations for an answer.

Instead, it was Sem who responded. 'Sleep.'

Fenna yawned loudly.

'I'm going to get the mill working again this spring,' Lotta announced. 'I haven't asked Edda yet, but I wonder if we could get it to generate more electricity for the theatre.'

Sem perked up slightly. 'I've had some more thoughts about puppet-making. Bram's designs are lovely, but I have ideas of my own.'

'We should make more of Fenna's whistling, too,' Lotta said. 'Imagine it: stories, puppets, light shows and our very own bird-songstress.'

Fenna let out a little giggle, her eyes twinkling in the lantern light.

'As wondrous as that sounds,' Milou said seriously, 'Egg and I have important shawl-identifying business to attend to first. It'll take us a while to knock on every door in Amsterdam.'

'It's a good job I have a map of the area already,' Egbert said from near the tree's trunk. 'We can cross each house off as we go.'

Milou couldn't see his face, but she could hear the smile in the stretchy sound of his words.

'This place is a dream,' Lotta said, kicking her trouser-clad legs happily. 'I never want to leave. There are so many possibilities; so much to do.'

'Right now, I really do just want to dream,' Sem said sleepily. 'For at least a week.'

A door creaked open behind them and Edda emerged from her farmhouse. She walked down the stone path towards them.

'I suppose you want the five of us tucked up in bed,' Lotta sighed, leaping down from the branch. 'It's very late. Way past our bedtime.'

'Um.' The clockmaker blinked. 'Yes . . . I'm sure that's very sensible, but actually I'd like to talk to Milou first if I may?'

Edda directed her question to Milou, her expression a little cautious. Milou nodded.

Egbert and Fenna hopped down. Sem toppled over, landing on one leg. Lotta caught him before he wobbled over completely. Fingers to her lips, Fenna whistled sharply and Mozart swooped down on to her shoulder from one of the upper branches. The five of them disappeared over the bridge and into Poppenmill, becoming hazy silhouettes behind the gauze curtains: a puppet show of stumbling tiredness.

Edda stood silently for a moment beside the flower garden, her expression hidden in the shadows. Her shoulders heaved once, heavily, then she scrambled up to sit next to Milou. 'I never was very good at climbing this thing,' she huffed as she settled herself on the branch, looking down as if she were on a cliff edge. 'Liesel and Thibault never teased me about it, and they'd even sit down here with me for a while, but, as soon as I went in to bed, they'd clamber to the very top to watch the stars.'

'I know,' Milou said with a small smile. 'I found their names up there.'

An awkward moment passed. The wind howled.

'You saw us through the window that first night, didn't you?' Milou asked.

Edda smiled. 'I did. I don't know what I was expecting to see, but, I can assure you, the sight of five children building a fake father was certainly not it.' She let out a big sigh. 'I'm sorry if my nosing around worried you.' Edda went quiet, her expression unreadable. 'You really don't like me, do you?'

'I didn't,' Milou admitted. She grimaced. 'But mainly because I thought you might be a werewolf.'

The Eyebrow of Curiosity arched like a pulled bowstring, then Edda burst out laughing.

Milou groaned. 'I know it's absurd.'

'Oh, Milou,' she said. Her chuckles subsided and she sighed heavily, turning serious. 'I think you're absurdly *magnificent*. All five of you. The past few weeks, watching what you children have achieved. The tenacity of it. The utter brilliance of it.' She smiled warmly. 'This world needs more absurdity like yours. Please don't ever change.'

Milou began to smile, then bit her lip.

Perhaps Edda was right. They had achieved a lot together, but that didn't stop her worrying that perhaps her friends wouldn't have been put in quite so much danger if it hadn't been for her wild imagination and silly theories.

'You being a werewolf is not even the most absurd thing I've ever convinced myself of.'

She took her Book of Theories out of her sleeve and handed it to the clockmaker. Edda smiled as she read the first few entries, then she closed the notebook, gave it back and reached into her own jacket pocket.

'That's why I wanted to talk to you actually.' She pulled out a piece of card and held it over her chest. 'As I said, I haven't spoken directly to Thibault in twelve years. I've certainly not heard of any werewolf-hunting or secret spying, I'm afraid, but he does have a sense of wild adventure in him. Just like you.'

She handed the card over.

'What is it?'

'A photograph he sent me a couple of years ago. No return address, of course, but I suppose it was his way of letting me know he's not forgotten me. You can have it, if you like.'

Milou lifted a lantern from above her head and held it closer. Her breath hitched as she realized what she was seeing. She blinked a few times, peering at the image, but it remained the same.

It was a hot-air balloon. It hadn't taken to the air yet, but seemed like it was about to launch. Hanging beneath the round black balloon wasn't a gondola, however, but a simple woven basket. She squinted at the photo, realizing it was set against a snowy landscape. Two figures could just about be seen inside the basket. One had a mass of midnight-dark hair and thick goggles over his eyes. The other was a large wolfhound.

She turned the photograph over. There was only a single line scribbled on the back:

You should see the night sky up here.

Edda flipped the photograph over again, then tapped the corner of the picture. There, in scratchy handwriting, were three words and four numbers:

Svalbard, Arctic Circle, 1890

Milou's scalp tingled and a smile tugged at the corners of her mouth. 'I wonder if he befriended any polar bears.'

'It wouldn't surprise me if that silly wolfhound of his managed to eat one whole.'

Milou jolted. 'Do you think he's ever been to Java?'

Edda shrugged. 'I don't know. You'll have to ask Thibault about it all one day. I'm sure you have many questions for him.'

'Yes, I do,' Milou admitted wearily, tucking the photograph into her Book of Theories. 'Several very *big* questions. But, for now, I just want to do gloriously normal family things. Like asking Sem to teach me how to ride that bicycle, watch

Fenna train Mozart, help Lotta make electricity and Egg . . . well, he needs my help the most and I intend to do everything I can for him.'

'And Bram?'

'My grandfather knows where I am if he wants to see me. And my father, well, perhaps he should be the one to find me. It's up to them if they want to remember the past or not, but I'll remember my mother with all my heart until the day that I die. And you can help me.'

'I certainly can,' Edda said, smiling. 'I have many stories about her.'

Milou jumped to the ground and held up a hand to help Edda down. The clockmaker stumbled only slightly less than Sem had, grabbing the tree for support as she slid down.

'Ow,' Edda said, sucking her fingers. 'Splinter.' She looked at the offending part of the tree. 'Oh.'

Milou followed her gaze. Carved elegantly into the trunk, next to where Egbert had been sitting mere minutes ago, were five new names:

Fenna

Sem

Lotta

Egg

Milou

Her heart fluttered. All thoughts of hot-air balloons, polar bears and wild adventures disappeared, replaced with a warm bubble of contentedness that spread right through her.

Milou really was *home*. It might not be perfect, or conventional, but it was *hers*. They were hers, and she was theirs.

'Come on.' Edda gave her hand a gentle squeeze. 'I hear it's way past your bedtime.'

They started back towards the mill, but the clockmaker stopped after just a few steps and frowned. For the first time since Milou had met her, Edda looked completely puzzled.

'What . . . I mean . . . how . . .' Edda shook herself. 'Should I make you all some warm milk first? And read you a bedtime story? Is that . . . is that what I'm supposed to do?'

'Yes,' replied Milou, grinning wolfishly. 'That's *exactly* what you're supposed to do.'

EPILOGUE

On a crisp, ambrosia-scented night, an owl patrolled its kingdom with sharp-eyed diligence. Its mismatched wings sliced through the star-strewn sky as it swooped and soared over fields and canals. Spring had been slowly but steadily tiptoeing its way across the land, breathing colour into the bleakest corners, teasing tentative tulip shoots out from the soil, and whistling soft lullabies to the three fluffy, newly hatched owlets snuggled in their yew-top nest.

The polder was emerging from a long, cold, dark slumber, yawning out new life, new wonder, new beginnings.

Even the crescent moon that night seemed warmer and brighter than ever before. And its shimmering yellow glow illuminated two very dissimilar, unfamiliar sets of footprints imprinted in the softening dirt, which the owl's keen eyes tracked with ease.

The longer and thinner set led, determinedly, in a ruler-straight line down the road. The other rounder set wove drunkenly in and out of the first lot, drifting now and again towards the canal edge, then towards a gate post, then back again, then off again, and so on.

The footprint trail ended at the base of the owl's own leafy yew tree. With a squawk of territorial fury, the owl spiralled towards its nest and peered down, round-eyed and sharp-beaked, to see just who was intruding so brazenly. It let out a shrill screech of warning at the man lurking ominously on the ground below, drenched from head to toe in the tree's deep shadows.

The lurker in question, however, paid the owl no mind. He stood, stiff-backed and unmoving, watching the windmill in deathly silence, his face lost to the darkness.

If the owl had been in any way knowledgeable about human fashion, it would have noticed that the man wore a long, Parisian-style jacket and a top hat unquestionably designed in London. His gloves were made of Peruvian wool and his boots of Bavarian leather. Around his neck was a silk neckerchief, decorated with a delicate batik pattern, and, in one gloved hand, he gripped a crumpled poster.

If the owl had been able to read, it would have noticed that upon this poster the man had circled, in bright red ink, four words:

Unaware of the eyes glaring at him from above, the man reached up to take his hat off, revealing hair that was a dark as midnight and eyes that were almost black. In all the years that he had been travelling the world, not once had he considered ever coming back to this place. It was nothing but pain to him or so he'd thought.

His shoulders heaved up and down as he watched the six hazy silhouettes behind the kitchen's gauze curtains; a puppet show of familial bliss, steaming mugs and cuddling bodies, so at odds with what he'd been expecting.

There was a scraping noise from behind the tree, and a huge grey wolfhound emerged from the gloom to stand beside him. Its jaws were wrapped round the head of the stone gargoyle it had just torn from a front gate, gnawing contentedly at it. The man remained silent and still, brooding and yet also bewitched by what he was seeing.

As if sensing her human's despair, the wolfhound dropped the gargoyle and howled, long and soulful, up towards the yellow slice of moon. It pierced through the quiet, startled the family of owls in the branches above them, and sent a single tear sliding down the man's left cheek, which curved under his chin and then dripped down on to his boot.

The howl echoed on, and a face appeared at the windmill's kitchen window. A small, heartbreakingly familiar nose pressed up against the glass, and eyes just like his own scanned the darkness. As the girl rubbed frantically at her ears, the man stepped tentatively out of the shadows towards her, beckoning the howling wolfhound to follow.

'Come, Andromeda,' he said, in a voice as rough as an Arctic storm. 'It's time we remembered.'

ACKNOWLEDGEMENTS

It really did take a village to raise this book-child of mine, and I therefore have a tremendously long list of people to whom I owe gratitude (get ready for the Dunglish).

First of all, my infinitely *wonderbaar* agent, Jenny Savill, who took these five little orphans on in their infancy and provided me with endless wisdom and encouragement to raise them properly. I'd also like to thank everyone else at Andrew Nurnberg Associates for championing this book and working so hard to find it a home with all my wonderful international publishers.

My editors on both sides of the pond: Naomi Colthurst, Kendra Levin and Maggie Rosenthal. *Hartelijk bedankt* for helping me shape this story, solve its never-ending plot-holes, and for generally being a joy to work with. *Dank u* to the entire Puffin and Viking teams, who have welcomed me into the Penguin Random House family and made this whole experience truly *magisch*. In particular, huge *dankje wel* to Stephanie Barrett, Janet Pascal, Jane Tait, Roz Hutchinson, Lottie Halstead, Lucy Upton, Kat Baker, Zosia Knapp and

Andrea Kearney. And to Ayesha Rubio, for bringing my characters and setting to life in her *prachtige* illustrations and cover art.

I also owe enormous *dankbaarheid* to the entire MA Writing for Young People Community. The tutors: Elen Caldecott, Julia Green, David Almond, Steve Voake, Janine Amos, Jo Nadin and Luce Christopher. Thank you for providing unrivalled wisdom, inspiration and support. And a *hele grote* thank you to C.J. Skuse, for being the first one to see potential in this story and encouraging me to drop all else and crack on with writing it.

My writing *kameraden*, Lucy Cuthew, who not only has the most beautiful hair, but also the sharpest eyes, kindest words and endless plot-fixing cleverness. Wibke Brueggeman, for the bleary-eyed, caffeine-and-Twix-fuelled writing sessions that got us both through our first drafts. Yasmin Rahman, who hates everything about the genres I write but reads my work enthusiastically, nonetheless. I'd never say this to her face, but she's pretty wonderful. Nizrana Farook, for reading an early draft and pointing out all the (owl-related) tangents I had gone off on. Sophie Kirtley, Alex English, Sue Bailey, Rachel Huxley, Kate Mulligan, all my workshop pals, Team SWAG (you know who you are) – I feel so lucky to have you all. And Caroline Ambrose for championing this book so loudly.

Rachel Betts, my all-time favourite Dutchie, who has been pulling my hair and cheering me on/up since we were in kindergarten. Vera Tooke: book research assistant, fact-fudging co-conspirator and *de echte beste moeder in de hele wereld*. My much taller siblings, for only ever looking down on me in the physical sense – you made writing about sibling-bonds much easier, so *dankie dankie*! And my father, who provided me with endless weird-spiration growing up, which I can now channel into all my stories.

Dylan: love of my life and chef of my dinners (the two being only 'coincidently' connected). I'm not sure there are words adequate enough. I wouldn't have got to where I am now without you. And Felix; my bluntest critic, fiercest supporter, and the funniest creature in this universe. Thank you for making me laugh every single day.

And finally, Maisy Moop, for warming my lap and keeping me glued to my chair so that I had no other choice but to keep writing.

ABOUT THE AUTHOR

Half Dutch, half English, Hana Tooke grew up near Amsterdam and moved to the south of England at the age of twelve. After completing a degree in music, and then a PGCE, Hana was a primary school teacher for several years. Hana also completed the Bath Spa University Writing for Young People MA, and *The Unadoptables* was shortlisted for The Bath Children's Novel Award 2018. She now lives in Bath with two humans and a cat.

ABOUT THE ILLUSTRATOR

Ayesha L. Rubio was born in Madrid. She studied Fine Arts in Spain and England before beginning her work as an illustrator. She has published three books of her own and has embarked on new adventures in the world of animation.

SUGGESTED
DISCUSSION QUESTIONS

In what ways are Lotta, Egbert, Fenna, Sem and Milou shown to be extraordinary throughout this book? What talents and skills do they possess? Are these abilities the result of luck or hard work? How do they help the children in their adventures? Which special skill would *you* most like to have and why?

Matron Gassbeek tries to upset Milou and her friends by calling them 'unadoptable', but her cruel label doesn't have the desired impact. What's their response to Gassbeek's insult? How do the children turn this label to their advantage throughout the story? Why doesn't Milou want to be adopted?

What have you learned about Amsterdam in 1880 from this book? How does the setting help bring the story and characters to life? Where would you choose to set a story? What would you tell your readers to help them imagine this location?

How much of this book do you think is historically accurate and how much is invented? Does it matter if it's not completely accurate?

The author uses exaggerated descriptions (*caricature*) to highlight people's faults or ridicule the world in which they live (*satire*). Can you find examples of how the author shows us who Gassbeek and Rotman really are using these methods? Are we meant to approve of their behaviour?

Beneath the humour and suspense of this exciting story, the author is asking questions about how people should behave. What can you discover about friendship, loyalty, the abuse of power and attitudes to difference in this book?

What do Lotta, Egbert, Fenna, Sem and Milou know about families? What do they imagine? How do they go about making a family of their own? How does this story explore the meaning of family in all its different forms? Why do you think orphans feature in so many books?

What role does Rose Spelman play in this story? Is it possible to do something wrong by following the rules? When should you follow your own judgement instead? Find examples of the children questioning authority and disobeying rules. Were they right to do so?

This book tells the story of the children's adventures but it tells other stories too. How many can you find? Who's telling these stories and why? What do the children want from their puppet performance, for example, or Rotman from his lies about *De Zeehond*?

Did you think the story would end like this? In what ways, if any, did this ending surprise you? What do you think will happen next? Who could be talking in the epilogue?

Thanks to castofthousands.co.uk for help in preparing these reading group questions.